FEISTY

JULIA KENT

FEISTY

I'm not to proud to admit that finding Mr. Right involves swiping right. Right? Welcome to dating in avocado toastland.

Here I am, on my first blind date, ever, courtesy of a smartphone app and my two annoying best friends.

So what is Chris "Fletch" Fletcher doing, walking across the room, looking at his phone like he's pattern matching a picture to find a real person he's never met before?

Oh.

Oh, *no*.

The guy I drop-kicked in seventh grade cannot be my blind date. The guy who earned me this infernal nickname.

That's right.

Feisty.

It was bad enough that last month all my old kickboxing training came in handy when a disgruntled noncustodial dad invaded my preschool class and tried to take one of my kids without permission.

That ended with news coverage of the closed-circuit

video that parents saw in real time as I beat him up and pinned his neck to the ground while waiting for police to respond.

We won't mention the part where I thrust my arm into the air in a power stance and, uh…

Roared.

Hey. HEY! Don't judge me. I protected those kids. And the kid most in danger was Fletch's nephew.

The same Fletch who just now noticed me sitting here.

Being noticed is bad.

Being his dating app match is even worse.

Why?

Because no matter how hard I've tried to avoid him since high school, every time I see him I have the same reaction.

I wish I'd never kicked him.

I wish, instead, that I'd let him kiss me.

Which it looks like he's trying to do.

Right now.

More from New York Times bestselling author Julia Kent as Fiona "Feisty" Gaskill gets her chance at love - drop-kick included.

Listen to the audiobook, narrated by the amazing Erin Mallon!

CHAPTER 1

"*M*iss Fiona, Jahra picked her nose and fed it to the hamster."

Mattie Fletcher-Lingoni's voice is even, calm, and perfectly blunt as he accurately recounts what I, too, just witnessed. No one in my master's program in child development ever explained the proper procedure for handling preschool-aged children who feed boogers to classroom pets.

"Did not!" Jahra tries to bend reality.

"Did too." Mattie is undeterred.

Jahra fails.

"And you didn't even wash your hands after. We're s'posed to wash our hands so the germs don't kill us," Mattie declares.

"Germs don't kill us." Jahra uses a time-honored tactic: Initiate conflict as a way to deflect.

"Do too! My daddy says germs are silent killers. They kill you *without* screaming!"

"Bad guys scream. Bad guys don't stay quiet," Jahra argues. "They scream when they kill you in the movies."

I make a mental note to tactfully ask Jahra's parents what she's been watching on Netflix lately.

"Jahra is a bad guy for feeding poor Piggly her booger! Boogers are not food," Janelle pipes up, her rainbow ombré the kind of cute touch on a little kid that is also a visual reminder of parents who can afford the elaborate hair treatment *and* a kid who will sit still for long enough to have it done.

"Boogers are not food!" Mattie echoes.

Jahra bursts into tears. Wet, sloppy, snotty, wailing tears.

Welcome to my classroom.

Twenty students age four or so, me, two assistants, and a hamster named Piggly, who now, apparently, has eaten the first-ever all-booger breakfast.

Scratch that.

I'm sure that at some point in the five years since I started teaching, one of my *students* had the first all-booger breakfast.

Piggly isn't all that original.

"Jahra," I say, giving her a hug as she sniffles and hitches her breath. "Please don't feed Piggly snacks from your nose."

"But... but he wanted it."

"He did?"

"He said so!"

"Piggly *talks* to you?" Mattie asks with the kind of skepticism that makes me just know he'll grow up to be an accountant. I taught his cousin, Max, two years ago, and *his* dad is an accountant, so maybe it'll run in the family.

I know the Fletcher family all too well.

I catch Michelle's eye. My twenty-one-year-old intern teacher gives me a smile that is more knowing than it should be. She's a natural with four year olds.

I smile back.

We're twelve minutes into the start of our day.

It's going to be one with a great story I can tell people.

Teaching preschool may not pay well, but the extras are *soooo* worth it. I'm blessed with stories.

Booger tales.

We-don't-eat-charging-cables tales.

Don't-use-tampons-for-craft-time-when-you-sub tales.

Wait. That one's for my best friend, Perky. She will never be subbing in my class again.

Ever.

"Piggly whispers to me," Jahra tells Mattie, eyes shifty. When four-year-olds are learning how to lie, they start in really obvious ways. "He told me he likes how boogers taste. Giving Piggly some of my boogers was being *kind.*" Dark eyes framed by long, curled-up eyelashes meet mine. "Miss Fiona always tells us it's important to be kind."

"Boogers are kind?" Janelle asks, clearly doubtful. She's a lawyer's kid, so the sneer comes naturally. "I don't think so. Who shares boogers and the person *likes* them?"

Michelle bites her lips to stop from laughing. We have plenty of students who like to dine on their own nose cuisine. Her toes curl up in her slippers, all of us wearing them, the change from street shoes to quiet, contemplative footwear part of the morning ritual.

What comes next is anything but routine.

The energy in the room changes before the sound hits our ears.

Squealing tires outside make me turn instinctively, the booger conversation on the back burner for a split second as protective instinct draws me away.

Our school is in a small strip mall. We're on the end, with a fenced playground off the back, the edge of the fencing touching thick woods with trails that are maintained by the town. The conservation land helps to make the school feel less strip-mall-ish. Unfortunately, sharing a parking lot with a coffee shop, a convenience store, a consignment shop, an insurance agency, and a women's fitness center means there's more car traffic than we'd like.

The front door is locked. Back door, too. Windows are latched but can be opened for quick evacuation.

Inventorying this takes a split second.

What feels like a century is my own awareness that a wave of bad energy is coming.

And I can't stop it.

"What was that?" Janelle asks, craning her neck around me to look at the front door, which is glass. You can see the parking lot between the painted flowers on the door.

"Just a driver going a little too fast," I say, hoping I'm right, knowing I'm not.

"Like Mommy when we're late for gymnastics?" she asks sweetly.

Mental note number two: Don't ask Janelle's mom to be a driver for our next field trip.

Our preschool has two big rooms with a single door connecting them. Two offices and two bathrooms are carved out of the space in the back. A small mudroom, made of a tiny greenhouse structure, is where we store boots and coats for recess time. Half the kids are in here with Michelle and me, while the other–I do a head count, nine–are with Ani, our other aide.

Bam bam bam.

Instantly, my eyes jump to the four cameras in the room, fisheye lenses strategically placed for maximum coverage. There are four in the other room, too, and two on the playground. Parents can watch everything we do via webcam, all day.

It makes separation anxiety so much easier.

The parents take longer to recover than you'd think.

I turn toward the banging to find Rico Lingoni, Mattie's dad, standing on the other side of the door, hands on his hips, chest rising and falling with huffing, angry breaths.

"Oh, boy," Michelle says, suddenly at my side, the two of us moving toward the door to act as a shield. "Candi warned us about this."

Candi Fletcher-Lingoni is Mattie's mom and Rico's soon-to-be ex-wife. Last week, she showed us a protection from abuse order, a new custody order for Mattie, and even asked the local police to keep an eye on Mattie's school and their home, in case Rico did, in her words, *Something worse.*

Without moving my mouth, I say softly, "Get the kids in the other room, get them all in the back office and evacuate if you can. Do it quietly and call 911. He wants Mattie." The words are surreal but they have to be precise.

"But Fiona, I–"

"*Now.*"

As if they pick up on the change in energy–because, *of course*, they do–every child in the classrooms looks up at us.

And Mattie's face lights up as he looks at the glass door.

"Daddy!" he shouts, fingers still on the small sticks he's arranging for his project, eyes bouncing between the door and his work. "Why is my daddy here so early?"

Bam bam bam.

Joy turns to terror on Mattie's face, color draining from him.

No four year old should ever, *ever* have that expression.

Any other intern teacher would panic. Any other intern teacher would clap her hands loudly, or call out an announcement. But Michelle isn't just any intern.

She's an intern who survived a shooting at her high school when she was fourteen.

So Michelle moves quickly, softly, and nearly silently.

Like an Australian shepherd, she herds the children into the other room by circling in a wide arc, only Mattie left with me as she gets everyone in with Ani, whose worried eyes meet mine for a split second, her frown so deep her glasses slide lower on her nose, short brown hair curling over the tips of her ears.

Rico smacks a paper against the door. "Today's supposed to be my day, Fiona. I got papers that say so."

I smile at him, nodding, holding up one finger to buy time. "Just a minute."

A tinkling sound, like small pieces of metal dropping on ice, comes into my consciousness as I put my hands on Mattie's shoulders. His neck is twisted, body facing away from his dad, eyes unable to not look.

"Sweetie? Go with Ani and Michelle."

"But–"

The metallic sounds get louder, and then I remember what Rico Lingoni does for a living.

He's a locksmith.

Normally, I turn off my phone during work cycles with the children, but we're not even twenty minutes into the morning. Our days have a rhythm and the rhythm has been interrupted, so as I hear notifications pinging in the air, I realize they'll only increase in intensity.

Because we're on camera, being watched by parents.

"Mattie. GO!" I hiss, his face crumpling as Miss Fiona turns from fairy-light goodness to firm, tense protector, his body ushered by my hands, my urgency vibrating out of my skin.

Michelle takes him in her arms just as Rico breaks into the school, a long pick in one hand, brandished as a weapon.

"You give him to me, Fiona. You give him to me *now*. Candi can't do this. She lied to that dumbass judge and you know it. He's mine and no stupid bullshit restraining ordah is gonna split up my family. I'm heah to take what's mine." A thick Boston accent punctuates his words. Bloodshot eyes with bags underneath and the bloat of a bender radiate danger.

Rico's past the point of no return.

Nothing in my child development classes prepared me for this.

But something much deeper in my past *did*.

Every second I buy means a greater chance that no one gets hurt. Hopefully, Michelle and Ani are leading the children out the back door, the police on their way, their response time swift because nothing bad ever really happens in Anderhill, Massachusetts, bedroom community to Boston, home of the Dance and Dairy festival every August.

A place where people send their four year olds to a tiny strip-mall preschool because it's *safe*.

Why wouldn't it be?

"You're right, Rico," I tell him, soothe him, pretend and friend him. That's what we do, right? When we're in danger? We say whatever it takes to defuse.

"I am?" His neck jerks back. He's expecting a fight. Boozy eyes, dark and oily, meet mine. Rico hasn't showered in days, I suspect, a heady, sour scent emanating from him as he takes his free hand and shoves his hair off his face, the other hand clutching the lock pick.

"Sure." My agreement makes him move closer, looking over my shoulder at the open door between the rooms.

"Then get Mattie ovah heah."

"I will."

More notifications *ping ping ping* through the air like bullets whizzing by. My eyes take in his body. The old jean jacket over a hoodie could hide anything.

It could be hiding a gun.

A phone in the office rings.

"Ignore it. Mattie." Rico jumps forward, the lunge setting my blood to nothing but electric current, shooting through me in a spray of shock. "Now!"

The texts and phone ringing blur out another sound, footsteps.

Little footsteps.

"Daddy!" Mattie shouts from the other room, out of sight behind the closed door but audible. "Don't hurt Miss Fiona! Not like Mommy! Please, Daddy!"

And then he's suddenly quiet, hopefully pulled to safety.

"You bitches," Rico screams as he points the long, thin lock pick—the kind that could skewer a heart or a throat with one careful plunge—right at me.

As he charges.

Sirens, dim and too distant to help me right now, turn into my own heartbeat as the thick, sour stench of alcohol and a primitive bloodlust assault my nostrils, Rico so close that the tip of his lock pick grazes my arm. He's taller, bigger, more muscular, and on a mission to harm.

In hand-to-hand combat, I'm not going to win, but if he breaks loose and chases after Michelle for Mattie, he's capable of anything.

Which means I have to be capable of *more*.

Until the police arrive and save us.

Please save us.

I pull back. He grabs for me, missing my arm but fisting the long, diaphanous sleeve of my dress. It billows in strips of purple, white, and silver, a beautiful style until it becomes a point of leverage for a man who wants nothing more than to push several inches of steel into my flesh so he can kidnap his own son.

I can't get away, can't escape his grasp. The fabric tears as I try, his hold resolute, his huff a grunt of victory.

"You bitches always think ya so smaht," he mutters as the fabric bares my shoulder, a burst of stardust on my skin from one of my fairy tattoos sending me a sign, a message – encouragement.

And so I drop.

The change in weight distribution shifts his center of gravity. His grip is strong, but the fabric gives enough, and the laws of physics make him lean over me. My hip rotates, muscle memory grooved into my bones so deep that it's become marrow. My knee stabilizes, psoas muscle curling, the gyroscopic twist of all that I am centralizing in one motion, one choreographed move, one full-body prayer.

I kick up.

I kick out.

I kick *all*.

He takes it square on his diaphragm, my slippered feet less effective than they would be with soled shoes, but the impact is enough. If righteous fury counted as force, he'd be hanging from the moon right now.

Instead, he's just dazed, on the ground, the lock pick across the room, under the Peace Table.

Blue and red lights flash through the windows facing the road, but I know how the stoplight works on Stately Road, and even blowing through it means the entrance to the building is still a full minute away for the police.

Sixty seconds.

I just need my higher self to carve out sixty more seconds to survive until they're here.

Leaping to my feet, I find myself facing him. His arms are spread, muscles straining against his jacket as he swells up, pumped by my kick, eyes murderous.

He rushes me.

Oddly, it's what I smell that strikes me most: the scent of bleach, coffee from the back room, a slight hint of crayons and markers. Instinct has turned me into a kinetic mass with a purpose buried so deep in my brain stem, it's like my core being is emerging through a fog to lead an army of truth. Without the time to ask for divine intervention, I process flashes of reality, the tree-like pattern of red vessels in Rico's eye, the grease in the cuticles of his right hand. He backs toward the closed door where we last heard Mattie's voice.

"Cops ain't takin' me nowhere," he growls, the words layered, an imminent threat. He reaches for his waistband and suddenly, I know.

I know what he's reaching for.

If he gets a gun in his hands, this is over.

Comical confusion crosses his face as I keep my knees loose, the lights from the cop car turning into the lot. Seconds pass like hours, but it's really only been three minutes since he banged on the door, according to the analog clock on the wall, the giant owl's eyes staring at us with a solemnity that is meant to be wise, but I find terrifying.

"What the–" Tearing his gaze away from me, he looks around.

I use my peripheral vision to find what he's looking for, neck turning when I realize what he's lost.

His gun is under a chair at the bubble station. My kick knocked it out of his pants.

Poetry comes when you least expect it, not mere words on a page but emotion that truncates because it's too big to convey any other way. Our bodies speak in silent poetry, too. Pain, grief, horror, terror, disappointment, dismay, regret, loneliness, evil–it all emerges one way or another.

Right now, my body's poem starts with one word:

No.

Diving for the gun, Rico doesn't bother with subtlety. The parking lot is suddenly screaming, just like me as I walk toward his back, twisting to do the mid-air jump and turn I need, every ounce of my *No* centered in my core, pushing energy from it to the ball of my foot.

Which connects with the back of his head.

No.

He goes down as the screech of tires fills the air, a parallel sound to the one his car made just three minutes ago. The scent of burnt rubber is in my nose, although that's impossible, and my throat is sore from warrior screams I don't realize I'm making until the video is reviewed.

The arch of my foot is on his neck.

The gun is still under the bubble table chair.

And every goddess in the history of the multiverse converges in me, their energy lent to me, feeding me, my body a furnace, an atom, a star, a fusion ball with a singular purpose: to save.

To protect.

To *win*.

And so I roar.

I roar, arm up in thanks to all that aligned to stop him as the police burst through the door, guns drawn on us. I roar in gratitude as Officer Capobeira puts his hands on my shoulders, his barrage of words meaning nothing, just gibberish I can't understand because I don't speak with my mouth anymore. I am pure energy, centered for one act, one move, one moment.

How do you unravel enough to remember words?

More cops.

More lights.

Cars and more cars are pulling in, frantic parents appearing, police officers and ambulances clustered in front.

"Fiona. *Fiona*," Officer Capobeira says, bending and kneeling before me like Prince Charming at the ball, his hands on my slippered foot, gently pulling up as another officer zip-ties Rico's hands behind his back. He's flat on his belly, body covering a train mat designed for play.

"Gun," I whisper.

The cops both freeze. "Where?" they ask in unison.

"Got it!" a female officer calls from the bubble station. "And some kind of pick over there." She points to the Peace Table.

"He attacked you with *that*?" Officer Capobeira asks as he stands, my foot now on the edge of the area rug, Rico hauled to his feet.

"Crazy woman attacked me!" he screams. "She broke my toof!" Blood clots along his lower jaw. "I was just here to pick up my kid. I got custody papers. And she went crazy on me!"

"Yeah, yeah, Rico. Tell it to the judge," the female cop says.

"MATTIE?" A man I know, wearing a paramedic badge and uniform shirt, appears at the glass door. His sharp green eyes catch mine, worried and frantic. "Fiona? Where's Mattie?"

"Get out of here. Crime scene," Capobeira snaps, eyes cutting over to someone behind the paramedic, a curt nod and a sudden burst of compassion confusing me.

The paramedic looks at Rico. "You piece of shit. If you hurt Mattie–"

Mattie? Why is this paramedic so worried about Mattie?

Oh. Right. Paramedic. Because that's Fletch. Chris Fletcher.

Tingling starts at my kneecaps, blooming at different points on my body, energy overloading my skin and pouring through me wherever it can, as fast as it can, my body too small to contain it. Nerve endings in my jawline fire up, sending starbursts into my vision, my diaphragm frozen, my chest a wall of bones held together with nothing more than residual fear.

Fletch.

The paramedic is Fletch.

Fletch from Mallory's wedding party.

Fletch from middle school.

The last time I dropkicked someone, it was *him*.

And it was in that moment, seventeen years and a lifetime ago, that I became *Feisty*.

"Mattie's mine!" Rico screams at Fletch. "You and your bitch mother poisoned Candi against me!"

He lunges at Rico, the officers anticipating it, a wall of dark-uniformed men and women appearing suddenly. Two paramedics grab Fletch's arms, elbows bent, his face hard to see with so many big, powerful officers surrounding him.

"Don't, man. He's not worth it." Capobeira's voice is calm, measured–and loud enough to make sure Rico hears.

"Besides," someone else says, their voices mingling as they all turn into energy threads, their bodies no longer real and distinct. "He got the shit kicked out of him by a chick. That's all the guys in lockup with him need to know."

Masculine laughter fills the air. I look at Fletch.

He's not joining in.

"Fiona?" he asks, stepping toward me. "Guys, I think she's about to–" Warm, strong hands hold my shoulders as my legs turn to rubber, energy whirling inside me, trapped in place, desperate to leave. Fletch's hand goes around my waist, his polo shirt collar brushing against my cheek.

I look up. Why do I hate him again?

"I'm sorry," I whisper, brushing my fingers against his short, brown hair. It's shiny and handsome, softer than I expect.

"For what?"

I can't answer, the room filling with blue light, not from cop cars but from some other layer of consciousness that makes my heart zoom, my skin grateful for his power, because his eyes care, his hands care, and his expression—oh, his face, his handsome, strong, clear-eyed, worried face...

It's the last face I see before I faint.

CHAPTER 2

"*Fi?* Fiona? You did it," Michelle says, tears streaking her face, raccoon eyes and blue-streaked hair distressing until I realize it's mascara and her hairdo and I'm not dreaming about a Marvel Universe movie.

I'm looking up. Behind her shoulder is the leaf mobile our class constructed just a few weeks ago, thirty-two different leaves from various deciduous trees creating a work of natural art.

"I did what?" I start to sit up and quickly recline. The world spins.

I need less spinning.

"You saved us! You—God, Fi, he had a gun. A gun! That asshole brought a *gun* into the classroom and—" Her hand on my forearm starts to shake.

Voice, too.

This time, I do sit up. "Where are the children?" A prickly feeling creeps along my skin from the palms of my hands to the soles of my feet.

"In the other room. The police are releasing them to their parents, one by one."

I look over, seeing only uniformed police officers and a paramedic who looks awfully familiar. One arm is around Candi Fletcher-Lingoni, the other on top of Mattie's head.

Fletch.

"Are they okay? The children?"

"Terrified, but yes—they're fine. They're unharmed. Ani and I took them out the back office window and through the alley behind the insurance agency and the consignment shop. We got into the woods and hit the swamp before the cops arrived, so it all worked out."

"What about you?" Compassion roasts me from the inside out, so fast and full, in a wave that makes me flush. "Oh, God, Michelle—the gun. The attack. You went through it before. Are you okay?"

"No." Her chin quivers. Swallowing hard, she squares her shoulders. "What're the odds, right?" A high, hysterical sound comes out of her. She sniffs and swallows again, suddenly looking considerably younger than her twenty-one years. "But the kids are fine. No one's hurt. No one died today."

No one died today.

My heart squeezes, like a million souls are hugging it, desperate to fill it with happiness again.

I grab her in an embrace and try desperately to refill her happiness, too.

"Where's Ani?" I whisper in her ear.

Michelle pulls back, wiping her eyes on her sleeve. "Being interviewed by the police."

"And Rico?" I shudder to say his name.

"Arrested. They took him out of here before Mattie's uncle could beat him up. They found the gun and that long spike thing. Did he use that on you?" Her fingers trace something on my arm that stings. "Is this scratch from him?"

"That's the same question I was about to ask," says another person with a paramedic's badge that says JOSH. "Hi, Fiona. I'm Josh. You fainted, but your vital signs seem to be fine so far. Blood pressure's a little low. Does it tend to be low?"

"What?"

"Are you having a hard time hearing me?" he says louder, eyebrows up, arching over his black-rimmed glasses. Like Fletch, he has on a polo shirt with the town logo on it, a paramedic's badge marking his role.

"No. Hearing's fine. Just–I'm just–" All I can do is blink. My throat closes up. My nostrils feel plugged. My pulse is in my ears, like the ocean gearing up for a nor'easter, the pounding waves growing.

And I can't breathe.

My lungs have decided that the world is too dangerous to make a move, utter a sound, do *anything*. I'm frozen, the pulse inside me growing stronger as time ticks away. My own shut-down system is the barrier to oxygen. The disconnect between what my body needs and what my tattered psyche can handle is causing my overload to leak out in a really obvious way.

"Fiona?" Josh says, shaking me gently, Michelle looking to him for certainty.

And then suddenly, Josh is out of my sight, replaced by two clear, calm, green eyes, light brown hair, and hands that feel like anchors.

"Feisty? Feis–Fiona?" Fletch corrects. The sudden pivot to using my proper name is jarring, given the fact that every atom in the world is buzzing inside my ears and nothing anyone does will help me to breathe.

I make a strange sound. I know it's strange because his

eyebrows turn down in the middle, his facial muscles pushing them low enough to show concern.

Concern for *me*.

"Breathe," he says slowly as he puts one hand on my diaphragm, fingers warm and firm.

I make a sound to indicate that I am confused and the speech centers in my brain have shut down. Empathy floods me as I realize this is exactly what my student with severe apraxia, little Myles, must feel like when he loses his words under extreme stress. For years, I've said "use your words" to four-year-olds having anxiety fits.

Never again.

"Breathe, Fiona," he murmurs, taking a deep breath to demonstrate, his belly expanding in a comical way, though I know his technique is strong. Hypnotic and commanding, his voice and body tell me what to do, guide me back from being lost in the woods to a cleared trail where I can find my footing, take a rest, and possibly feel safe again, knowing I can find my way home.

I inhale, the insides of my nostrils cold, the air hitting my nasal passages a welcome assault, diaphragm spasming and sputtering back to life.

"That's my girl," he whispers against the curl of my ear, his breath like coffee, his hard forearm muscles all I can see, the ripped cord of his strong lines drawing my gaze. "You just breathe. It's over now. You did it. You saved them. It's okay to breathe." He inhales, then slowly exhales. "Let's do this together now."

The back of my throat thickens, my ankles tingling, blood rushing to my extremities as the truth of what just happened in my classroom starts to course through me.

"FIONA!" someone calls out. "Brad Johnson, NECN. Were you injured in the attack? Is it true the assailant had a gun? Do you have martial arts training? We have questions, Ms. Gaskill!"

I look over to see flashes, cameras popping, people with video equipment crowding around the front door as police lights outside blind me, turning into a purple haze.

"Hey," Fletch says softly, drawing my eyes to him, turning my focus to something sharper. He's all I see now, the cacophony behind him just a buzz. "Come here." Shielding me from the worst of the media circus that's taken over our parking lot, he curls me into him, becoming my shell, giving me his heat, his peace, his energy.

I let him.

I've received so much today, why not a little more?

"Is it true you're specially trained for this?" someone shouts from the media horde. "You're a ninja nursery school teacher!"

"Oh, God," I groan.

He glares in the general direction of the cameras. "The police want to interview you. I think you need to go to the hospital first." He's not hugging me. We're not intertwined. He's just there, a solid wall between me and the cameras.

Between me and the world.

"Michelle says everyone's okay. The kids are okay? Tell me they're okay. Why am I saying the word okay all the time? Is that okay?" I ask, my mouth apparently detached from my brain.

"*Shhhhhh.*" Lips barely moving, he keeps his eyes on mine, watching me with his chin down, eyes up, as if he's ready to restart my heart at any minute.

"I'm fine."

"You're anything but fine."

"Hey! I'm great in an emergency. I'm fine."

"You're *damn* great in an emergency. That still doesn't make you fine."

"But–"

"Thank you."

"For what?"

"For keeping Mattie *safe*." His emphasis on the last word makes my knees buckle as the reality of what I did sinks in. The kids *weren't* safe. Hearing Fletch acknowledge that makes my stomach melt into my toes.

"Fiona? Fi? Feisty?"

"Don't call me..." My voice winds down as I pitch forward into his arms.

It's the last thing I remember until I wake up to find my body on a stretcher, a warm blanket on me, and the sight of Fletch, whose expression makes it clear he's overwhelmed with gratitude.

And pissed as hell as he bounces up and down, leaning suddenly to the left.

"They were supposed to back off," he mutters as the ground beneath me lurches to the right. I realize we're in an ambulance.

A *moving* ambulance.

"They?"

"The media."

I nod. "How long was I out?"

"A few minutes. We're getting you to the hospital now."

"Hospital? I don't need–"

"You're getting evaluated. Your blood pressure is low and you experienced syncope twice. That's enough for a doc to take a look at you. You got someone I need to contact?"

"Huh?"

"Boyfriend? Husband?"

"You know I don't have either! We're in Mallory's wedding together. If I had one of those, I'd bring him!"

"It's a formality. For the paperwork." His amused side eye doesn't help matters. "And good to know you're back."

"Back?"

"Back to being Feisty."

I kick him. He's just out of range, unfortunately, so my foot goes into dead air.

"Careful. Those things are lethal." He grabs my slippered foot, hand so warm, the grasp full of a caring possession so different from what Rico Lingoni just did to me.

"I didn't kill him." I move my hand so it's under the white blanket, the warmth very welcome. "Even if I wanted to."

Eyes flashing with emotion, Fletch leans toward me. "I wouldn't have blamed you if you had."

"I used the least necessary force."

"That takes skill. Composure. Deep awareness."

"Yes."

"And compassion."

"*Compassion?* I pressed my entire weight into his neck."

"But you didn't break it. See? Compassion."

My laughter makes me feel guilty.

The ambulance slows at the exact moment that a rush of energy infuses me. Closing my eyes, I touch it, drawing on my higher self, my wiser mind, to help me during this time. I need the positive power of the universe to support me.

Feed me.

Take *care* of me.

"You okay?" Fletch asks, his voice filled with concern.

I open my eyes. "Yes." I'm trying to catch the essence of my core self. His sexy forearms aren't helping. I close my eyes.

"What are you doing? Meditating?" This time, his voice is curious, not concerned, but I still don't open my eyes.

"Something like that." Trying to explain my energy

healer, Jolene, to a guy like Fletch is just begging for teasing.

"I meditate," he says.

My eyes fly wide open. "You do?" Through the small windows in the ambulance doors, I catch a glimpse of a large sign, glowing white and red, that indicates we've arrived at the emergency room. I'm suddenly embarrassed to be brought in via ambulance.

"Sure. Lots of people do. Helps keep me focused at my gym." The ambulance stops. "And here."

"I'd imagine being a paramedic requires a lot of grounding."

Pain flashes through his eyes like a flipbook. "Yeah." He closes himself off, all professional composure. "Look, I'm still working my shift. This is where we part."

"My phone!" I gasp. "My purse! Where are they?"

He reaches behind him. "Here." He hands me my purse. "I already called Mallory and Perky."

"You *what*?"

"Mallory insisted we all have each other's numbers because of the wedding. Remember? Something about the wedding party needing to be able to contact each other in an emergency. This counts," he says with a grimace. "And Perky's still in town." One side of his mouth goes up. "We have that dance lesson tonight."

My composure disappears. "I don't think I'll be making that."

"No kidding. Me, either. After my shift, I'm spending my time with Mattie and Candi." He grabs my hand, the feeling white-hot lightning. "You did a good thing."

"Did I?" A shiver ripples through me as the danger sinks in.

And then I just tremble, unable to control it, my abs tightening without end.

"Of course! All those kids, Feisty–"

"You know my name is Fiona," I bite.

"Yeah. I know. But damned if you didn't turn into the girl who kicked my ass in seventh grade. Rico got what he deserved. And you deserve a goddamned medal."

The back of my hand buzzes as he kisses it, so soft and gentle, it's almost not there.

And then his arms are wrapped around me, his lips on my ear as he whispers, "Thank you."

The back doors of the ambulance slam open just as he pulls back and grabs a chart, reciting my vitals as if the last thirty seconds didn't happen.

Now I'm trembling for completely different reasons.

The gurney is moved forward, then released so the wheels hit the ground, every face a blur as I clutch my purse.

Fletch's face isn't one of the blurs.

"Fi! Fiona!" Perky screams, her voice distinct, my eyes unable to focus as various medical personnel ask me questions, orienting me in space and time, my friend's voice a comfort until I'm taken back behind a curtain.

"Dr. Chan," a doctor younger than me says, shaking my hand, his skin smooth and hot. "Looks like you had two episodes of syncope. Any history of–"

"FEE-OH-NAH!"

"Uh, excuse me, doctor, could my friend come back here with us?" I ask.

"You *want* her here?" The way he says *want* makes me smile.

And shake.

"Yes. Please." Finally, the tears start, bubbling up like hot springs, like an overflowing bathtub, like a tsunami wave that just keeps coming. "Please. *Please*," I beg.

"Of course," he says gently, surprising me with wise

compassion, his youth triggering assumptions in me that aren't fair.

Perky barrels in, all long, honey hair and wide-mouthed grimaces as she takes me in, squeezing me in a hug. The tiny, curtained-off area has a television in it, the channel turned to a news station that suddenly cuts to a news report about Rico's attack at the preschool.

And then, video of me fighting Rico.

The doctor's eyes flick up, following our gaze. He crosses his arms over his white coat, eyes intrigued, bouncing from the television to me. I'm riveted, and horrified that someone gave the news stations the footage from our password-protected webcam system at the school.

I relive what happened to me just an hour ago.

Rico banging on the door, Michelle herding the kids into the other room. The door opening. My conversation with an angry Rico, his body language dangerous, frightening. Rico charging me. As we watch, I feel my blood pressure rise, my brain reliving it biochemically, pulse racing, chest tightening.

And then I do the roundhouse kick and Rico goes down.

My foot. His neck.

Perky shouts, "YES!"

"*Shhhh*," the doctor chides, turning it off.

Perk turns to me, her eyebrows tight with concern, mouth twitching with mixed emotions.

Then she sighs, her hands cradling my face, eyes tightly locked with mine as she says:

"The roar was just showing off. You're so *extra*, Fi."

I can't laugh.

"What are you doing here? I thought you and Parker were on a flight."

"He is. I'm not. We saw the breaking news coverage of

what happened while we were grabbing a final coffee at Beanerino, before our flight, and suddenly, my best friend is Wonder Woman and I shooed Parker off to Texas."

"But Perky, you were – "

"Hush. Parker will be there forever. You need me more right now." Her hug makes me cry.

"Thank you."

"And he said your roundhouse kick was exquisite in its simplicity, whatever the hell that means."

I sputter-snort through the hug. I guess I *can* laugh.

A little.

The next few minutes are a blur. Perky is forced to go to the waiting room while the doctor examines me. Dr. Chan has short, black hair cut tight at the neck and ears, longer on top, with straight, angled bangs that cover one eyebrow. The hair bounces as he checks my heart rate, eye tracking, and other basic vitals.

I assume he's an intern. A dawning horror fills me as I realize he's *much* younger than I am.

How can I be older than the *real* adults, like doctors, lawyers, and engineers?

"You seem perfectly fine other than this long scratch on your arm," he says with a puzzled look. "Is your tetanus shot up to date?"

"I'm a preschool teacher," I explain.

"And?"

"Yes. It is."

His eyes cloud as someone raps hard on the wall next to the curtain exactly twice, the sound more a command than a request.

Dr. Chan gives me an apologetic look as he goes to answer. Someone in a suit, another in a cop uniform, and Perky's bouncing head behind them are all I need to see.

It's interrogation time.

"Hey!" a low voice says in the hall. "Quit jumping like that. You'll take out someone's foot."

"I'm worried about Fi."

I realize Perky's arguing with Fletch out there. Why did he come back?

"We need to question her," the suit says to the doctor. The uniform looks bored, cocking one eyebrow at Perky and Fletch, eyelashes flicking up and down as he surveys them. His hands are on his belt, arms akimbo, biceps straining against the sleeves of his uniform.

Fletch's arms are bigger.

Why did *that* thought pop into my head now, of all times?

" … kick isn't something you just learn in a cheesy gym–" someone out there says.

"Hold on!" Fletch says loudly, turning away from Perk, standing right next to the uniform, who I realize is Officer Capobeira. "Did you just say 'cheesy'?"

"People don't just bust out moves like that unless they have training," a deep male voice says.

"Or if you're Feisty!" Perky adds.

What the heck is going on out there? I sit up, my head spinning.

I sit back.

A hiss, a rumble of low voices in the hall, and some kind of reprimand for Dr. Chan by a nurse who looks like she eats interns for lunch lead to everyone suddenly coming into my little area. Two cops, one best friend, one middle-school nemesis, and a student doctor all crowd my little curtained area.

"You two." The suit looks at Perky and Fletch. "Out."

The last thing you want to do with Persephone Tsongas is issue a direct order that contravenes her need to protect a bestie. Detective Suit just made a grave error.

"Make me," she challenges.

"You realize I can do that whenever I want, miss."

"My boyfriend is a congressman."

"And me mum's the queen of England," he mocks. The suit is a tall dude, lanky and weathered, with thick wrinkles that run in vertical lines along his cheekbones. I get a deep vibe off him, one that makes me feel safe yet puts me on edge.

He trafficks in sarcasm and uses it to filter the world.

"I'm staying." Perky crosses her arms over her chest, which is currently covered in a t-shirt with a message about the ratio of blood in her caffeine stream.

"Then you're being cuffed."

"Hold on," Fletch says calmly, like he's placating someone dialing 911. "She's Fiona's friend."

"Next of kin, practically," Perky persists. "Fiona's parents are out of town, so I'm it." She doesn't mention my older brothers, Dale and Tim. They both live in the midwest, so I really don't have any family nearby, and if anyone's my next of kin now, it's Perky and Mallory.

"I'm here for her, too," Fletch tells the suit, his words making me freeze, my skin taking on a fire-like quality it really shouldn't.

Certainly not over Fletch.

Seventeen years ago, when we were in seventh grade, Chris Fletcher tried to kiss me. I didn't want to be kissed, but he persisted.

So I dropkicked him.

My real name, Fiona, became the basis for my nickname, Feisty. The word became a taunt, uttered in over-the-top hisses from popular boys who banded together to tease and torment me.

But no one ever tried to kiss me again without my permission.

By high school, the nickname stuck, as did the hardass reputation, which meant I was labeled. Stereotyped.

Contained.

When someone else decides your identity out of spite, it sucks.

When that same someone turns out to be your source of help in your greatest time of need, it rocks your world to the core.

"We need to question her without you here." The Suit's words shake me out of the memory as Fletch gives me a funny look.

"Especially if this involves the feds," Capobeira adds.

"Feds?" I ask.

Capobeira gives me a flat look. He makes eye contact with the suit. "She's good."

"Good?"

"No one takes a perp down like that without some serious training," he says. Suit shoots him a STFU look, but Capobeira goes on.

"I trained when I was younger. Kickboxing," I try to explain.

Fletch reflexively massages his neck.

"Not that kind of training. You know," Capobeira challenges.

"I... don't know."

"That's how you're trained. To pretend you don't know. I got it."

"Cap, this isn't the way to go," the suit says to him.

"I got this, Moe."

"Got what?" I ask as Dr. Chan slips out of the area, avoiding my gaze. I hear him in the hallway, a flash of a security guard's uniform, the words "private room" and "media" floating into my hearing range.

"Which alphabet soup you with?" Capobeira asks me. Suit cringes, fingers twitching like he needs a smoke.

"Alphabet soup?"

"You know. FBI. CIA. NSA."

"You think I'm–you think I'm an agent? A *federal* agent?" I look down at my dress, a torn series of pastel shreds of diaphanous cloth that make me look more like a human maypole than a CIA operative.

Fletch and Perky start laughing.

Hard.

"Hey! I *could* be," I snap at them before realizing that's the worst thing I could say right now.

Capobeira's eyes narrow. "That's right. You could."

"But I'm not! I'm just a preschool teacher."

"You're not *just* anything," Perky says, suddenly serious. "How many times have Mallory and I stood behind you when people say you're *just*–"

"That's it. Get out," the suit orders her.

"You two Keystone Kops seriously think that Fiona Gaskill, the woman who uses a divining rod to find free parking wherever we go, is a CIA agent? What's next? Is she a vampire slayer, too?"

Fletch snorts. The suit's mouth purses, like he's taking a drag on an imaginary cigarette. Perky, who is keenly attuned to All Things Nicotine, catches his energy and starts chewing on her lower lip, a telltale sign she wants a ciggy, too.

"Vampires are vastly underrated and extremely misunderstood spirit beings," I protest, shaking off the ex-smoker vibe.

"How did you do it so gracefully?" Capobeira asks.

"Kill a vampire?"

He rolls his eyes. "Take down the perp. With a Muay Thai

te tat roundhouse kick. The economy of movement is the tipoff," Capobeira persists. "You even got the hair-combing movement. The clips of you fighting Lingoni are all over social media now. I reviewed the tape a few times. You know what you're doing. Trained so well, it's in muscle memory, but plenty of guys train like crazy and never accomplish what you did. Your body has the mark of an experienced operative," he emphasizes, eyes on my chest and legs as he says *body*.

My dress is in shreds from Rico tearing it, though it still covers the important parts. A few spots of blood from Rico's injured mouth have started to dry, the burgundy like wine stains, which seems more possible than what it really is: a result of violence.

Violence I enacted.

Fletch tenses, taking a step toward me, his energy loud and clear, pulsing with a blue light that my skin drinks in like I'm parched.

Before Capobeira can say more, Perky adds, "Fiona's always been like that. Remember when you took Fletch down in seventh grade? Fi just does shit without thinking and it works. Some asshole threatened her kids. She *acted*. That's more than you cops do half the time here in Anderhill."

A bright red flush starts along Fletch's neck line, his hands curling into fists, eyes shifting.

I wince. It's not from physical pain.

The suit sucks in air past his back teeth. "That congressman boyfriend of yours better have bail money at the rate you're going."

"Money means nothing in the face of principles," she counters.

"Ah, God. We got ourselves a live one here."

"You have no idea," I mutter.

"Tell us what happened today. We got your other two

teachers' statements. Now we need yours." Suit stares hard at Fletch and Perky, then turns to me. "You want them present?"

"Do they have to leave?" I ask.

"No. You're not being interrogated. Just making a statement."

"Then I want them to stay."

As if they synchronized it, Perky and Fletch both have notifications buzz on their phones. Heads tipping down, hands in pockets, they extract their phones and look.

Fletch's mouth tightens. "My sister's down the hall with Mattie. He's having an asthma attack. Gotta go."

"Is he–tell him I'm thinking about him and what a brave boy he was today." Some piece of my heart seizes as I imagine the terror and elation he felt today, seeing his dad at school.

And then...

"I will." Fletch's eyes go soft. "I'll tell him what a brave teacher he has, too."

With that, he disappears.

Perky looks at her phone. "Huh. My text wasn't nearly as dramatic. Just my mom's app-based litter box telling me it needs to be cleaned. I really need to delete that."

Fletch's words linger in me, piercing the protective shell of energy I keep trying to weave around myself.

Brave.

What does that word really mean?

"Was I brave?" I blurt out, startling Suit and Capobeira, who turns to Perky in a near panic, as if my emotional question is out of his range of training. "Was it brave to do that? In the moment, it seemed so clear. He was going after Mattie."

"Tell us what happened," Suit says, his voice soft but eyes blank.

So I do.

And then the tears start and don't stop until he puts his pad of paper away and leads Capobeira out the door, Perky's arms around me, my body shaking with an uncontrolled frenzy that is more biological than emotional.

But there's a surplus of those, too.

Getting the whole story out takes time, but it's all on tape, so this is a formality. By the time I'm done, the two men put to rest the idea that I'm some kind of superspy, the Suit muttering in a curmudgeonly tone to Capobeira, who defends himself with the sagging confidence of someone who knows they've made the wrong assumption but can't let it go.

I'm just a preschool teacher.

Just.

But today, that *just* meant something so much more.

CHAPTER 3

"*I*'m sorry."

"Quit apologizing."

"I'm sorry for apologizing so much," I reply.

"God, Fiona. STOP IT."

We're pulling into Perky's driveway, a long, rambling path that takes us to her parents' mansion and her two-bedroom cottage, which is a large pool house behind the main house. My ER trip turned out to be short on the medical side and long on the police side.

I'm *drained*.

I need to soak in her parents' hot springs mineral bath. I need to recharge, and what better way to do that than to have every square inch of my body covered by hydrogen and oxygen galore?

"Where's Mallory?" I ask.

"On her way. She was working on one of Will's proper-ties to turn it into a destination event house for twenty-five people. It's on the water, in Salem. Gorgeous place she's considering for the wedding shower or bachelorette party." Perky turns off the car and stops, hands on the wheel, eyes widening as she stares ahead. "God. Who cares about all that now? I can't believe the last few hours."

"Same."

I see the silver side strip of my phone in my purse. Perky turned it off in the ER. Before she did, there were hundreds of notifications, most of them news stations, lots of them offers for money. Jobs. Dates.

Marriage proposals.

But not a single one is a message from Fletch. I'm really worried about Mattie.

We climb out of Perky's car and walk into her little house, an adorable place that is decorated like someone just threw fingerpaint all over the place and then brought in cloth furnishings in the same colors. "Mal can meet us here and we'll go over to the big house together," she explains. "Want a sparkling water? A coffee? Cookies? A half gallon of vodka?"

"You're getting closer." I plop down on a purple beanbag chair, a four-foot-wide hug in furniture form.

"Weed's legal in Massachusetts now. We can get some special brownies and you can access all those past selves Jolene tells you are guiding you via divining rod to the free parking spaces you find."

"Don't mock my energy healer." My voice is muffled by the gooshy goodness of the purple embrace. The long scratch on my arm where Rico did something with the pick throbs. I know it'll sting going in the hot springs, but I don't care. In a way, it'll cleanse the wound.

Exorcise this day in a ritual bath.

"Not mocking. Trying to find a way to get you to eat the magic brownies."

"You don't need me to do that."

"Good point." She reaches for a bottle of white wine and holds it up, shaking slightly. "This work?"

"Yes."

Two glasses are poured, one handed to me as I sit up. I sip slowly, moving carefully to a standing position at the small granite island that bisects her kitchen. Sighing heavily, I lean into the cool stone, willing it to anchor me.

"That asshole," Perky blurts out.

"What did Parker do now?"

"Hah. I meant the guy who attacked you."

It's only when other people say it like that—when they bluntly state the obvious—that it sinks in. Someone attacked me. Someone tried to hurt my kids.

Someone almost succeeded.

And it was me—and only me—who fought back. Who stopped him.

Who *won*.

"Perk," I say in a low moan, free to emote here, allowed to acknowledge what I've held off with everyone else leading to this point. "He–he tried... oh, my God, Perky, what if I *couldn't* stop him?"

"But you did."

"But what if I couldn't?"

"But you did."

"What if I'd missed? What if he'd used that gun? What if–"

"But. You. *Did*."

Just then, Mallory walks right in, dumps her purse on the floor by the door, and makes a beeline for me. Her arms are around me before I know it, her clutch so strong that it's hard to breathe, wine almost sloshing over the rim of my glass.

"Don't you ever scare me like that again!"

I start laughing. It's hysterical.

"You listen, Fi! I don't have time to get another bridesmaid. Do you know how hard it is to schedule seamstresses for fittings?" She hugs me harder. "You're a hero!"

"I'm a wreck."

"You can be both."

Shaking, I bring the wine to my mouth and guzzle the rest down, carefully setting the glass on the counter by the stem, fingers pulling back as if I'll break it otherwise.

"I *am* both."

"My mom asked if you need anything. She knows your parents aren't here."

Of all the times for my parents to be out of the country. Three years ago, they planned a massive, six-week world cruise, the culmination of years of saving. They left last Sunday.

Rico's timing *sucks*.

"My parents are on a cruise ship, and Mom refuses to pay the crazy prices for internet access. It'll be weeks before they find out."

"You're not going to contact them? Tell them?"

"I will," I say faintly, mind freezing at the thought of managing my mother's reaction. Like any loving parent, I know she's going to freak.

I don't have the strength to manage someone else's freakout just yet.

"You want us to do it?" Perky asks. "Because we can."

"If I don't, my brother will. I'm sure he's one of the people trying to call me. If he can't, he'll reach out to the cruise line to contact them."

"Honey," Mal says with concern, "they're going to find out somehow, and – "

"I will. I *will*. Promise. But right now, I just want to be a wreck in the hot springs." I don't know why I'm drawn to it, but I am.

Perk grabs the open bottle of wine and marches to the door. "Let's go."

Mal holds my hand like I'm a child needing guidance, and we walk outside along a stone path bordered with ivy. The small Japanese maples add accents of burgundy, tidy and sedate, beautifully ornamental. Perky's parents won $177 million in the lottery about ten years ago, and the grounds reflect carefully cultivated luxury.

A stone archway built into a hill has a huge, carved oak door with a rounded top. Mal opens it, revealing a stone staircase that drops down two levels.

It smells like aged sediment, the prehistoric scent of an underground cavern with stalagmites. There aren't natural mineral springs here, but Perk's mom, Sofia, hired a team of designers and architects, stone masons and landscape architects, to come in and create the ultimate replica of one.

It's like the ancient baths in England. Like Mammoth Cave with a spa attached.

I stand in the doorway, a deep hum moving through me, as if the stone itself were conducting a chant from the Earth's core.

"What's wrong?" Mal whispers.

"*Shhhh,*" Perky replies. "It's one of Fiona's moments."

She's right.

I've learned to pause when I feel overwhelmed, to be a conduit for energy rather than trying to generate it myself, or ignore it. Years of seeking out a higher vibrational truth has pulled me away from my thinking mind and into my intuitive mind. Mallory's volition lives in her head. Perky's volition lives in her spine.

Mine used to live in my core, but now it's in my aura.

Savoring the silence, I let my breath guide me, my shaking inner being needing to release the fear that almost took over, the anger that made me fight back. Righteous instinct turned me to violence to protect children who couldn't defend themselves. The mixed morality of what I did today means that doing right–*being* right–isn't enough.

I had to use violence against another soul.

And that is making me shake.

Then I realize – I used violence against Fletch when we were younger, to get him to take my no seriously.

I shake even more.

"Do you want to be alone?" Mallory asks softly, her hand on my shoulder, the grounding both appreciated and difficult. "We can let you soak in the hot springs by yourself."

Politeness dictates that I tell her *no, I'm fine, it's okay, I want my friends here*.

Truth dictates something deeper: that I accept her loving offer to give what I actually need.

"Yes," I say, grateful she's put it into words so I don't have to. "Just for a little bit? Maybe twenty minutes?"

"It's fine," Perky soothes. "Just don't overcook."

"I know. Your mom thought of everything when she had this designed. Plenty of water to drink and places to climb out and cool off." I swallow, hard. "You're sure this is okay?"

"Totally. Gives us time to go out to the cabana and find my mom's Tim Tams stash." She and Mallory share a glance I easily interpret: They're worried about me.

"Your mom has a secret Tim Tams stash?" Mallory coos as they leave, the sound of their conversation like warm breath on ice as it fades to a whisper with their departure.

I take a deep breath.

I move forward.

I'm *pulled* forward.

Steam rises as I descend, recessed lighting muted and warm, giving the already cavernous space a womblike feel.

My breath, every sound I make, echoes, and then I reach the water, where stone columns rise up around a huge, zero-entry pool that bubbles.

I strip down, naked, immodest, unmoored.

The water feels like a mother's womb, the slow lapping of waves caused by my entrance like love in liquid form.

"Please heal me," I whisper. "I invite you to bring me what I need."

Working with Jolene has taught me this simple grace: Ask the universe for help. Be specific.

Be *open*.

I'm in the water to the tips of my breasts, the hot springs sending off waves of steam, the heat caressing my chin, then the lower tips of my earlobes. I sink down, pinch my nose, and go under, holding my breath as my closed eyes shield me from the world.

I could stay down here forever.

Alas, I am mortal, and oxygen is a must.

Breaking the surface, I inhale in a controlled manner, then exhale until every last molecule of air is gone, nearly choking as I splay my arms, palms flat, like starfish with their bellies to the ceiling. Holding my diaphragm in place, flat against my third chakra, I inhale slowly, feeling a controlled fire inside that has no name.

Rebirth is hard. Renewal is harder.

Regret is the worst.

Did I do everything I could to save the kids? Were my actions more traumatic than they needed to be? If Mattie was in the ER with an asthma attack, was it anxiety induced? Were other children harmed today? The collective weight of their little psyches is like having the ceiling cave in on me, my lungs too small to breathe for all of them, my arms too short to wrap around them and protect them from a world where an angry dad with weapons shows up at their preschool and nearly shatters *everything*.

"Did I do right?" I finally gasp, the words wrong but the feeling too intense not to express. I close my eyes and float, needing the water to support me, my sense of responsibility so heavy that my bones cannot hold it up any longer.

I have to be aided.

I have to be upheld.

I have to ask for mercy.

As the hot water holds me dear, the minutes with Rico rush through my mind's eye. With intent, I freeze-frame each moment, thinking to myself: *I am only here to love people*.

When I kick him, I freeze the picture and think: *I am only here to love people*.

When I see the gun under the Peace Table, I freeze the picture and whisper aloud:

"You fucker."

Sputtering, I stand suddenly, wondering where the hell *that* came from.

So much for serenity. I'm not nearly as evolved as Jolene tells me I am.

"What the hell?" I mutter.

"Hey, sorry," a deep voice says from behind me.

Oh. Wow. I've entered a completely different realm. Jolene told me that over time, if I raise my vibration, I can access other planes of consciousness.

Has it finally happened?

"Who's there?" I ask, dipping down so my shoulders are in the hot water, but my back still turned. The entity could be anyone–no one–a Master from the spirit world, or a long-dead relative coming forward to chide me or thank me for what I did today.

It could be my soul, reaching from within me, taking on a different form.

Or it could be–

"Fletch," he says. "Perky's mom said you and Mallory were down here, but I didn't realize you were, uh..."

I'm *really* inventing voices, aren't I?

I stand, brushing my hair off my face, the water up to mid-buttock, steam billowing off my skin as I laugh, a throaty, deep chuckle that feels good.

"I must be losing my mind," I say aloud, spinning around, "because I swear I just imagined Fletch–"

Our eyes meet.

We both freeze.

Except for his eyes, which take me in, running down my body like the sure touch of a spirit who was once part of my soul.

For a few extraordinary seconds, we stand like this, the steam forming a curtain that tries to be modest but fails. My will, his will, our collective sense of connection, all gathers in the steam as the shock of being seen–fully, nakedly, rawly *seen*–sinks in.

And I drink in his gaze.

Until I scream and drop down underwater, this time forgetting to pinch my nose, the shriek still half out of me as I go under.

He's not *really here*, right? Why would Fletch be here?

I come back up.

Still there.

"What are *you* doing here?" I gasp, keeping my body below the water, the surface at my neck.

"You weren't answering your phone. Neither were Perky or Mallory. I guessed Perky might have brought you to her house, so I pulled up and knocked on the front door. Perky's mom said you guys were down here. She pointed to the big wooden door with the stone arch. Offered me a suit, even."

That's a *lot* of words in a row out of Fletch.

Hungry eyes meet mine, then dip to the water. "I assumed you would be here with them. And that you'd, uh, have a suit on."

"Well, I don't!"

"No kidding."

All I can hear is the sound of the water splashing against the rocks as I flail underwater, uncertain but needing to move. He doesn't speak, eyes on mine, so piercing.

So earnest.

So *tempting*.

I clear my throat. "Would you mind turning away?"

"Yes."

"Yes, you'd mind, or yes, you'll turn away?"

"Both."

"FLETCH!"

A short sigh, then he turns away. "Perky's mom said to remind you to hydrate."

"What are you now? The hot springs police?"

"I came to see how you're doing. And to tell you Mattie's fine. Had a nebulizer treatment and he's doing well."

My throat tightens, the beginning of tears creating a sour taste in the back of my mouth. "Thank goodness," I whisper, the sound carrying through the cave.

He walks over to a water dispenser. Sofia's too environmentally aware to stock individual water bottles. Filling a plastic glass, he sets it down near me on the edge of the pool. "Drink."

"I'm fine."

"Fiona, let people help you. You don't have to be strong and bossy all the time."

"I'm not bossy!"

He smirks. "Then drink."

"I'll drink when I want to."

"I'm turning my back. I won't look at you if that's why you don't want to get the drink."

But a part of me likes having him look at me.

And that's why I don't want to be one inch closer to him right now.

Slowly, I move closer, secretly grateful for the hydration as I grasp the glass and chug about half. Then I say, "This is awkward."

"Yes."

"You're not leaving."

"Not yet."

"Why not?"

"I don't know." His wide back tapers slightly to a thick waist with zero fat on it. Fletch owns a boxing studio and is a trainer. The cut of his t-shirt, a simple white one with sleeves that curl around thick biceps, reinforces that he's in fine shape.

How had I not noticed before?

Scrambling to find something to say, I settle on "Thank you," mind flashing back to the moments after the attack, when Fletch breathed with me. Breathed *for* me, it felt like.

"For what? I didn't do anything."

"You grounded me. It takes someone with a connection to their higher self to do that. You gave me a piece of that self and I appreciate it."

He starts to turn around. Is his need to look into my eyes as great as mine right now?

A commotion upstairs makes it clear Perk and Mal are on their way, likely with a package of Australian cookies and another bottle of wine.

"Oh, my GOD!" Mallory gasps as she reaches a point in the steam where she has visibility. Eyes jumping from my obviously naked, wet form to Fletch's dressed self, turned away from me, she makes a speedy calculation before adding, "We're going to need more Tim Tams."

"I was just leaving," Fletch says, giving them both a smile. "Stopped by to make sure she's okay and to tell her my nephew is fine. Take care of her."

"We already were," Perky says, giving me a look that questions everything.

And then he's gone, the steam swallowing him like a magician's trick.

"What. Was. *That?*" Perky demands, stripping out of her clothes, the steam showing a leg, a breast, the ends of her hair, as it flutters around her like a burlesque dancer using large white feathers. She's in the water quickly. Only sound tells me that Mal does the same, the steam thicker than ever.

"That was Fletch."

"Hah. No. I mean, what *was* that? The sexual tension between the two of you was so thick, you could scoop it out of the air and use it as lube."

"Ewww! Perky!" Mallory shouts, suddenly next to me. "That's gross."

"What? It was a compliment."

"Only you could turn a dirty lube joke into a compliment."

"It's a skill."

Mal drops underwater and comes up, wiping her face. "He came to check on you?"

"Yeah."

"He's a good guy, Fiona." Years of hearing me complain about him are etched into her words. She's imploring me to go easy on him. To accept that he helped me in a crisis.

To change my opinion of someone who represents a past identity he forged for me.

"You know, my first instinct was to say, 'he's an

asshole,'" I inform her. "But he has more good to him than I admit."

"Ooooo, Fiona likes Fletch! We've got ourselves a new couple here!" Perky jokes, poking my shoulder as she noshes on a Tim Tam.

"I do not *like* him. But he did help me today. And Mattie adores him, so he has to have some redeeming qualities. You can't fool a four year old."

"The guy stumbled across you naked in a hot springs and didn't jump your bones. He's a gentleman, too. Turned away and everything before he saw you naked," Perky pushes.

My silence changes their energy, like deer in the woods during hunting season hearing a twig snap.

"He... *did* see you naked?" Mallory asks.

I sigh.

"Oh my God! What did you do?"

"I thought he wasn't real. Thought I was hearing voices from the spirit realm."

"You hear voices?" Mal's tone is one of deep concern.

"No. That's the thing. I've tried, but never succeeded. I thought hearing his voice meant I'd crossed over! That my spirit guides were finally speaking to me and I could hear them! So I stood in the water and–"

"And Fletch got the Full Fiona Monty."

I grab the entire package of Tim Tams from Perky and start shoveling them in my mouth.

"Hey! Those are mine!"

"No," I mumble around the chocolate and caramel. "Not anymooo."

Mallory steps out of the pool and refills my water glass plus two more for her and Perky. We drink it down, sitting in peace, the two cookies I just ate sitting like a stone in my stomach.

"Guys?" I sob, the emotion too hard to contain. "What am I supposed to do? I feel like I lived a lifetime in the last ten hours."

"Maybe that's how time works," Mallory says, suddenly next to me. "Some minutes are longer than others. We think of time as an objective measure of space, but maybe it's not. Maybe it's more fluid. Maybe emotion turns it into taffy, something we can stretch and compress."

I'm struck dumb by the thought.

"That's very metaphysical of you," Perky marvels.

"Thank you," Mal says simply. "The Tim Tams make me smarter."

"Fi stole the rest of the box."

I eat another one to prove her point. A wave of dizziness hits me.

"I have to get out," I inform them, pointing to the towel rack. As I step out of the water's embrace, I expect a chill, the steam's slight temperature drop a pleasant transition. Shivering slightly, I dry off, remembering Fletch's eyes.

The curl of his mouth.

The seriousness of his gaze.

My mind flips to Rico's murderous face.

And I shiver more.

"Let's go get the rest of your mom's stash," Mal says as she steps out, too, grabbing a towel. Five minutes later, we're ascending the steps, holding glasses full of water. My body is boneless, my brain filled with a million tiny pieces of sliced-and-diced memory.

And my soul full of so many questions.

CHAPTER 4

*M*allory has the best apartment of the three of us, with gorgeously designed shiplap walls, a whitewashed exposed-beam ceiling, and pale seaglass colors. Best of all, her fiancé just bought the house attached to her in-law apartment and they'll be settling in there after their wedding.

Perky lives in a two-bedroom pool cottage with a living room full of beanbags and bright colors, her aesthetic more like a preschool teacher's than mine–although, unlike *any* teacher, her budget is nearly unlimited.

Me? I live in a matchbox.

An apartment box like all the other ticky-tacky boxes in my mega-complex that makes me feel like we're all controlled by IT from *A Wrinkle in Time.*

But it fits my budget and until my student loans are paid off in the year 2131, it's where I live.

Of the three of us, my apartment sucks the most, so we barely ever spend time here. No, it's not a dump, and I've done my best to make it homey. Truth be told, I love the décor, I just hate the structure.

Decorating is on my mind. High on my list of must-dos, even, because it's a serious distraction.

And right now, I'll take all the distractions I can get.

It's the morning after the attack, a sunny fall Saturday. Just shy of twenty-four hours since Rico Lingoni banged on that school door and altered the course of my entire life. The video, leaked by a parent, has taken over everything.

The enormity of it is one big cloud of black mist.

When I turn my phone on, it buzzes for so long, I fear it's dying.

When it stops, I look.

879 notifications.

Not a typo.

Eight hundred.

Seventy.

Nine.

Notifications.

My email, which I proudly clean out every day to achieve Inbox Zero (because who wants all that unfinished energy?), has unread messages in the hundreds. This is my personal email.

I cringe to imagine my *work* email.

Booting up my ancient laptop, wondering if I should go into the office instead, I see that my work email and all school-related social media accounts are on fire. My eyes jump to the email titles in my inbox. It's a mix of freaked-out parents and local and national media outlets. One that's clearly from England, another from Germany, jump out at me.

What the hell?

Tap tap tap

Someone's here? At my door? Mal and Perk always text before they come.

"Fiona Gaskill?" someone calls out from the hall. "I'm from Anderhill Flowers? I have a delivery?" The inflection at the end, plus the higher-pitched female tone of the voice, makes me answer the door.

A giant–and I mean peacock-in-full-feather-glory-level giant–flower arrangement threatens to topple the poor woman holding it.

"I've seen Vegas showgirl headdresses that are smaller," the delivery woman says as I reach out and try to help. "No, no, dear. Just point me to your nearest flat surface and I'll unload this."

As she passes, I see gold-foil chocolate balls on thin, clear spikes. There must be fifty of them, tucked in between peonies, orchids, roses, and assorted greenery.

A card stands tall in the center, like the star on a Christmas tree.

"Someone is really happy with you!" the merry woman says. I can finally see her face. Short hair, a little salt-white around her ears. Wrinkles at the corners of her bright blue, nearly lashless eyes. She's petite but in great shape for someone who looks like she's on the northern side of sixty and barely south of seventy.

I reach for my purse, wondering what you tip after someone delivers half a greenhouse full of flowers to you.

"No, no, dear. They already took care of it." She smiles, eyes glistening. Her energy changes, a misty vibe passing in the air.

Is she about to cry?

"They?" I ask, holding the shake from my own voice. Emotion is so contagious for me.

"I'm not supposed to say this," she whispers, reaching for my hand, the jolt of her feelings making my hand go numb, "but this is from the parents of your preschool class.

They've been trying to reach you, but understand if you want privacy."

"Oh."

"And what you did–thank you." Big drops pour down over her lower lids. I sense loss. Heartache. Pain. Something deeper than her words, but I don't ask. *Can't* ask.

I literally can't.

Because now I'm crying, too.

The hug is wholly expected but my reaction to this bizarre moment isn't, her scent all sugar and cloves, with an undercurrent of roses.

"Oh, my goodness. I'm a mess. How unprofessional!" she says, backing out my open door. "I'll leave you to your privacy, and don't let those pushy camera crews get to you!"

And with that, she shuts my door.

Camera crews?

Walking past the gigundo arrangement, I make a beeline for my window.

And gulp as I see three news vans in the parking lot.

I rush to my phone and tap until I see my voicemails.

Mom's number.

Eighteen times.

I hit Play:

"Fiona? Fiona, please call and leave me a message! Dad and I are worried sick about you. We have internet and phone service now on the ship, but we can't reach you at all! I'm paying for internet and phone every single day until you get ahold of me. We called the police and they said they'd just seen you and you are safe but please! We love you and we're so worried. And Dad says to add we're proud as hell, too! You kicked that mofo's ass!"

Oh, no.

I imagine the other seventeen voicemails are the same.

I hit Call Back and leave a message, assuring her I'm fine. I add *I love you* for good measure. I don't think I've heard those words from her since I graduated with my master's degree. Mom's about as emotionally demonstrative as a Vulcan. Her way of showing she cares is to do my taxes for me.

More tears come. I'm a mess.

The flower arrangement is a great distraction. A card pokes out from the middle. I slip my index finger under the flap and pull out what appears to be a check.

In the amount of $2,145, from the personal account of one of the parents in my school.

I drop the check.

I read the card:

No flower arrangement, no chocolates, no collection taken up by the twenty families of the precious children in your class can possibly be enough to show our deep appreciation and gratitude for what you did yesterday, Fiona, and what Michelle and Ani managed as well. We know that you're busy with the police and with your own recovery, but please reach out to us when you can. Rest first. Every single child is safe and whole because of you. We could not have chosen a better school or a finer teacher to guide our children. In gratitude, The Grounded Child Community

My eyes are as wide as moons.

The folded check is on the floor, the endorsement section a thin line that stares up at me, as if asking a question I can't hear. My heartbeat thrums deep in my throat, under earlobes that itch. My heart double thumps, then goes back to regular rhythm, a cough resetting it.

I need to center.

I need to ground.

I need to *think*.

My students are priority number one. They must be so

scared. Michelle and Ani are my first calls, though, because I need to make sure they know how much their acts of heroism mean to me. I may have incapacitated Rico, but none of the children would be as safe as they are today without my two assistants.

I dial Michelle's number. Voicemail.

"Michelle? It's Fiona. I'm sure you're screening your calls, too, so I'll just leave this message. The long weekend means we have an extra day off from school, but I need to see you and Ani. Could we meet somewhere quiet when you get a chance? And thank you." I start to choke up, my free hand rubbing the roses all over my leggings. "Thank you so, so much for everything you did yesterday. You're amazing."

I hit End.

The check looks at me with a gimlet eye.

No one goes into preschool teaching to get rich. *No one.* That collection, that $2,145, covers four months of student loan payments for me.

It gives me breathing space.

It brings financial relief.

It fills me with guilt.

Ring!

I jump a foot as the ringer on my phone goes off, surprising me. I look.

It's Ani.

"Fiona? Oh, my God, finally. I've been trying since the ambulance took you away to find out how you are! The police wouldn't tell me anything and your parents are on that damn cruise and—"

"I'm fine. Really. Just fainted a couple of times and the police and paramedics were being extra careful. What about *you*?"

All I get in response is a series of heartbreaking sobs.

"I'm–I'm sorry! I need to get a h-handle on this! I'm fine. Michelle and I got the children out the back office window. We–we were worried if we took them on the playground we'd be trapped by the fences. We went behind the dumpsters in the alley and over to the strip of woods at the end of the building, and then Michelle couldn't find Mattie. That's–that's when she realized he'd wandered off."

"How is Michelle?"

"Her parents have her on complete media blackout. After what happened to her in high school, she's–she's having a hard time, Fiona. I have her mom's number, though. I'll text it to you. Her mom wants to talk to you."

"Is she angry with me?"

"*What?* No! She's so grateful. But I think she's as protective of Michelle as we were–*are*–of the kids."

"Right. Any mom would be."

"Your parents must be freaking out."

"I–I ignored my phone and email until now. I couldn't handle it. Called my mom's number and left a voicemail."

"You must have so many messages. And did–did you get the flower arrangement and check from the parents?"

"You got one, too?"

"Can you believe it?" More sobs. "I feel like I'm cursed and blessed at the same time."

"Cursed?"

"What were the chances that a deranged parent would be a *locksmith*, Fiona? We followed every safety procedure. None of those plans ever accounted for a guy who could pick a lock."

"Yeah." My voice is high and hoarse. "That's pretty crazy."

"The media are here. Asking me for interviews."

"Have you done any?"

"Not the ones for money, no. Just one from my hometown newspaper so far. Fi, there are major news shows asking for us to appear. That video of you, though..."

"Who leaked it? Do you know which parent did it?"

"I don't know. But it's someone without tech skills, because it's a cellphone video of someone's computer monitor."

"Low tech skills. That rules out two-thirds of the class parents. So many of them work for Big Data."

She laughs. It sounds like snot bubbles popping.

I sigh, the sound deep and hollow as it echoes back to me through the phone. "It doesn't matter. The damage is done. I have more than a thousand notifications on my phone and email."

"I only have a few hundred. I can only imagine what you're dealing with. We don't even have a boss to handle this stuff. The one time it sucks to work for a co-op school."

"Amelia Wissen must have organized the flower arrangement and collection. I wonder if she's getting hit up by the press." Our preschool is a co-operative, which means the teachers and the parents run the entire program. Amelia is the president of the board. There's no director, no principal, no head of school.

Technically, that's *me*.

Created more than forty-three years ago, The Grounded Child was a tiny nursery school devoted to individualized learning. The woman who founded it, Cecily Wissen, died ten years ago. She left a few million dollars in a trust, and the income goes to the school. Her granddaughter is president of the board. It's why we're able to stay small, but our jobs are secure.

And our waiting list is always full.

Another call beeps in on my phone. It's Perky.

"Ani? I have to go. Let's plan to meet for coffee tomorrow. I'm–" I look out the window. There's another media van there. "How about Beanerino, maybe at ten?"

"Sounds good. We need to talk with Michelle, too."

"I'll handle it. If she can't be there, that's fine. I'll reach out to the parents, and Michelle's mom. I've got it all under control."

Perky's call beeps in again.

"I know you do. You did yesterday, and you do now."

That makes me want to run away screaming.

"Thanks. Talk to you later, Ani. Another call coming in. Stay safe and grounded."

"I will. You too."

I click over.

"My mom insists you let her call our PR company and they'll manage all the media contacts and the negotiations for the endorsement offers you must be drowning in," Perky says with zero polite intro, her voice a *rat-a-tat-tat* of punctuated authority.

"Hello and good morning and how are you, too?"

"No time for that. How many thousands of notifications and emails and voicemails do you have?"

"Not as many as Two-Dogs-Humping Girl."

"Well, *someone* has to be the star, right?"

We laugh.

I start to cry.

"Oh, Fi. I'm coming over."

"No, no."

"Then let my mom do this."

"I can't afford a PR company!"

The check looks at me and says, *Bitch, please.*

"Mom will pay for it."

"My brother is the one who helped you with your reputation management! I can ask him for help." Tim left a message on my phone already. Three of them, in fact. He lives in Canton, Ohio now, renovating his fourth old Victorian home in some up-and-coming neighborhood where he lives with his boyfriend. Four old homes there are cheaper than even one in the Boston area, and he's been able to retire at thirty-three.

He's one of those hardcore early retirement guys.

But he'll come out of retirement if I need him.

"He was only good at removing pictures of my boobs, Fi. He can't help after the fact. What you need now is an experienced PR firm where someone steps in and acts as your shield from the press, companies with offers, that sort of thing."

"I can't keep taking charity from you guys."

"It's not charity and yes, you can."

Too much energy, directed in the wrong places, is as sickening as too little.

"Fi, let Mom do this. It stresses her out to know you're going through so much and have so little help. The media inquiries and offers are a huge deal. Those jackals will invade your life nonstop if you don't have filters. You *need* a filter."

Tap tap tap

I jump and scream, the sound small but full of panic.

"What's wrong?"

"Someone's at my door."

"See? Filter."

"Fine! Yes. Tell Sofia yes. And thank you. And yes. And I'll pay you back."

"Saying *yes* is payment enough. I'll get the ball rolling. Keep your phone on so they can reach you. PR woman's name is Rafaela. And I'm coming over in a few hours."

"Okay."

End

"Delivery!" a guy shouts through the door.

Another one? I stare at the small forest on my dining table and wonder where I'm going to put anything else.

I look through the peephole. Normal looking guy. About my age, round black glasses, sherpa-fleece-lined plaid flannel hoodie. He's holding something in his hand.

I open the door.

To discover that to his left, there's a guy with a film camera rolling.

"Fiona Gaskill, I'm John Griswold with Metro News." He holds up what looks like a coffee mug with a pack of convenience store candy in it, inside a ziplock bag tied with a bow made of string. "Let me have a quick interview?"

I start to shut the door. "No. Stop. I don't want–"

He inserts his foot in the door, suddenly so close, I can smell the coconut lime deodorant he's wearing. I recognize the scent because it's the same natural brand *I* use.

"This would be a huge scoop, Fiona. You set the narrative. You pick the questions." He has that overeager, too-slick attitude that makes my intuitive receptors go nuts.

He's a user.

I'm his use-*ee*.

"No. Leave me alone," I say firmly, pushing on the door. I'm barefoot, so I can't use my foot to shove his out of the way.

The camera rolls on.

"Or what? You'll dropkick me?" Excitement rolls off him like a green wave of fun. He likes intimidating me. He revels in conflict. I suddenly doubt he's with Metro News, whatever that is, and I'll bet his name isn't John Griswold, either.

His vibes are so bad, they're starting to stink.

I recoil, trying to close the door. "No! Why would I–"

"John" stays in place, moving closer, hot breath

smelling like sour coffee. "Someone's going to get your story. Might as well let it be me."

"Go away! I said no!"

"You sound really angry, Fiona. What if I don't back off?" he hisses, the back of my neck prickling with a feeling I know all too well. It's an energy that transforms from fear into something harsher with each passing second.

"I'll call the police!"

"You rolling?" he asks the camera guy, who makes a sound of assent.

"Maybe you should fight me," he says in a low voice, the set-up clear: He wants clickbait.

"She won't, but you keep this up and I might have to."

We both turn toward the sound of *that* voice.

"Who are you?" John asks.

"Your worst nightmare." Fletch shoves the guy, just hard enough to make his feet move, just light enough to carry the threat of more force if he doesn't respond to this first, polite push.

"He's my trainer," I lie, trying to friend and pretend, to de-escalate, my heart going into palpitations at the craziness of it all.

"Trainer?" The guy lights up. "I knew it! You're a trained MMA fighter, aren't you? No normal nursery school teacher can do what you did." He snaps his fingers and looks at the cameraman. "That's right! She's the Ninja Nursery School Teacher. NINJA NURSERY!"

"Get the hell out of here and leave the lady alone like she told you," Fletch growls, inserting his body between me and the cameraman, who holds steady, but takes a step back. "Respect her *no*. I can get a cop here in three minutes."

"That would be great!" Smirking, he holds his hands

open, like he's taking on the world. "The more drama, the better. If it's clickable, it sells."

"Fiona's had enough drama from being attacked by assholes," Fletch says to the guy as he moves back, his right arm behind him, wedging himself in my door. "She doesn't need you, too. Stay away from her and the other preschool teachers. Leave the families alone. These were little kids. Have some decency, man."

Click

Fletch shuts the door.

Thump thump thump

Heavy footsteps fill the hallway as Fletch looks through my peephole, grinning.

"You got a permit for that?" I hear.

"Who is that?"

Fletch turns around, smiling. "I lied. I got the cops here in under a minute, because I brought them with me."

I put my hand on his arm and he moves so I can look through my peephole.

"Officer Minsky," says a woman I vaguely remember. Minsky. Wasn't she Mallory's jerky babysitter when we were little? The one who caught her on the porn set not quite two years ago, where she met Will again? She's in uniform, standing next to another uniformed cop I don't know.

"That's Michel Saad," Fletch whispers in my ear. "He's a hardass. I warned them you'd be inundated, so they figured they'd do a drive-by."

"It's not illegal to pursue a story!" "John" shouts in the hall.

"Did you put your foot in the door to block Ms. Gaskill from closing it?"

"What? No!"

I open the door and poke my head out, like Jack Nicholson in *The Shining*, minus the axe.

"Yes. He did."

"She's lying!"

"You're trespassing. Ms. Gaskill, did you invite these men in here?"

"No."

"I know my rights!"

"Good. You can explain them to me at the station. Let's go down there for a little questioning," Officer Saad says.

I shut the door.

I press my back to it.

I stare at Fletch.

Who is plucking a chocolate ball from the flower arrangement with an amused grin on his face. He holds it up, one eyebrow cocked, asking permission.

"You have a funny way of appearing everywhere in my life."

"Your life has a funny way of making that necessary."

"What are you doing here?"

"Candi told me some of the parents have been trying to reach you. They're so grateful, and they're all worried. Thought I'd stop by."

"You're out of luck this time. I'm wearing clothes," I joke.

There's a smile in his eyes but not on his mouth as he just maintains our gaze, the moment sinking deeper into emotional territory that is unfamiliar, dangerous, and disturbingly delicious.

"There's always next time, Feisty."

That nickname.

That *damn* nickname.

Invoking it brings all my past irritation with him to the surface. A part of me is grateful, the immature part that has been waiting for a chance to take over. Anger flashes through me, my body an oil fire in a cast iron skillet.

"Don't call me that. And don't you dare tell the press that name!"

"I'm pretty sure you're Ninja Nursery School Teacher now," he jokes, finally eating the chocolate.

"If you're here to make me feel better, you're failing."

"I'm here to thank you," he says around the sweet in his mouth.

"You already did."

"Maybe you deserve *more* thanks."

Ring!

I leap out of nervousness, grabbing the phone to find a number I don't recognize, but for some reason, my intuition tells me to answer.

"Fiona? My GOD! Are you okay? What on earth happened? You beat a man up on live television?"

My mom, I mouth to Fletch, who nods and starts browsing my paperback book collection. I'm pretty sure he's not desperate to borrow my copy of *Many Lives, Many Masters* or *Self Care For Modern Feminist Witches*, but if he wants to, no problem.

"I – hi, Mom." Tears fill my eyes suddenly, the emotion expected but still catching me offguard.

"Your father and I have been worried sick! Tim called the cruise line and somehow, one of the staff members found us and gave us a phone to use. Dale's been frantic, too. Fiona, dear, what happened?"

"Fiona?" Dad says, his voice deep with concern. "I wish we were there."

"I'm fine, Dad. It's all over. Don't come home. And I'm sorry about Tim and Dale. I swear I'll call them as soon as we're done. But don't come home."

A rustle, then Mom's voice. "But we should! You'll need a lawyer, and – did you spend time in jail? In the hospital?"

"Yes, I – "

"Jail?"

"NO, no. The hospital. Not jail."

At the word *jail*, Fletch smirks.

Or maybe it's because his eyes are now on the book *Grimoires and Your Inner Child*.

"HOSPITAL?" Dad thunders. "Beth, we need to go home. Now."

"I told you, Geoff, we needed to get off at the next port and – "

"STOP!" I shout into my phone. "Both of you! No one is coming home! I am a twenty-nine-year-old woman who had a non-custodial parent come to my class, pick the lock, threaten me and my staff and children, and I put an end to it. I went to the hospital because Fletch made me."

"Fletch? Who is Fletch?" Mom gasps into the phone.

"The paramedic?" Dad clarifies. He's the CFO for a security firm and knows all the local paramedics and fire-fighters.

"The boy you dropkicked when you were in middle school? Chris Fletcher? Was he the attacker?" Mom shouts.

My eyes cut over to Fletch, who seems not to have heard. He's now perched on the arm of my sofa, a paper-back in his hands, open as he reads. I can't see the title.

"No, he wasn't," I say, trying to be vague. "It was his brother-in-law."

"They ganged up on you?" Mom says in a confused voice.

"Of course not, Beth," Dad corrects her. "We saw the video. It was only one man Fiona took down. Nice work, by the way," Dad says to me. "Attagirl."

"GEOFF!"

"What? All those years of training paid off for Fiona. When the time came, her instincts kicked in. Haha. Get it? Kicked in."

"I want to know more about this hospital trip. Fiona, are you okay?"

"I'm fine. Just a scratch from the attacker, but the doctor treated it and I'll be fine."

"That Chris Fletcher is a fine, upstanding young man," Dad adds. "Was he first on the scene?"

"Yes."

"What does that have to do with anything, Geoff?"

"He's the kid Fiona's hated all these years."

I look at Fletch and realize the book he's reading is called *Release That Which Does Not Serve You.*

"And if he made you get medical attention, it means you got good care," Dad continues.

"You must be overwhelmed! Tim says the social media coverage of the attack is everywhere. Have you spoken with him yet, honey? I'm sure he'll help calm all this down," Mom interjects.

"He left some messages. I was just about to start calling everyone. I have to deal with the parents in my class, the kids, the media – it's a lot."

"You need us there," Mom says firmly. "I'm sure this qualifies as an event for trip insurance, Geoff," she says in a softer voice. "We could call the insurance company and see if we can reschedule this cruise."

"NO!" I bark into the phone, hating my voice. This is what my parents bring out in me.

All my sharp edges.

"Stay," I plead. "I have friends here."

Fletch looks up and catches my eye.

"Plenty of community support. I don't need a lawyer, and the guy who attacked me is in jail."

"We love you, Fiona. We feel like bad parents if we don't come home," Mom admits.

"And I'll feel like a failed adult if you do."

Folding the book shut, Fletch replaces it on the bookcase and moves on.

"Oh, Fiona," Dad says in a voice that says he doesn't know what to do with me.

"You're – well – there's a logic to that," Mom says with a nervous laugh.

"Please," I reply. "Really. Stay on your trip. You two spent all those years saving and scrimping. Has it been fun so far?"

"Yes," they say in unison, then laugh.

"Your father's a lobster. I don't think I've ever seen him with so much sun!"

"And your mother is taking cha cha lessons on board. Haven't seen her hips move like that since college."

"We never danced in college, Geoff."

"Who said anything about dancing? I'm talking in bed."

"GEOFF!"

But she giggles.

More tears fill my eyes, and for some reason, I look at Fletch and smile.

He smiles back.

"Stay," I repeat. "If I need you, I'll call."

"We have free Internet now! The staff told us the cruise line wants us to have it so we can contact you," Mom says.

"Nice!"

"We can stay in touch daily. Hourly, honey. And I really think Tim or Dale should come back to Mass and be with you."

"They have their own lives, Mom. I don't need to be rescued."

"You clearly don't," Dad says with a chuckle, alluding to what I did to Rico.

"Whatever you need," Mom says. "I – I guess you're a grown up and you know what you – "

"That's right. You raised me to be independent, remember? What I need right now is to answer hundreds of calls and emails."

"Hundreds?" Mom squeaks.

"It's a big deal, Beth," Dad says. "Our daughter did a big thing."

"She did the *right* thing. I'm so stinking proud of you, Fiona!"

Now I'm pretty sure all of us are crying.

Everyone but Fletch.

"So, um, you two need to go have fun, and I need to deal with the... whatever you call all this," I say, knowing I'm facing thousands of notifications and emails and all I want to do is crawl into a hole.

And I have a very hot, very curious, very *present* man to deal with.

"I love you so much," Mom sniffs.

"Me, too," Dad adds. "But if this is what you want, we'll honor it. We'll toast to you tonight at the champagne and lobster midnight buffet."

"GEOFF!"

"Ouch! You're getting one hell of a right hook, Beth."

"Behave better and I won't need to use it!"

I shake my head. Fletch cocks his, questioning.

Parents, I mouth.

He rolls his eyes in solidarity.

More *I love yous* and I'm off the phone a minute later,

shoulders slumped, so much of my energy already sucked out of me by a short call.

How am I going to handle having even more drained? Every parent, every media request, every child in my classroom is attached to an emotion I am tracking.

I feel so helpless.

"You okay?" Fletch asks.

"No."

"Glad you're being honest."

"When am I not honest?"

He holds up his palms. "Hey, hey. I never said you weren't. Most people would say they're fine. I like that you're not playing that game now."

"I don't play games."

His eyes take in my face, then my body, coming back to my eyes as I smolder from his gaze.

"Neither do I."

One of the gold chocolate balls is begging to be eaten. I snatch it off the plastic stick, unwrap it, and start chewing. Filled with caramel that oozes out one side of my mouth, it's a flavor explosion that gives me a single frequency to focus on.

One thread.

One sensation.

One sense.

Until Fletch reaches over with the pad of his thumb and slowly, sensually wipes a drop of caramel from the corner of my mouth. He closes his lips over his thumb and sucks on the sweet drop, eyes on mine the entire time.

Heat and frequency converge between my legs, too much energy finding a single spot to consolidate, hot eyes on mine, his body so close, so raw, so–

Ring!

"My–my phone!" I gasp, moving around him to grab it.

Amelia Wissen.

"It's the head of the school board. I have to–"

He gives me a thumbs up. "Got it. You're busy. Go. Do what you need to do. My work here is done."

"Thanks!" I say, hitting Accept, closing my eyes as I start the call with Amelia.

Even after he leaves, the throbbing between my legs continues.

Done?

Hell, no.

I think he's just getting started.

CHAPTER 5

"*I* can't believe how many men think sending a dick pic is a great way to break the ice. Some of them even use it to start a marriage proposal," I say as I take a bite of my turnip, cauliflower, and heirloom rainbow carrot mix, simmered in bone broth and whipped into the perfect texture by the chef at this new paleo restaurant Mallory insisted we try. Paleo2Clean is about as trendy a name as you can find, but the food tastes wonderfully old-fashioned, like I'm absorbing calmer nutrients from a bygone era before everything came in a vacuum-sealed pouch with a website, "natural flavors," and a hashtag.

"*Pfft.* I could have told you that from long experience," Perky says as she chews on a coconut-covered chicken strip, holding it like it's a cigarette. If it had an ash, she'd tap it.

"Anonymous dudes on the internet sending me dick pics doesn't make sense."

"I wasn't talking about the anonymous ones. I was talking about Parker."

"Wait–he proposed to you with a dick pic?" Mallory

asks before sipping her beet-kale-ginger-raw honey-jicama drink.

"Were any of them good?" Perky asks, moving on to cucumber sticks dipped in roasted cauliflower hummus, avoiding Mal's question.

"How would I know? Rafaela weeded through everything. I just got a quick highlight reel for fun."

"Staring at dick pics is not fun!" Mallory protests.

"You're looking at the wrong dick pics, then," Perky says with a snort.

"Thank you, by the way," I tell Perky, pointedly ignoring Mal. "Rafaela's been great. It's been two days since that jerkface journalist tried to shove his way into my apartment. Rafaela was there a few hours later and she's been a fabulous shield."

"How is everything?"

"Define *everything*."

"The kids at school. Michelle and Ani. The parents. The media."

"Every child seems to be fine. Our board president hired a crisis counselor to go to everyone's house, to check in. They recommend I *not* do the same, that I wait and see them when we're back to school. Keep life routine and normal for the children."

"It's killing you, isn't it? To hold back and not see them?" Mal asks. She knows me well.

"Yes."

"You're dealing with so much."

I shove my food away and focus on my green drink, shoving my hair over my shoulder. "What felt like a firehose of energy to the face is now all the same energy, just less tangled. Rafaela has someone who is helping me with the money offers."

"Money?"

"Yeah. Endorsements." That word is so hard to say. It feels like bragging and tastes like shame.

"Endorsements? For what?"

"Products. I guess," I say, reluctant to even talk about it but knowing I have to. "The video of me has been turned into an empowerment meme. Loads of kickboxing companies and athletic apparel companies want me to be in Instagram videos. Remember my Insta account? The one with a few hundred followers, most of them the parents of kids I taught?"

"Yeah," Mal and Perk say in unison.

"I have 74,000 followers now. And I'm adding a few thousand a day."

"Wow!" They sound like twins.

"Rafaela says we'll have a meeting soon. She's using these offers as leverage to get more out of other companies."

"You're serious?" Mal gasps. "You're going to take... money for this?"

I shrug, the embarrassment in my bones. "Maybe?"

"Why shouldn't she?" Perky asks. "Fiona's got all this crazy student loan debt. I've tried and tried and *tried* to get her to take money from me to pay it off."

"That's your money. Not mine."

Mallory nods in solidarity.

"My money is unearned! I did nothing to deserve it!"

"That's how this feels, too," I confess. "Rafaela says I have high-five-figure endorsement offers from kickboxing companies. That would clear out all my loans," I whisper, reaching for chamomile tea to calm my belly. "And the extra could go to the preschool endowment. Or for other charities I support. Think about all the good I could do for the Boys & Girls Clubs if I had the money."

"How what feels?" Mallory asks gently, taking me back

to my emotions. What a role reversal. Normally I'm the one doing it for her.

"Like it's unearned money. I'm being offered huge sums for a tragedy."

"You *did* earn it, Fi," Perky says somberly. "Honey, you saved those kids. You averted tragedy! You literally used your body to protect them. And you succeeded. Those parents took up a collection for you, Michelle, and Ani for a reason. Because you *earned* it."

"But this isn't how I want to earn anything!" I explode, my voice loud enough to make several diners at other tables turn and look. "I'm more worried about the children than about making money!"

"Speaking of money, where's the check?" Mal says, looking for our server. "It's my turn to pay. And even if it wasn't, I'd pay, because you *earned* it."

"Hey, hey there," Perky chides her. "Slow down. We haven't had dessert, big spender!"

Mallory's look of shock is replaced by her neck craning to find the dessert case. "Sorry! You're right!"

"Say that again," Perky asks.

"Sorry!"

"No. The other part."

"You're right!" The comment comes with an arm punch.

I slump back in my chair. "Everyone is so revved up. It's hard to feel the separate forces in the world."

"I thought you said energy works best when it's synergistic and integrated?" Perky's words make me smile in spite of myself. She's internalized some of this, even if the quiet light needs to shine a little harder to get inside her skin.

"Unless it's the wrong kind of energy," I explain, turning serious. "Then it's like a tangle of old Christmas lights that someone plugged into an unsafe outlet. Touch the wrong bulb socket and you're electrocuted."

"That's how life feels right now?"

"Yes."

The server appears, a huge smile on her face. "No check. It's taken care of. And they want you to have dessert, too."

"You can't do that!" I protest.

"I didn't." She points to an older couple, sitting to the right of a large table of ten people, the ones facing us all about college age, those with their backs to us hunched over in conversation. "That couple did."

They stand and come over, the woman about my mom's age. As she approaches, I realize I know them.

"Fiona, my word!"

"MOM?" Mallory stands up and gasps, staring at her parents, Sharon and Roy.

Walking right past her own daughter, Sharon grabs me in a big old mom hug. I'm only halfway up, so I have to engage my glutes to handle the physical contact. Sharon smells like something from the Estee Lauder counter mixed with beef tallow and unrefined organic coconut oil.

"You are a hero," Sharon whispers in my ear as it hits me: This is going to be every conversation I have with every adult in my life for the foreseeable future.

I'd better come up with a go-to answer.

"I just did my best," I reply. "I knew what needed to be done, and I did it."

I sound like Coach Belichick at a post-game press conference for the Pats.

Perky practically chokes on her laughter and the protein bar made of ground crickets she's eating.

"That's right, sweetie, you did it," Roy says to me as Mallory stands and gives her parents perfunctory hugs.

"What are you doing here?" she asks.

Roy pats his belly. "Lunch."

"No, I mean–aren't you working? Are you closed for the Monday holiday?"

"I own the business. I'm the boss. Taking my best employee out for a treat." He winks at Sharon, who giggles.

Mal makes a fake gagging gesture.

We're still thirteen when we're around our parents, aren't we?

"How are Beth and Geoff?" Sharon asks me, concern knitting her brow. She has auburn hair, a few shades darker than Mallory's brighter red, but Sharon's comes out of a bottle. Kind eyes, brown with a sable ring around the edge, tell me she's worried about me.

It's nice to have someone worry about you when the stakes are lower. Right now, I feel like the world is either worried about me or wants a piece of me.

"They're fine. I talked to them last night, again. They call every day now that the cruise line gave them free Internet, just to check in. The timing of the attack was terrible," I say with a silly laugh that feels stupid the second I do it. "Mom and Dad are the embodiment of delayed gratification, and they finally sprang for this world cruise."

"Rico Lingoni should have thought of that before he lost his damn mind," Perky snarks.

A guy whose back is turned to us, sitting in the middle of the long table of people, suddenly stiffens.

I lower my voice. "I just don't want attention."

Sharon pats my hand. "It's a little too late for that."

"At least you're getting positive social media attention," Roy says, Mallory's face going pale as she predicts what's about to come out of his mouth.

"Dad–"

"Perky is social media famous because of her, uh..."

One eyebrow arches perfectly on Perky's face.

Roy turns bright red.

"Um, and then there's Mallory and that picture of her sandwiched between Will and Beasty."

"Beastman," Mallory corrects, unable to help herself.

"Well, now, look at the time!" Sharon chirps, tugging so hard on Roy's sleeve, she's about to rip it off. "We have that meeting with the main office. Can't be late!"

"What meeting?" Roy asks as she speeds him out of there.

"Why can't *my* parents be gone on a six-week cruise of a lifetime?" Mallory wails as they leave. Her eyes land on the vegan dessert case. "Mmmm, coconut key lime pie."

"It's really good," says a male voice I've come to know all too well.

"Are you stalking me?" I ask, looking up at Fletch, who I realize is the same guy who was sitting with his back to us at the long table.

"I could ask the same of you. I'm here with my staff from the gym. What're *you* doing here?"

"Being tortured by my parents," Mal murmurs as she stands. "Is that a sprig of lavender on that chocolate cake, Perky? Let's go look," she says in an arch tone. Perky frowns, then the lightbulb goes on.

"Your mom and dad got the check, so let's gorge."

They disappear, fast.

Fletch is staring down at me expectantly, hands on his hips, biceps peeking out under a tight black workout shirt. He's fit beyond belief, with the kind of body that naturally draws good lighting to it. For someone I've been avoiding since seventh grade, he's turned out to be incredibly hot.

And even more incredibly annoying.

"I'm eating," I finally answer.

"Aren't we all. How are you doing?"

"I'm fine. You just saw me two days ago, Fletch. Nothing much has changed since then."

"You're the biggest social media story in Anderhill since Mallory was a porn star. I'd say plenty has changed."

"Mallory isn't a porn star!"

"And you're not fine."

He's right.

I *hate* that he's right.

"Why are you suddenly meddling in my life like you know me? Because you don't," I inform him, moving closer, one hand rising up, my index finger pointing as I assume a power stance that seems otherworldly. Some self inside me is coming to the forefront.

And she has something to *say*.

Two of the people at his table turn and look at us, then start whispering. Fletch's eyes cut over.

"Can we talk in private?" he asks.

"Why? Afraid of being called out in public?"

"No, but you're about to get a bunch of cellphones pulled out. You really want more recordings of you floating around on the internet?"

I spin on my heel and move to the hallway in what I think is the direction of the bathrooms. Paleo2Clean is new to me, but before this incarnation, it was a soup restaurant, and before that, a froyo place.

Yep. Guessed right. High chairs and bathrooms.

"Look, Fletch," I say, grabbing his arm hard. "Until our reunion last year, I hadn't seen you in forever. And when Mal and Will chose us both to be in their wedding, I wasn't happy, but I plastered on a fake smile because that's what you do when your friends are getting married and you used to hate one of the groomsmen."

"Hate?" A smile tickles his lips, his amusement infuriating me more than any other response he could possibly have. "You," he says, looking at my hand on his skin, taking a step closer into my space, "*hate* me?"

"No. I said I *used* to hate you. Before I worked on evolving and being a better human being."

"How, exactly, have you done that?"

"By increasing my vibration."

"You are a better person because you use vibrators?"

"Who said anything about sex toys?"

"You did. Just now."

"No, I didn't! I said *vibrations*!"

"What's the difference?"

"Enlightenment!"

"Pretty sure enlightenment comes from enough orgasms, too, Fiona."

An espresso machine hisses in the distance, cutting through the sound of our matched breath. He's inches from me, heat pulsing off his rock-hard body, the close-fitting black cloth of his shirt rippling only because of curved muscle. My hand on his arm feels like heat itself, our bodies some sort of element that conducts energy on a wavelength science hasn't discovered yet.

And I'm wet, wanting, and so, so confused.

"Why are you turning this conversation into a sex talk?" I finally choke out, pulling back as he leans in.

"You started it," he replies, the smile fading, replaced by something intensely seductive. He bites his lower lip for a moment, looking at me. Then, in a whisper that makes me lean in to hear, he adds, "Maybe you wouldn't hate me so much if I helped you with those vibrations."

Is that an offer? I almost ask, before I mentally smack myself.

"I am not having this conversation with you," I say tightly.

Releasing me, he takes a distinct step back, still deeply amused. "Fine. But hate? You *hate* me?"

"You gave me that horrible nickname."

"That was seventeen years ago. You're carrying around resentment from seventh grade? Can't be that evolved, can you? I really think you need more work on the vibrations, Fiona," he says with a wink before turning toward the dining room. "Might make you less uptight about me."

I am speechless.

I am agog.

And I am *fuming*.

Angry in all the wrong parts of my body, and hot in all the right ones.

Using the opportunity to get my act together, I go to the bathroom and take my sweet time. It's a single stall, the kind with a pedestal sink, a filthy mirror, and a toilet that won't allow you to flush anything thicker than a spider web. As my body cools off, my temper sure doesn't.

Why am I letting Chris Fletcher get to me like this?

Tap tap tap

"Fi? You okay?" It's Perky.

"I'm fine. Just finishing up," I lie as I turn on the faucet and wash my hands.

"He's gone. Coast is clear."

"Who's gone?"

"Fletch."

"Why would I care if he's gone?"

"Because he walked out of the hallway with a shit-eating grin on his face and I figured you were a puddle of boneless goo from some hot bathroom boning."

"BATHROOM BONING?" I screech, then clamp my wet hands over my mouth. Who am I? What am I saying?

"I wouldn't blame you. Have you taken a look at those

arms? Dang. Now I miss Parker," she whimpers through the door.

Ripping three too-short pieces of paper towel off the automated dispenser, I finally dry my hands and mouth, opening the door to find Perky standing there, her shirt unbuttoned to below her bra line, strategically angling her camera to take a picture of her cleavage.

"I'd have thought you'd learned your lesson about sexy selfies by now," I lecture her, grabbing the phone and taking a picture of a high chair, hitting the up arrow to send the pic.

"OH MY GOD, FI! NO!"

"Serves you right."

"But Fi! Before you sent that, I texted him the words *Ready for this, Parker?* Now he thinks I want a baby! We're not even married!"

Bzzz

"Shhhh!" Mallory appears, finger over her pursed lips. "We can hear you out there, Perky! What's wrong?"

"I can't look!" Perk screeches, covering her eyes, flinging the phone at me.

"It's an email shipping confirmation from ItAlwaysFits for some kind of device called a–"

She snatches the phone back. "Never mind."

Mal plucks it out of her hands and taps the screen. She gasps.

"You bought a dildo with Parker's head on the end? His actual–" Squinting, she spreads the image on the screen with her pinched fingers. "His actual head?"

"That's right. I shrinky-dinked a sitting member of Congress and attached his still-pulsing head to a sex toy. You wouldn't believe the blood cleanup. Come on, Mallory."

"I wouldn't put it past you."

"Give that back!" She shuts the phone off and shoves it in her pocket. Huffing. "Besides, it's not like I'm the first one. Turns out they had five others. Parker has a personalized dildo groupie club. The customer service person was a little too forthcoming about *that*."

"Why?" Mal groans.

"Because it's cute! And they follow Fair Trade practices." Perky turns to Mal with mischief in her eye. "That might make a good bachelorette party gift for you."

"The only dick I want attached to Will's head is his real one."

"That... sounds like something from a horror movie."

"You know what I mean!"

"Easy to be smug when you don't have a long-distance relationship."

"You don't have a long-distance relationship anymore! You're about to move to Texas!"

Perky waves her hand dismissively as she wanders off to the dessert case.

"At least you both have regular sex," I groan as we head back to the table. Fletch and his group are gone, our server washing off their table.

Speaking of sex...

Wait! No! Sex and Fletch don't go together. Ever. Never ever ever. I don't like him. I go out of my way to avoid him. I cannot associate Fletch and sex in my conscious mind, because that thought will invade my subconscious layers. The last thing I need is for *my* spirit self to try to connect to *his* spirit self and ruin my equanimity.

"You need a date."

"What about Fletch?" Mal asks slyly.

"Anyone but him."

"You seemed... flustered talking to him."

"Because I can't stand him!"

"If you say so."

"ANYONE but him!" I insist as Perky appears with three selections of baked goods from the vegan case. I see coconut cheesecake with blueberry compote, something very chocolate, and a raspberry mound that covers something made from coconut ice cream.

"Then do the app," Perk insists.

"I don't want to swipe right! I'm not out for a virtual booty call."

"What's wrong with virtual booty calls?"

"Hold on," Mal says around a mouth full of macadamia nut crust and blueberry. "I thought we were here to talk about my wedding shower. Not Fiona's defunct vagina."

"Defunct!"

"Out of order," Mal adds with a blue-stained grin, her teeth perfectly aligned from years of orthodontia.

"In need of a reboot," Perk contributes.

"Temporarily out of stock."

"Are you two quite finished?"

"No." They flash mirth-filled eyes at each other. "Available in two to four years," Mal quips.

"So popular, we ran out!"

"Hey! My vagina isn't some refurbished Apple product you buy on Groupon."

"But it could be. Bet that's in their business plan for 2023," Mal deadpans.

"Can we get on with this and just sign me up for blind-date hell? Anything is better than this conversation."

Perky leaps at the chance, grabbing my phone, punching in the password, and immediately downloading the app.

"Just avoid NiceGuysFinish," Mal mutters. "Stupid David and his conversion-consultant snare."

"Huh?"

"Remember the guy who secretly works for the dance studio and made me think we were having a date for dance lessons?"

"Oh. Right. Block him," I tell Perky.

"This is why I hate those dating apps," Mal grumbles around a mouth of chocolate mousse. "Too many perverts and con artists."

"You're really selling it," I inform her as I steal the chocolate candy sculpture sticking out of the mousse and lick the tip.

"I'm sure it'll be fine for you," she soothes.

"Perverts and con artists are in my dating pool. Multi-millionaire real estate heirs who are Rhodes Scholars and former quarterbacks are in yours."

She rolls her eyes playfully. "Looks like you have a paramedic gym owner in your dating pool if you want him."

"There is only one way I will ever date Chris Fletcher," I announce, then stuff my face full of raspberries.

"How?"

"When her third chakra aligns with the moon in the seventh house of Aquarius under a geopathically sensitive female lemur giving birth during a meteor shower," Perky says.

"That doesn't make any sense."

"Neither do your energy things."

"My answer has to do with energy, but not that," I correct her.

"Then what would it take for you to date him?"

"Signs."

"Signs? Like, he needs to go make up a big banner and fly it above the town common?"

"No. The universe would need to send me signs. My higher power would have to guide me to him."

"Weren't you just complaining that he keeps finding you?"

"That's different. That's *him* manifesting his *own* intentions. I'm talking about–"

"Fate," Mallory declares. "She's talking about *fate*. Coincidence. Uncanny moments when neither should be there but they are. You know," she says with a grin, teeth still purple. "Serendipity."

"Exactly," I say, taking the last bite of cheesecake.

"That's stupid." Perky taps on my phone, squinting. "I'm going to make fate work *for* you with this app. You're athletic, right?"

"Sure."

"And you like coffee?"

"I prefer tea, but–"

"Coffee *and* tea," she says loudly, as if overriding my heresy. "Kids?"

"Huh?"

"You like kids?"

"I'd better. I work with twenty of them every day for a living."

"Wants kids," she says under her breath. "Kinks?"

"What?"

"Any sexual kinks?" For good measure, she pumps her hips up and down, sacrum arching off the booth seat.

"Uh, what does that mean?" I imitate her. "Like, strap-ons? Because no."

"No kinks. Camping is next. You like camping?"

"Camping is next to Kinks on the app?"

"They spell camping with a K."

"The developers make six figures a year but they can't bother with an English major on staff," Mallory grouses.

"No. It's Kute. Spelled K-U-T-E. Everything on the app is spelled like that."

"How K-stupid."

"Make sure you mention the fact that she dips French fries in *mayo*," Mallory stresses with a shudder. "Any potential mate needs to be warned."

Before I can respond, Perky's face screws in confusion.

"Wait a minute. The app won't let me create an account for you."

"Which app?"

When she names it, I realize the problem.

"You'll have to use my old Yahoo email address."

They both look at me, stricken.

"What did you do on this dating app to get your regular email address *banned*, Fiona?"

"I encouraged people to vote."

"Huh?"

"On election day in 2018, I swiped right. Had a script I used to encourage people to vote."

"You used a booty-call app to lecture people about voting?" Perky gasp-laughs.

"I used a piece of technology that reaches the average person in ways nothing else can to nudge them to do their civic duty."

"How many guys did you do this to before they shut you down?" Mal seems fascinated.

"Six hundred and twelve."

"And how many dick pics did you receive with 'I Voted Today' stickers on the tip?" Perky asks, as if her question is perfectly natural.

How did she know? "Seven," I reply. "Eight if you include the guy who put it on his waxed butthole."

"I don't know whether to have you committed or marvel at your ingenuity," Mallory declares.

"Both," Perky says flatly. "Using your old Yahoo address now. FirstChakraBlueLight90 is the email, right?"

"Yes."

Once she's in, she sets up my profile. "Can't use Fiona Gaskill. What name should we use?"

"How about Cassandra? My middle name. And my mom's maiden name is Jones."

"I can't believe Fiona the preschool teacher was kicked off a dating site for Get-Out-the-Vote efforts."

"They said I violated their terms of service. I didn't tell people *how* to vote, just that they were letting the world down by *not* voting."

"There," Perk declares. "Cassandra 'Cassie' Jones. I uploaded an old pic of my sister in case their system is sensitive."

"I look nothing like Ditie!"

"It's that picture from back when she did female body-building competitions."

"Didn't she do one? *Just* one?"

"Yeah. Turned out she's allergic to spray tans. We had to hear her complaining about her labia itching for weeks."

"Why would female bodybuilders spray tan their labia?" Mallory asks.

I cut off the answer. "You put up a picture of your Insta-gram-influencer-wannabe sister on a dating site so guys will find 'me' hot? No way. Change the pic to me."

"Fine. The only one in your Photos folder on your phone that works is an older one, before you dyed your hair. Back when it was your normal color. And it's in profile."

"Good enough!"

A few taps later and we're done.

"Excellent. That's settled." Mallory pulls out a three-ring binder the size of New Jersey. "Now, let's talk about wedding planning. We have a dress fitting coming up, and a shower and a bachelorette party to plan."

"I need more cheesecake," Perky and I say in unison. Is that a set of color-coded spreadsheets and pens Mal is pulling out?

My phone buzzes.

"Date?" Perky asks hopefully.

"Just Rafaela. Told me to add her to the new dating app account."

"How did she know?"

"I guess she's tracking my phone."

"That feels stalkerish."

"So does Fletch."

"See? You can't stop thinking about him."

You know how guys think about baseball stats to keep from ejaculating prematurely? Or they imagine their mother, to come up with the most repulsive image they possibly can to strip away all sexual arousal?

Wedding planning with Mallory is my version.

Then again, I have to admit to myself that every time there's some wedding-related event, I think about *him*. I realize I get to see *him*. We have dance lessons coming up, and Mallory speaks constantly about Will's bachelor party plans, how his cousin might not make it as a groomsman, how Parker's status as a congressman complicates security – and it's all rolled up in being around Fletch as we both celebrate our respective friends' happiness.

Her wedding has become a touchpoint for being near Fletch.

And as reluctant as I am to admit it, I like knowing I'll see him.

"You're right," I admit. "I can't. I can't stop thinking about him, and I know I shouldn't."

"Why shouldn't you?" Mallory asks, her fingers flipping through a tiny set of pointed Post-it note flags.

"Because I've spent all these years filtering him out of my life. Trying to make him a non-entity. And I succeeded."

"Did you?" Mal's brown eyes seem wise in a breathless way as she looks at me. I hold my inhale, feeling seen but questioned at the same time.

"Hmm?"

"Did you succeed? If you spent so much energy filtering him, maybe you failed. Maybe you should examine why you spend so much time on him."

"Time?"

"It takes effort to make someone be unimportant, Fiona. Why has it been so necessary?"

"You know how much I hate that stupid nickname! And how people viewed me as my old self."

"So?"

"So... what?"

"Who cares what people think. You know you're not Feisty. You know you're a wonderful preschool teacher with a master's degree and a soul-perfect career you're really, really good at. Even Will thinks so."

"Will?"

She blushes. "We were talking about kids the other day, and he said he'd want you to be our kids' preschool teacher."

Just then, Perky comes back with one of every dessert option.

Mal's eyes are big as the macarons on the plate.

"Perk! We just ate three desserts!" Mallory pats her belly. "And I have a wedding dress to fit into."

"Hey – Sharon and Roy are buying to thank Feisty here for her brave service to the community. Can't disrespect your parents."

For that comment, I snatch what I know is her favorite macaron, a lavender vanilla, and shove it in my mouth.

"But!"

"To the fighter go the spoils," Mal says, flipping to a page in her binder that says, RIBBON.

Just... RIBBON.

As I chew, I listen to them bicker and think about Mallory's energy comment. She's right. It takes a lot of energy to avoid Fletch. To stay angry at him for something he did all those years ago. To keep up the forcefield around me that I think protects me from being hurt even more.

What else could I do with that energy?

Then there's the fact that he's not an asshole. Not even a little bit. Every interaction with him since the attack in my classroom has been nothing but kind. Caring. Sweet, even.

And a little sexy.

Okay. Fine. A *lot* of sexy.

"Wait," I say after swallowing, holding up one finger as I drink water, my friends looking at me in anticipation. "Am *I* the asshole?"

"Yes," Perky says immediately.

"We haven't even heard why she's asking!" Mal points out.

That elicits nothing more than a shrug from our friend.

"What if," I say, eyeing the RIBBON page, wondering why Mallory has an entire page of scribbled notes on that topic, "I've been wrong all these years?"

"I told you the word *tits* is terrible!" Perky crows.

"Not about that."

"Your taste in coffee?"

"Nothing is wrong about my taste in coffee!"

"Shhhh," Mal admonishes. "Let Fiona speak."

"Thank you." I look at my water glass, the drops of condensation reflecting the restaurant's soft light. "What if Fletch is a really good guy? What if I've been mad at him for doing something that stuck me with a nickname I hate, but the problem isn't him? It's my inability to let it go?"

"Then that's easy – just become Elsa and let it go."

"If it were that easy, I just would!"

"Maybe it is that easy, Maybe you're right – it's you. Not him," Mal says as she taps the tip of her pen on the RIBBON page.

"He was a jerk."

"Sure. In middle school and high school."

"And a little at the reunion."

"That was well over a year ago, and he'd been drinking. He was boisterous, but I don't think he was a jerk," Mal says gently.

"You don't?"

"I think you're a little biased," she ventures.

Perky snorts.

"A little?"

"Says the woman who spent five years being miserable because she wouldn't take a single text from the guy she was wrong about," I snap at her.

"And you should learn from my mistake."

"Learn what? I assure you I never, ever sext or take nude photos with guys or allow dogs in the bedroom when I'm – "

"Not *that* mistake."

"Which one? Because when it comes to you and mistakes, there's a list longer than the contents of Mallory's wedding binder."

"How did you feel when you saw Fletch? Just now?"

My heart flutters.

"See?" Perky pops a piece of pie in her mouth.

"See, what?" I demand.

Mallory answers for Perky. "You look smitten."

"Smitten? Mallory, you've been spending way too much time with your mom."

"We're planning my wedding!" she taps the word RIBBON. "Speaking of which, we need to talk about the ribbon we're using."

"For what?" Perk asks.

"Everything! I need to decide on colors for the flower arrangements, the goodie bags, and the – "

Perky shoves a macaron in Mal's mouth.

"I can't like Fletch! I can't change my mind about him!" I blurt out.

"Why not?" Perky challenges.

"Because – because – because he…"

"If you bitch about being called Feisty yet again, Fi, so help me God," Perky says, using a pirouette cookie like it's a cigarette. She takes a drag off the end, tapping it like she's ashing. "He's a hot, nice, hometown guy who did a really good thing helping you after the attack. When we were at the ER waiting to see you, he even brought me a coffee. Asked if I knew how to reach your parents and brother. Sure, he was kind of a dumb jock in high school, but you can't be mad that he gave you a nickname that doesn't represent who you are anymore and then put him in a box and do the same to him."

"Whose side are you on?"

"The side that gets you laid."

"This isn't about sex."

"Every time you look at him, your eyes say otherwise."

"So do other parts of my body," I admit.

"Can we get back to my wedding?" Mallory asks kindly, the look on her face making it clear she's not selfish.

She's doing me a favor.

"Ribbon!" I chirp. "So excited! So many colors!"

A grimace is her reaction.

"I liked you better when you were questioning your life," she snaps, sliding the binder to Perky, who thumbs through it.

"You have an entire page devoted to lighters and long matches?"

"The colors of the handles and the boxes matter, Perk."

"Where's your page on color-coordinated bottles of lube?"

Mal blushes.

"You have one, don't you?"

It all boils down to this, I realize, as Perk and Mal argue over... lube.

We're all on the side that gets us laid.

CHAPTER 6

*T*he first day of classes every school year is the scariest one for kids and teachers. So many unknowns.

This year, though, the scariest day has a completely different date attached to it.

I arrived early today, ready to give each child as much time as he or she needs. We've created a special schedule, with the twenty children coming in pairs, two at a time, five minutes apart. It means the first hour of school will be calmer, more methodical, less chaotic. Some kids will need to arrive a bit late, but not one parent complained.

Truth be told, I needed to build a little time in there for the parent hugs, too.

Mattie and Jahra are the first kids to arrive. Jahra hands me a big, rolled-up paper.

"What's this, sweetie?" I ask her as she fiercely hugs my neck, legs wrapping around my waist. We generally don't hold the children like this, but her grandmother's face spreads with a weepy grin and suddenly, I'm enveloped by a sari-wearing, grey-haired woman named Nisha, whose grip on my shoulder rivals her granddaughter's.

"Bless you," Nisha whispers as we hug so tight, I think a rib will crack.

"Nani!" Jahra shouts against my chest. "I can't breathe!"

Stepping back, Nisha looks at us, her weathered hand coming up to my face, cradling my cheek. Her eyes capture mine, the old, grounded energy in her making me feel so heavy, like a rock that weathers everything, never needing to move, mere presence more than enough.

"You," is all she says before spotting a very excited Mattie, who is jumping up and down with eagerness, a wrapped present in his hand.

"Thank you," I whisper as Nisha nods, turning back to walk the five blocks to the home where she lives with Jahra, her son, and daughter-in-law.

"FIONA!!" Mattie shouts. "This is for you!" Shoving a present at me, he beams.

I take it. Small pieces of tape cover every possible surface, the wrapping paper lumpy.

"You wrapped it yourself!" I exclaim.

"How could you tell?" he asks as Candi stands next to him, quivering and sobbing. Mattie looks up at her and frowns. He pats her hand.

"It's okay, Mommy. Daddy didn't hurt her like he hurt you. Fiona stopped him. Uncle Chris says Daddy can't hurt people anymore. He's not a bad man. He just did a bad thing."

The words come out of his mouth just as Fletch appears behind Candi, jaw setting tight as he overhears what Mattie's just said. Our eyes meet, his full of unspoken pain. The fact that he's here, his hand resting carefully on his sister's shoulder, means so much.

"Fiona, I'm so sorry," Candi chokes out, face crumpling as Mattie ping-pongs his attention between me, his mother, and his uncle. They don't know this, but I built in an extra buffer for them, the next pair of kids coming in ten minutes, not five.

Before I say anything to her, I bend down, one knee touching the ground, my leggings covered with brightly colored donuts and my tunic a pink, frothy thing with piping the color of the icing on one of the donuts.

My new slippers have hard soles on them.

"Mattie, thank you."

"Open it now," he insists.

Candi nods, and Fletch offers her a handkerchief, an honest-to-God old fashioned one, ironed neatly in a square. She makes a hand motion that says I should open the gift.

When I do, I stare at it, dumbfounded.

"It was Mattie's idea," Candi says, uncomfortable.

Fletch's throat bobs with emotion as he realizes what Mattie gave me.

"Is this a lock-picking kit?" I ask, the case designed to hold the same kind of long, thin metal tool Rico used to break in.

"Yes! That way, you have your own if someone tries to come here again and do a bad thing," he says, hugging me.

And then he runs off, waving to Michelle, who looks like she's about to crawl into a heating vent.

"I'm so, so sorry!" Candi says, chest rising quickly, her hands ice cold as I reach for her, trying to reassure her. "The–the counselor the school sent to talk to him told me I should let him give you that, because he's working through his feelings and–"

I pull her into a real embrace, chin on her shoulder. Fletch's helpless look is one of raised eyebrows and a keen sense of frustration that he can't rewind time and make it so Rico didn't do what he did.

In my classroom, and to Mattie and Candi long before.

It's okay, I mouth to him. He nods, then takes in a long, deep breath. The urge to comfort him is overwhelming.

The *need* to comfort him is almost unbearable.

"Jesus, Fiona, I can't believe you did whatcha did," Candi says, chattering. It's not a cold day, but she's freezing, a semi-shock state making me worried for her.

"I did what I needed to do, Candi. And I don't want you or Mattie to ever, ever think any of what Rico did is your fault. Don't you ever tell me you're sorry. You have nothing to be sorry about. You and Mattie are important members of our school community and we love you."

Her grip on me is fiercer than Jahra's.

We're both sobbing as Fletch turns away, and–is he wiping a tear from his eye? The way he coughs makes me think so.

"I'm, uh, going to be in the car," he says to Candi without turning around.

As she pulls away, Mattie comes running back to us, tugging on the hem of her shirt. She looks down, pain and love pouring out of her.

"Yes, honey?"

"Uncle Chris is staying, right?"

"Uh huh. I have to go to work, but Fletch will be right there." She points outside, to a small black compact car. Fletch has the door open. He waves.

Mattie waves back. I have to curl my fingers into a fist to stop myself from doing the same.

"What's he doing?" I ask as Mattie runs back into the other room to play with Michelle. Ani's busy with Jahra.

"Mattie cried and cried and refused to come this morning," Candi whispers. "We explained that his dad is in jail and can't come back here. But he wanted to give you the locksmith kit, so that was the first sign he might be willing to try. Fletch came over when I called him and Mattie said he'd come to school only if Uncle Chris was there to guard everyone." Finger quotes punctuate the word *guard*.

"Fletch is going to sit in his car *all day*?"

A light laugh, the first sign of anything not traumatic, comes out of her. "Yeah. My brother's a good guy." More sniffling, more tears. "Why couldn't I pick someone like him? But nooo. I have to pick an abusive fu–"

Bzzz

Her phone startles us.

"Shit. That's my first client. I must be late already." Candi is a home health aide. "Oh. No. Just need to add gluten-free bread to her shopping list." Candi smiles through tears. "It's gonna be one hell of a day."

"Mattie's safe here, Candi. You don't have to worry. And you can always watch the webcam."

"No," she chokes out. "Hell, no. You have any idea what that did to me? Getting a text from other parents about what was happening and logging into the app to see *that*?" Profanity fills the air between us. "If you don't mind, Fiona, I'm done watching webcams. I'll just take your word for it when I pick him up at the end of the day."

A squeeze of my hand and she's off, climbing into a small red SUV, waving at Fletch as she drives away.

I stare at him.

He doesn't look up from his phone.

Janelle and Myles are my next two students.

For the next hour, I greet the other eighteen kids and parents, everyone nervous, all of them overwhelmingly grateful, emphasis on overwhelming.

By the time the kids are all settled, the parents assured, and the classroom in order, I'm ready for a nap.

Too bad naptime isn't until 12:30. Today, I'm grabbing my own mat and catching some zzzs with the rest of them.

I walk into the other room where Michelle and Ani have everyone in a circle, already speaking in hushed voices. Miguel, a little boy with big brown eyes and a crooked smile, looks at me.

And points.

"You scared me. When you roared."

"I did?" Controlling my expression, I seek to affirm. Validate. Confirm. "You heard me?" Silent questions pour out of me as I catch Ani's eye.

One shoulder goes up. "We could hear you in the woods," she says softly.

"You were really, *really* loud!" Miguel squeals.

"Like a dinosaur." Lisa nods her head so hard, her blonde braid flops against her back.

"No–like Sully from *Monsters, Inc.*," Miguel corrects.

"No! Like the big furry guy in the *Star Wars* movie," Jahra replies. "The big monster." She makes a Chewbacca roar.

"Monster?" Myles asks, trying so hard to join the conversation. "Pond monster on Steven Sharer channel on *YouTube!*" he cries out, using the only concept he has about monsters that connects to language he knows.

That's also the longest sentence I've ever heard out of him. His speech pathologist is going to be so thrilled with his mean utterance length expansion. Normally, I'd take time to appreciate the huge gain this represents, but the situation in my classroom is spinning wildly out of control.

All because of my *roar*.

"Nuh UH! Miss Fiona roared like a T-Rex!" Janelle shouts.

"She screamed like the dinosaur in Jurassic Park!" Miguel counters.

"Okay, okay, everyone, let's settle down—"

"If Jahra points a stick at me, can I step on her neck?" Janelle asks, eyes narrowing as if she suspects Jahra has considered this.

"What? No! Of course not." My stomach drops.

This welcome back is *not* going as planned.

"But Mattie's dad pointed a knife at you and *you* got to step on his neck!"

"I think Miss Fiona needs to sit at the Peace Table with Mattie's dad and hold hands until they can be friends," Lisa says firmly.

Twenty pairs of wide eyes look to me.

"My daddy's in jail. He can't come to the Peace Table," Mattie says, lip quivering.

"That means he can't hurt people now." The set of Janelle's chin makes it clear she approves of Rico's current residence.

"He didn't hurt anyone *here*," Mattie defends.

"My mommy said she knew you when you were in high school and she showed me your picture. You used to shave your head. Why'd you cut all your hair off like that?" JoJo asks, red curls covering perplexed eyes.

Ani and Michelle give me nearly identical looks that make it clear they want to see those pictures. I look down at my slippers and feel a sudden craving for my old Doc Martens.

"Did you have cancer? My cousin had cancer and her hair all fell out. Even her eyebrows! She looked like an egg," Lisa declares.

Michelle and Ani shoot me looks that say, *What do we do now?*

I shrug.

Hell if I know.

"Like Humpty Dumpty?" Myles asks Lisa.

"No. She wasn't broken."

"Took picture with Humpty Dumpty at Storyland last summer with my grandma!" he adds.

Go Myles!

"I want to go to Storyland! Miss Fiona, can we do a field trip to Storyland?" Lisa enquires.

"No, honey. Storyland is almost a three-hour drive from here."

"Then how about Chipotle? I like Chipotle!" Mattie chimes in.

These children are members of Generation N.

The N is for *negotiate*.

For the next two hours, as we transition to routine activities, I do my best to soothe and calm, to speak in age-appropriate ways about what happened with Rico. Preschoolers are remarkably simple *and* complex beings. Simple in needs, simple in thoughts, complex in emotions.

Which makes them, well… *human*. Like the rest of us.

By noon, after a story and an art project, they've mostly moved on. We settle them at their various tables, Myles, Laura, and Miguel at the peanut-allergy one, everyone else eating peanut-free lunches but sitting separately.

Michelle waves for me to go eat in peace.

Coffee first. Lunch, second.

I'm brewing my cup in the cheap office machine when it dawns on me.

Fletch.

Having no idea how he takes his coffee, I make him one in a spare travel mug, grabbing some sweetener and sugar packets. If he needs cream, I can always pop back in. Careful not to disturb the class, I go out the back door, walking down the alley behind the insurance agency, suddenly seized by the emotional residue of what the children, Michelle, and Ani were feeling as they escaped this way.

Swaying, I lean my back against the building wall, both hands full of travel mugs: mine and Fletch's. Why did I bring mine?

I recover quickly and find my way to his car. His eyes are closed, head leaning against his seat.

I tap awkwardly on the window. He snaps to attention, gruff and frowning.

When he realizes it's me, he cocks one eyebrow, tilting his head. The window has condensation on it, and as he lowers the glass, he comes into full view.

"Here," I say, handing him a mug with Bailargo's logo on it. The local dance studio handed them out at last year's Dance and Dairy festival on the town common. "It's black. Do you take cream or sugar?"

"No. Thanks. Thank you," he says, voice filled with growing gratitude as he realizes what I'm doing. "I told Mattie I wouldn't leave at all, and now I'm in a pickle."

I laugh. "In a pickle? Haven't heard that phrase since my great-grandma said it." Mallory's use of the word *smitten* comes to mind.

Which makes me realize I am.

Smitten.

With *him.*

One shoulder shrugs. "Isn't this your lunch time?"

"Yeah. What about you?"

"Brown bagging it. But I forgot coffee." He holds up the mug and gives me a grateful smile. "Thanks again."

I nod, hovering and realizing that with each passing second, he's become more attuned to me. Fletch looks mighty fine no matter where he is, broad shoulders stretching the cloth of his shirt, his alert eyes focused entirely on me.

"Can I ask you a question?"

"Shoot."

"How do you – how do you do it? The paramedic work, I mean. It's been hard for me, since the attack. Falling asleep. Closing my eyes and not thinking about all the 'what ifs.'"

His head tilts slightly, attention sharpening. I've taken a light-hearted conversation and gone deep, fast.

He's going deep right along with me.

"What ifs?"

"You know. People getting hurt. Not being able to save them from pain. I've imagined a thousand times all the ways that day could have gone wrong, and then it occurred to me that you do this for a living. You see what happens when things *do* go wrong."

"You think about me?" he replies with a half smile, eyebrows lifted, eyes serious.

"I do. I mean, I did. I just – "

He reaches out the window to place his hand on my forearm. "I get it. Sorry to make fun like that. I didn't mean to – well – it's a serious question." The smile fades.

The hand stays.

"Because sometimes things do go wrong," he says in a low, troubled voice. "And we have to live with what we see, what we did, what we didn't do – what didn't work. And it's in your mind and memory forever." The pad of his thumb is on my pulse, as if he's checking on me even in this moment, marking me safe, his steady presence so centering.

Even as the topic most certainly *isn't*.

"Right." The word comes out in a pained rush. "Like when you worked on Dancy that time at Bailargo, when we were taking dance lessons. The entire time, I kept praying he would live. And you did it. You knew what to do and you saved him."

He shrugs. "That's my job."

"It's more than your job and you know it."

"I know. But if I talk about it, it's hard to do the job, you know?"

"No."

"You know the Mr. Rogers thing?"

"The what?"

"The quote. About how Mr. Rogers said in times of difficulty, his mother taught him to look for the helpers?" Fletch pulls his hand away, but not his eyes.

"Oh, yes. We use that a lot in my class."

"I think about that when I'm on a call that goes wrong. When the person we tried to save dies. When an injury causes severe pain I can't stop or help. When we have to white-knuckle our way through a horrible tragedy, second by second." He pauses to take a sip of his coffee. "And I'd be lying if I didn't tell you that the moment the 911 call came in from your classroom, I went straight to worst-case scenario mode in my brain."

"Oh, Fletch." Wrapping my arms around my waist, I lean closer to his window.

"I didn't – I couldn't get Mattie out of my mind."

He doesn't have to share the kind of images that plagued him, the half-crazed sequence of what could have been.

Because I have those thoughts, too.

"But," he says, clearing his throat and shaking his head. "None of that happened. Because of you."

I inhale, open my mouth to say something, and freeze.

I have been such an idiot.

My bladder starts to tickle me, the kind of intrusive body sensation that makes it impossible to think.

"If you need to use the bathroom, feel free to come in," I blurt out, instantly regretting my words.

He laughs, though the amusement dies out quickly. "I don't think having a man appear at the door, knocking, is a good idea, Fiona. Today of all days."

"Good point."

"I don't want Mattie looking out here and not seeing me."

"Is he looking out here?" I can't keep the surprise from my voice.

Fletch points. Mattie's in the window, hands cupped around his eyes, clearly checking in on Fletch.

"Yeah. He's... well, I think it'll be a while before he's okay."

"Children are remarkably resilient," I say lamely, regretting the words the second they're out.

"Sure they are. But this isn't your normal, everyday problem, you know?"

Candi's cold hands come to mind. "Yes. I know."

Bzzz

My phone surprises me. I pull it out of the big pocket in my tunic.

Have you checked your dating app? Perky texts.

"Go. You've got kids to teach," Fletch says, shooing me.

I look at the text.

Look back at him.

Take a sip of coffee.

And then I wave as I go back inside.

Through the back.

I haven't given the stupid dating app a moment's thought, but as I settle in for a quick lunch in my office, facing the dating app sounds way better than answering hundreds of emails.

Huh. Nine people interested. I look.

Six dick pics. Left, left, left, left, left, and *ohmyGod*, where would you fit that thing?

Definitely left.

That leaves three. Guy #1: a picture of a bloody deer between his legs. Obviously a hunter. I have nothing against hunters, but that is not sexy.

Guy #2: says he's thirty-five. Maybe in dog years.

Guy #3: outdoorsy type. Long blond hair. Minus points for the man bun in one picture. Plus points for mentioning buying local. Works for a nonprofit that places first-generation college students at small liberal arts schools. His photo is not taken in his car–that alone makes him stand out from the crowd.

What makes me swipe right, though, has nothing to do with anything the guy says, or any aspect of what he looks like.

What makes me swipe right, and spend the next half hour chatting–finally settling on a date tomorrow evening at Beanerino, the coffee shop where Perky works–is this: He seems grounded. Stable. Settled.

And he's *not* Fletch.

If I'm going to stop being defined by my past, to let go of letting other people tell me who I am, I have to act.

I have to take risks.

I have to be anyone but Feisty.

The pull of Fletch's goodness (and, I confess, hotness) takes too much of my past and blends it with my present.

I need to look to the future.

And Man Bun, the dude in the app, represents something pretty close.

So I say *yes* to coffee.

Yes to a stranger.

Yes to risk.

And maybe, just maybe, when I say *yes* to the unknown, I take some of that energy Mallory noted that I spend filtering out Fletch, and I filter in something worthwhile.

Maybe.

But that *maybe* makes me open my email.

And say *yes* to someone else.

Someone important.

Someone I've been avoiding.

CHAPTER 7

"*I* am so glad to see you," Jolene says as she opens her front door and steps out barefoot, moving with me toward the spot where we will earth. In anticipation, I've already removed my shoes, the crisp grass making my toes curl against it, to grasp a bit more of the anchor that I desperately need.

You won't find a website with Jolene's name or business on it. Perky calls her place The Quantum Cottage. You become a client through word of mouth only. I was fortunate, a few years ago, to have a friend of a friend of a friend suggest me to her.

She is pure energy.

"I should have come sooner," I admit as we stand before each other, right hand on belly button, left over the heart, bare feet connecting with the electrified charge of dirt and stone, dust and dead leaves, of energy and home.

Kind eyes meet mine. "There are no shoulds. Only what pulls you toward."

"I thought I could wait. I thought I was fine. But the children and the parents and then there's Fletch and–"

"Breathe. Let's breathe together. Your energy grid looks like a time-lapse photo of Los Angeles traffic at night. Just... inhale. Exhale. In. Out." A breeze pushes my long hair against her arm, the curtain of lilac and platinum like gossamer on the wind.

Tangled gossamer that hasn't had a decent deep-conditioning treatment in too long.

The brush of my own hair against my bare wrist feels pleasant. Soothing. A reminder that I'm a body as well as a mind and heart. Our energetic layers need attention and kindness, just like our physical bodies and emotions do.

It's so easy to spend your entire life unaware, always a bit on edge as we pick up on energy but don't understand or see it. I'm grateful that my life has brought me to teachers who encourage me to let intuition be my guide. Dad calls it gut instinct, which is the closest he's ever going to come to the idea of a higher, wise self.

But I'll take what I can get.

"Open yourself. Accept love. Accept power. Accept and take from the world what you need, Fiona. You've given so much. It's time to let the rebalancing feed you. Refusing what the universe offers will only keep you unstable. You must *receive*."

A rush of tingling ripples through me, filling my mind and soul. I am nothing but breath.

Breath that brings in.

Breath that lets go.

When my mind settles, thoughts melting into a puddle of water that turns to a rushing brook feeding a beautiful waterfall of shush-shush-shush, I open my eyes.

Jolene's hair, long and braided behind her back, has grey and white frizzies that frame her face as the sun caresses her back.

"Better?"

"Yes. I feel so blocked."

Her brow knits. "That's not what I see. You have no boundaries now, Fiona. The world has reset them. You need to feel the edges. Find your perimeter."

"My what? I thought I was supposed to stay open to receive."

"To receive energy, yes. And love. But if you don't have the protection of the light around you, it flows right through you. It never recharges you."

"Being open is what makes me one with everything."

"But trying to do that before you've learned what you need to learn in this lifetime means you learn nothing."

"I am so confused."

"Good! It's in the confusion that we find serenity." Pulling gently, she guides me by the hand back up the stairs of her small deck and into the giant, multi-story solarium attached to her house. Smelling of cedar, the room is filled with light, a simple structure of glass panes between large wooden beams. Inside this room, we stand and face south.

"Ask for what you need."

I try. Words fail me.

Jolene turns to a table next to her, covered in small wooden boxes. Each holds a different set of energetic substances: flower essences in one, essential oils in another, mineral drops in a third, dried herbs in a fourth, and so on. I don't know what's in the other boxes, because Jolene has never given me anything other than those first three, but now she reaches for a bright red box.

This is new.

Opening it, she extracts a crystal, a muted purple form that is lumpy and unpolished.

"Before I give this to you," she says, cradling it, "I ask that you do not seek out its name."

"Why not?"

"I cannot tell you. It is my only request, though. Hold it on the right side of your body. Weave the light around you for protection. Do Celtic knots and envision them in blue while holding this." Warm fingertips slide against my open palm as she hands it off.

Heavy and light at the same time, the crystal does... nothing.

Normally, I sense energy in a stone with as much power as a crystal. A low-grade hum, a warmth, a tingling, or a heaviness that belies its actual weight.

Hollowness is all I sense. A nothing feeling that disturbs me.

I want it out of my hand.

Jolene is perceptive, her eyes on mine. "What do you sense?"

"Nothing. It's empty."

"Yes. It holds space."

"What does that mean?"

"You have too much right now, Fiona. You have the gratitude of so many in this realm. All those children are unharmed because of you. Your attacker is harmed at your hand—"

"Foot, technically," I mutter.

"Foot." She smiles. "But taking so much on has left you with no space. The energy is piled in layers that tangle and twist, serving no one. It's trapped."

"That's why I come here. So you can help me release it."

A firm no comes from her head shake. "This is different."

The stone's nothingness pulls me down, making me feel dark and cold.

"Different?" The soles of my feet itch to go back outside.

"Only you can do what needs to be done. In the moment

when your body knew what to do, it was the vibration–the higher one that let you access your wise self–that guided you. Now that you're no longer in crisis, the energy of everyone around you is clouding that central self. You need to hold space. I can't do that for you."

"But this crystal can?"

"If you let it."

"This is *not* what I wanted to hear."

"You don't trust space to take you where you need to be?"

"I don't–I don't know. I thought that nature abhors a vacuum."

She smiles. "Space isn't a vacuum."

"You want me to carve out emptiness."

"No, space."

"What's the difference?"

"That is for you to discover."

"This feels very cryptic!"

"When we change our patterns, everything feels like a mystery. Because it is. That's what living fully feels like. One big, joyful mystery."

I'm starting to identify with Perky, who thinks Jolene is full of nonsense. My irritability is understandable–and completely manufactured by some piece of me that doesn't want to do the hard work Jolene is pointing me to do.

Self-awareness is a double-edged sword. After a while, I can sense when one self inside me is fooling another self. You would think the clarity would help.

Instead, it just threatens the piece of me that is avoiding pain.

"Fiona," she says gently. "You are in the middle of a massive identity shift. Old Self and New Self. Part of your struggle is that you've tried so hard to close Old Self off.

"Old Self?"

"Feisty."

I bristle. She catches it, instantly.

"See? You put up a wall when someone calls you that. Why?"

"Because I hate it."

"You hate yourself?"

"No! I hate the nickname. I'm not that person anymore."

"Aren't you?"

"I'm not! I don't shave my head or do kickbox training or pour myself into stripping all the color out of life so I can put up walls! I don't put up a shell of anger and hold people back by refusing to participate in the world. When I was younger, that's all I did! I poured myself into being kickass."

"Can't you be kickass now?"

"Preschool teachers aren't kickass."

"You were. You are. Why can't you be both?"

"Because… because… "

"Spoiler alert: You can. You *must*. Otherwise, the fight you fight won't be in the world. It will be inside yourself."

"You're saying I have to go back to being shitkicking Feisty? The girl who dropkicked Fletch when he tried to kiss me in seventh grade?"

"Fletch." The way she says his name sends shivers up and down my spine.

"What about him?"

"You see him through the eyes of your Old Self. But I think New Self is starting to pay attention to him."

"What? No! He's just–he's popped back into my life. It's all Mallory's fault."

"What did she do?"

"I'm a bridesmaid. Her fiancé, Will, asked Fletch to be a groomsman. So now I'm stuck in the wedding party with a guy I've actively avoided for nearly seventeen years."

"That's a lot of energy to spend on someone."

"I'm not spending any energy on him. I'm avoiding him."

"Avoidance uses plenty of energy. More than we think."

"I–"

The crystal in my hand begins to pulse.

Either that, or my blood pressure is skyrocketing.

Bzzz

"Oh! I'm so sorry," I gasp. "I forgot to turn the ringer off." My phone feels hot in my hands as I drop the crystal and tap on the screen. "My date. It's a reminder."

"You have a date with Fletch tonight?"

"Fletch? What? Of course not!"

"Are you sure?" Clear eyes meet mine.

"I think I would know if I had a date with Fletch."

"Fair enough." Smiling, she stands, reaching for both my hands. "Rejecting Old Self causes you pain, Fiona. Embrace her."

"She stands for everything I don't want to be."

"But she *is* you. And she helped you when you needed it most. When your classroom needed it. That Old Self joined forces with New Self and defended vulnerable people. You should be proud."

"Proud?"

"Yes. Proud. Have you told your selves how proud you are of them? All of them?"

"Proud." Mom and Dad have said it. Sharon and Roy did, along with Mal, and Perk, and half of the town. All the classroom parents.

But not once has it occurred to me to say it to myself.

"I'm proud of me," I whisper, closing my eyes, my seventh-grade self with bony shoulders, baggy pants, and a bound chest rising up, standing taller, heels anchored and knees unlocked.

"Say it again."

"I'm proud of me," I intone, this time envisioning my current self, pink glasses and lilac-platinum hair.

"Say it to all of the pieces of you until it feels true."

Bzzz

She laughs. "And go have your date with Fletch."

"It's not Fletch!"

She smiles and repeats, "If you say so."

THE TABLE at Beanerino has a few advantages:

It's in a quiet corner.

It's not too close to the bathroom.

It's not under a stereo speaker.

And most of all, I'm out of Perky's line of sight at the barista counter.

"I can't believe you picked up a shift just so you could scope out my date with Tom," I hiss at her as she brings me a giant mug of chai, cinnamon sprinkled on top in a pattern of latte art that—hold on.

"Is that a penis?" I accuse, peering closely at my cup.

"Yes. Glad you can still recognize them."

"HEY!"

She smirks. "You said the dude has a man bun, right?"

Soft jazz plays from the coffee shop's speakers, the glow of streetlights outside making the inside feel more sophisticated. After five p.m., Beanerino turns into a wine bar, a change the owner, Thiago, made about six months ago. You can still get the full menu of coffee and tea drinks, but also grab a glass of pinot noir or Chablis.

Raul comes over, holding a glass of water, looking

around the sparsely occupied shop. Wednesday nights are pretty slow. Two couples sit near the windows. One lone woman sips a glass of white wine at the counter, reading on her phone.

"Man bun, right?" Raul says to me with a twinkle in his eyes.

"You told *him*? Perky!"

"I told everyone."

"That's not a good defense!"

"Who said I needed a defense?"

"Don't you feel a shred of guilt for violating my privacy?"

"Uh," Raul interjects. "Have you *met* Perky?"

Breathe, I remind myself. *Just breathe.*

"You two need to give me and my date some privacy," I inform them both.

Raul looks at my drink. "Is that a penis?" His big, brown eyes cut over to Perky. "My dad did not send you to artisanal latte art classes so you could draw genitals in the milk!"

"Genitals were half the class! You should see my clitoris!"

"I have no desire to see your–you know!"

"Why not? It's beautiful!"

Raul turns redder.

"And it tastes like heaven," she adds. "A little bit of cinnamon, some vanilla, and–"

Raul turns a dusky shade of red, an adobe color that sets off his topaz eyes. "Perky," he says in a low voice. "Remember the sexual harassment training?"

"Not my actual body part–I meant my artistic rendering on a latte!"

"I will take a pass on *both*," he says firmly.

A tall man in a suit walks into the coffee shop. Long

face, pinched, slightly worried expression. He's familiar, but I can't place him. The woman at the bar turns, glances at her phone, then gives him an expectant look.

"Cheryl?" he asks. She beams, pushing a long wall of blonde hair off one shoulder and onto her back as she stands. An awkward hug ensues.

First date. App date.

"Isn't that the asshole cop from the emergency room last week?" Perky says out of the corner of her mouth. The guy settles in at the counter, Raul moving off to wait on him.

"I think so. Now leave."

Two women, not together, trickle into the shop. Business is starting to pick up. A guy alone at a table looks at his phone, then at the women.

"Why would I leave?"

"Because you'll scare off Tom."

"Man Bun's name is Tom?"

"See? Leave."

"Look at him. Go, dude! Get up the courage," she says under her breath, the random guy's unasked-for cheering section.

"What are you doing?"

"The wine bar is nothing but a meat market. This is where all the men on that dating app tell women to meet them."

"What?"

"We need to rename Beanerino the Bootycallerino."

"Perky!"

"What? It's not my fault Man Bun asked you for a first date where there's more jizz in the bathroom stalls than in a dirty sock at Boy Scout camp."

"PERKY!"

The door opens. I look over, searching for Man Bun... I mean, Tom.

And instead I see Fletch.

"Fletch?" I gasp as Perky smiles and walks away, abandoning me in my time of need.

"Hey, Fiona. What're you doing here?" He looks down at my drink. "Nice penis."

"Excuse me?"

He points to my chai latte. "Perky did a good job. I was in here last week and she made some beautiful flower patterns on my latte." He frowns, then his eyebrows shoot up. "Hold on. Those weren't flowers, were they?"

I laugh.

"Wow. And they seemed so... detailed. And gorgeous."

My sides are splitting.

"Please... stop... flowers..." I gasp.

"That latte did give me a sudden desire to go to a Georgia O'Keeffe show, though."

I rush to take a sip of my chai latte and make the penis go away. Fletch watches me, mouth spreading into a wider grin, his green eyes shining as he crosses his arms over his chest.

It's only then that I realize he's wearing real clothes. A crisp, light purple dress shirt, open at the neck, tucked into khakis. He has actual leather shoes – and not for weight lifting or cross-training – on his feet. His hair is styled but not sticky, and he has a close, clean shave.

His aftershave is *divine*.

"You're not in workout gear. Or a paramedic's uniform," I say as I blot the foam on the tip of my nose, wondering if it's ruined my makeup.

"And you look lovely tonight. A little overdressed for a Beanerino latte with Perky," he says, waving to her from across the room as she swings a hand towel in the air like she's a date-night air traffic controller.

"I have a date."

"So do I."

"You don't have a man bun, do you?"

He looks down at his crotch. "Is that like camel toe for guys?"

Bzzz

I look at my phone. It's Tom.

Running late. Couldn't get a train that had room for my bike. Be there in ten.

"Your date ditch you?"

"What? No!" I lick my lips, tasting sugary penis residue. "What about you? You're meeting someone?"

"Blind date. New app." He shows me his phone. It's the same app I'm using.

My heart sinks. "You didn't use a fake name, right? Call yourself Tom?"

"No. Why?"

"Whew. For a moment there, I thought the app matched us up. That would be crazy."

He laughs. "Nah. I'm not here to find a Fiona. My date's name is Cassie."

Soft jazz changes over to a darker funk orchestra. "Huh?"

"Cassie Jones." Craning his neck, he looks around. "Dark hair, longer than yours. Beautiful profile shot. Says she likes–"

"You... how... you're not really here for her, right?"

"I am. She's been sexting with me for days. You think I'd pass up an offer to meet her here at Beanerino? This place is where dating app desperadoes come for quick sex. Don't touch anything in the bathrooms," he whispers under his breath.

I look up at Perky. Did she sneak into my app and sext with Fletch, posing as my alter ego?

"Uh, I hate to break it to you, but *I'm* Cassie Jones."

"What?" Shock makes his jaw drop. He leans in. A whiff of his aftershave makes me swoon.

"I'm Cassie."

"You're the one who's been sending me all those beaver shots?"

"Beaver?"

"Naked pictures of your–"

"I KNOW WHAT A BEAVER SHOT IS," I say a little too loudly.

Perky snickers.

I'm going to dropkick her so hard.

"And no, I did not send those to you!"

"Then who did?"

"Perky!"

"Yes?" She's suddenly there, bringing Fletch a black coffee. "Depth charge, just how you like it. Added some macchiato-level foam to cut the strength."

"Thanks."

"Perky, did you send crotch shots to Fletch?"

"What? God, no. Why would I do that? My phone's tainted enough. I would never send naked pictures of myself to anyone, ever."

"I mean beaver shots of me!"

"Of you? When would I have taken pictures of your vagina?"

Two guys at a table nearby lean in. So does a woman.

"Not *my* vagina! *Your* vagina posing as *my* vagina!"

Fletch takes a long sip of his coffee and watches us.

"My vagina doesn't need to pose as anyone else's vagina, thank you very much. It has its own identity and has no need to be Fiona's Fake Flaming Lips."

Fletch sputters, shooting the tight blob of foam on his coffee all over my neck.

"That's the strangest pearl necklace I've ever seen,"

Perky says as I snatch the hand towel from her apron and mop myself.

Deep breath, I tell myself. *Deep breath*. Reaching into my pocket, I grasp the lump of crystal Jolene gave me.

And I ask for space.

Or a giant sinkhole.

Either will do right now.

"Why on Earth would you ask me that question, Fi? Why would I use my vertical taco to pose as your flesh tuxedo?" Perky seems genuinely confused, and Fletch is now doubled over, half grunting about his scalded uvula, half wheezing with uncontrolled laughter.

"Because Fletch claims he's here for a date with Cassie Jones!"

"Who is Cassie Jones?"

"MY FAKE PROFILE! I'M PRETENDING TO BE CASSIE JONES, REMEMBER?" I shout, all pretense at calmness long gone.

Unfortunately, as I shout that out, the front door opens and in walks a guy with a man bun. He stares at me.

"Tom?" I manage.

"Shortest first date ever," he mutters as he leaves, the door closing slowly, the sound as the air pressure equalizes sounding not unlike a queef.

"Oh, my God," I say, head in my hands as Perky half punches Fletch.

"Hey! You're up to something. Why did you just sabotage Fiona's date?"

"I did nothing!" he protests. "Just told her my date is Cassie Jones."

"The app matched you two? You're Tom the Man Bun?"

Fletch can't stop howling. He has one of those contagious laughs, and if I weren't so discombobulated, I'd laugh, too.

"Not Tom," he gasps. "But the app suggested 'Cassie' to me this morning. I immediately realized who it was and swiped left."

"What? Why would you swipe left? I'm a good catch!"

"And she sends great beaver shots," Perky adds.

"You're not helping."

"No one sent me shots of any animal, mineral, vegetable, or *flower*," he says, giving Perky major side eye. "I'm just messing with you."

"So you're not really here for Cassie Jones?"

"No. I'm meeting someone named Ariana."

"Oh."

The space this crystal is supposed to give me fills instantly with sadness tinged with shame. My date ditched me. Fletch is seeing someone else.

Someone else.

Jealousy, wholly misplaced and fiercely consuming, rises up in me like a green cloud of lust with no place to go. I have no right to feel this, but I do.

I do.

It fills the space, overflowing into the rest of me, the mist spreading far beyond where it should.

Respecting no boundaries, it is opportunistic. It stops only when forced.

"Hey," Fletch says, hiking his pants up slightly at the thigh before bending down, the gesture giving me an eyeful of those powerful legs under well-cut cloth. "I'm sorry about your date. I was just joking with you about Cassie, and it looks like it all went to hell. Want me to track that guy down?"

"No."

"Okay." He looks around. "Can I sit with you until my

date arrives?" Grimacing at his own words, he has the decency to backpedal. "Forget I said that."

"When is she supposed to be here?"

"Any minute."

Bzzz

Groaning, he reaches for his phone. "So help me, if I get stood up again..."

"Again? Women stand *you* up?"

He gives me a funny look, one eye on his phone. "Sure. Enough to make a last-minute text like this–yep. Sick cat."

"Who would lie about having a sick cat to get out of a blind date with *you?*"

"Why do you keep saying *you* like that?"

"Because look at you! You're a paramedic who owns a boxing studio. You have arms the size of tree trunks. You save lives for a living and you're super sweet to your nephew. You're the whole package. Why would anyone *not* want to date you?"

Every sound in the universe disappears.

The crystal in my hand lightens and begins to hum.

It's all I can hear.

And Fletch's eyes are all I can see as he holds my gaze with an intensity that feels like all the space in the world is taken up by *us*.

I stand, flustered. "I'm leaving. It's been a long day."

"Hey, Fiona, if things were different, I'd–"

"You'd what?"

"I'd ask you out."

But things aren't different, I say to myself, the words like a snake's hiss.

Frowning, he looks at his phone. "But Ariana says she'll be here twenty minutes late, so..."

And then I'm out of there, rushing into the dark night,

running to find my car, Jolene's words haunting me: *Go have your date with Fletch.*

So much for opening space in my life. You know what space feels like right now?

It feels like seventh grade.

CHAPTER 8

"*F*iona," Rafaela says in a surprise call, the phone ringing on my nightstand, next to my glasses. For some reason, I grabbed the phone first, which makes the sound of her voice more acute. I'm half blind without my glasses, and I hate contacts.

"Hi, Rafaela. Everything okay?" She's never called me out of the blue. Fear spikes through me.

"It's great, actually. Remember that workout-wear company that offered you a high-five-figure contract? MPOWR2Q? They're ready to sign."

"Sign?"

"Yes! And if you take the offer, they want to donate half a mil to an early childhood literacy organization. Or that Boys & Girls Club you mentioned."

"Half a what?"

"Half a million dollars."

As if having my eyes able to focus will help my brain comprehend, I search harder for my glasses, finding them but accidentally nudging them off the edge of my nightstand. Nimble fingers catch them in time. Opening the stems, I slide them on.

Bliss! Acuity is my friend.

"Say that again," I beg. "They're offering me *what?*"

She quotes a figure that wipes out all of my student loans and leaves enough to repair my car. Or even put a down payment on a new one.

"And half a mil to charity. The sponsor knew you wouldn't do it just for your own gain."

"Awwww."

"Don't take that personally. It's a PR stunt."

"Uh... thanks?"

"Here's the deal, though: Your video will be out of the news cycle shortly. Don't get me wrong—it was brave and all. But someone else is going to do something brave, and then the endorsement clowns all start chasing the new shiny."

"Okay?"

"Which means we have to act. Now. Can you do a photo shoot in four days?"

"Four *days?*"

"Yes, on Sunday. They'll find a local gym. Photographers will set it all up. Lighting, set design, you name it. The client wants the initial pics and short videos for Insta to be in rotation within two weeks, to get ahead of the holiday attention-grab rush. We're already headed toward Halloween and after that, it's a mess in terms of getting eyeballs. Can you do it?"

Every word out of her mouth sounds like the marketing jargon I spent my entire college career avoiding. "I don't know. Can I? You're the one who knows this industry. Not me. I defer to you."

"God, I love you, Fiona. You are so easy."

"That's good?"

"It is for me. So, here's the deal: an electronic contract is coming your way. Sofia already covered the legal once-over."

"The *what*?"

"She paid for a lawyer to go over it," Rafaela says in a slower, more deliberative voice. "It's strong for you. You do this, and more endorsements may come."

"But what if I don't want—"

"*Shhh*. Be easy, Fiona! You want this one. Trust me. Being debt free will feel great. Not that I would know," she adds. "But you have to strike while the iron is hot."

"Will people think I'm a sell-out?"

"The half mil is designed to give you cover. Makes the company look good, makes you look like you did the endorsement to help kids. Win-win. And the lawyer said there's no conflict of interest with your teaching job. No morals clause in your contract."

"*Morals* clause?"

"We've had clients who lost endorsements because their employers prohibited it."

"Dang."

"Yours doesn't."

"Good!"

"And I made sure the contract doesn't specify nudity."

"Nudity?" I gasp, sitting up and throwing off the covers. I open my texts on my phone and shoot Perky an emergency one.

Can I trust Rafaela? I tap out and send.

"No nudity. That's what I'm saying. I've made sure there's none."

"Absolutely not!"

"Then we're on the same page."

Bzzz

She's great. Seriously. Take the workout-gear endorsement, Perky replies.

"Uh!" I gasp, outraged.

"You want more money?" Rafaela asks.

"What? No. Hang on."

You knew about this? I text Perky.

Of course. Take it.

"You're texting Persephone, aren't you?" Rafaela asks with a knowing laugh. "She told me this would happen."

"You two talked about me?"

"She cares, Fiona. We all do. I wouldn't act as the world's biggest attention sifter if I didn't care. This is a lot of money for a one-day photo shoot. The company is leveraging your viral success. Take it. Give a charity half a mil. Move on in a better financial position."

For once, I wish Mom and Dad were here. I've been raised to be extremely independent. Unlike most of my friends, they didn't pay for college. I've been financially independent since I graduated from high school, and I'm proud of being able to live on my own. Perky's been shoving money at me for years, but it tastes like failure to take it.

This endorsement deal tastes like something else. Bitter and–

"I got them up to a flat mil," Rafaela declares.

"Huh?"

"Told them you were wavering. Considering going with their competitor. That your fee didn't matter, but the donation did. A million dollars for children's programs, Fiona. Do it for the kids."

"Now you're just guilting me."

"Yep."

"You're not even going to pretend you're not?"

"Nope."

"You're hardcore."

"That's why Sofia hired me for her daughter. And now, for you."

Closing my eyes doesn't erase the sound of her clipped expectation. I pick up the vibe of her triumph at getting another half a million dollars donated to a worthy cause with a single text. Perky can feel electrical fields, the charged hum of transformers, the vibration of geopathic grid lines underground. That's not what I pick up.

Emotional energy is my kryptonite.

Rafaela is stoked, hungry, and eager to close this deal. Does she act as a filter for overwhelmed clients? Sure. But far beyond that is her real mission: going in for the kill.

Only instead of death, the end result of her hunt is corporate dollars.

"When you worked for Perky, how did you handle endorsements?" I ask softly.

"I didn't. Who the hell would want an endorsement from a half-nude woman with two dogs having sex on the pillow above her head?"

"I can think of plenty of web companies that would, but they all have the word 'porn' in them."

"Exactly. We went for settlement money." Speaking her language has turned this conversation into deep shorthand.

"Settlement?"

"Corporate bucks. Letters straight to legal threatening copyright-infringement suits. They coughed up to keep it out of the courts."

"Money? Perky's family has plenty of money."

"Money is never about money when it comes to corporations. This was about teaching people lessons. And Persephone donated it all to organizations that help labor conditions for women in South America."

Of course she did.

"You're not really a PR filter, are you?"

"I *am*. Of course I am. But if I can also help turn injustice into a lever for cracking open the wallets of corporations to help real, living human beings, then so much the better."

"Saving the world, one negotiation at a time."

"A mil is nothing to this company, Fiona. It's a lot to a Boys & Girls Club that gets full funding for after-school tutoring programs for a good, long time. Think of all the lives you'll change."

She's right.

I'm fully awake now, for sure. I get up and walk to my computer.

I open the electronic document and look at the signature section. *Click*

Click

Click

Finally I click Finish, and then–

"Yes!" she says. "Got it. Congratulations!"

My hands begin to shake.

"Thanks."

"Don't sound so glum! Think about the giant wire transfer coming your way soon!"

"And the million-dollar donation."

"And that. You did it again, Fiona."

"Did what?"

"The right thing."

"Did I?"

"Absolutely. You did it when you took down that attacker, and you're doing it now."

We hang up. I'm still shaking.

The crystal that Jolene gave me sits next to my computer mouse. I pick it up.

I close my eyes.

And I try to make space again.

FOUR DAYS AGO, Rafaela changed the course of my financial life.

Four days ago, a company offered to donate one million dollars to a cause I believe in.

Four days ago, I said *yes* to a photo and video shoot of me in a gym.

Four days ago, though, I didn't realize which gym they'd chosen.

"Hey," Fletch says with a smile as I open the door, half blinded by photographer's lights that are being turned on by an assistant. "Welcome."

"This is your gym." Too embarrassed to admit I didn't even look at the gym's name and address until twenty minutes ago, I blurt the words out, feeling a bit sick.

"Yes, it is. You like what you see?"

One of the assistants jerks her head up at his words, the side of her mouth curling in a knowing smile.

"I always do." Did those words really come out of me? "I mean, in gyms. Kickboxing gyms, at least."

"This place is more boxing than kicking, but we have something for everyone." Are these double entendres? The photographer's assistant is in full-blown grin mode now.

"I didn't realize we'd be filming here," I confess as a man dressed all in black turns his head like an eagle hearing a mouse scratch against a pine needle.

"Is that Ms. Gaskill?" His voice is low and measured. "I am Michael DelAmbrosio." Sleek black hair with streaks of silver at the temples frames a wide face, the slightest hint of jowls showing me his true age. Fit like a professional cyclist, he's small, tight, and uses compact movements to accomplish what needs to be done.

We shake hands. He looks at Fletch, then at me.

"You two know each other."

"We go way back. Fiona was the first person to knock me out."

"You didn't pass out!"

"From embarrassment, I sure did," Fletch mutters.

"Maybe if you hadn't tried to kiss me, you could have spared yourself the embarrassment!"

"Oh, dear," Michael says curtly. "You two *do* have a past." He looks Fletch up and down. "Did she bruise you?"

"Only my pride."

Michael's eyes narrow. "You two have *chemistry*."

"If you mean being around him is like pouring battery acid all over my body in chemistry lab, then yes."

Fletch laughs. "You're bitter. What's going on?" His eyes have questions his chuckling can't hide. Is that hurt I see?

The last time I saw him was at Beanerino, four days ago. He told me he would ask me out if it weren't for his date.

What was I supposed to do with that? Other than spend the last four days drinking obscene amounts of basil tea and clearing energy by burning herbs. Every inch of my skin smells like sage and I'm pretty sure that weird crystal Jolene gave me is some sort of voodoo.

"Not bitter," I snap.

"Your vibrators not doing the trick?"

Michael's hand goes to his throat, thick, dark eyebrows up over his rimless glasses.

"My what?"

"You know. Those vibrators you're working on elevating."

"*Vibrations* and vibrators are distinctly different."

We're now the focus of the crew's attention. Every person in Fletch's tiny gym is looking at us.

"One makes you feel like every part of the world is perfectly aligned so you can be happy," Fletch says, surprising me with his wisdom and insight.

"That's right."

"And the other one takes batteries."

"YOU!"

"What about me?"

"I don't think this gym is the right place for this shoot," I tell Michael.

"Oh, my dear, I think it's the perfect location," he purrs. "Your anger is razor sharp. You look ethereal *and* street tough. How do you manage both?"

"I, uh..."

Fletch is pulled away from us by a crew member who has some questions about lighting. The snippets of their conversation I overhear are hard to grasp as Michael bull-dozes through, saying something about the contract, my dewy skin, and...

"–have the two of you do some face-off stances, and–"

"Two of us? You hired a model to work with me? Rafaela said it would just be me."

Michael holds up one long, pale finger. I pause.

Waving Fletch over, Michael leans in, hand on his shoulder, the two eye to eye as Michael says something, Fletch nodding, his gaze cutting over to me twice.

"Sure," he says with a slow headshake. "If that's what you want."

"I can pay you a model fee. Nothing like what Fiona's getting, but–"

"Can you feature the gym in promos? Give me some free publicity? If yes, then no fee needed."

Neither of them is trying to be quiet. They're speaking in a normal tone of voice, and as it dawns on me that Michael wants Fletch to be in the video and photo shoot, my irritation becomes a full-blown body flush.

The guy I've spent most of my teen and adult life avoiding is about to be in the spotlight with me for this endorsement deal.

"Hold on!" I call out to Fletch. "You could get way more money than free publicity."

Michael gives me a murderous look that only serves to heighten my anxiety.

"I got it covered."

"What does that mean?"

"It means I'm fine."

"But why would you–"

His fingertips press lightly against my lips, shushing me.

That full-body flush becomes a blazing fire.

"It's fine, Fiona. You're the one who always says that and expects other people to believe you. I'm fine. Everything is fine. Now get your ass over to one of those bags and start treating it like Rico."

"You're not my trainer!"

"Not what you told that journalist at your door a week ago."

"I said that to get him to leave!"

"Maybe it wasn't just a distraction. Maybe it was a prediction. Don't you believe in signals from the universe? Could your vibrators–er, *vibrations*–be telling you something that brought you here to me?"

Jolene's words echo inside the cavern of emptiness that is my mind: *Go have your date with Fletch.*

This isn't a date.

Just like the coffee at Beanerino wasn't a date.

But the universe is definitely telling me something about Fletch.

"You have the only boxing gym in a half-hour radius of Anderhill. This isn't fate. It's pragmatism."

He hoots. "Since when did New-Agey woo-woo Feisty get pragmatic?"

"The minute your brother-in-law tried to hurt Mattie and my kids."

All joking drains out of his body. We're in a stare-off, anger at the tips of our fingers and toes, a richer, deeper awakening taking the overexcited atoms that smash against the walls of our skin and moving them faster, harder, the heat exquisitely unbearable.

"Just like that!" Michael says, shutter clicking. "Now I want you to take off your coat, Fiona, and Dia over there–" He points to a young woman with a headful of box braids, wearing a jean jacket like a second skin, way cooler than I've ever been, "–will get you dressed in our sponsor's gear."

My pulse has migrated to my belly, the second chakra pounding like a jackhammer as Dia escorts me to the women's locker room. The place is empty, and I recall Rafaela telling me something about the gym being rented for the shoot, exclusively.

I change into the skin-tight garments, leggings fitting like a glove, the spandex cotton cooling my skin as I slide into it. The sports bra doesn't constrict like most, and the crossover-back tank, a shade of lilac that seems chosen specifically to match my hair, gives the whole outfit a feeling of the surreal.

Only my pink-rimmed glasses stand out.

"Makeup and hair will deal with you next, Fiona," Dia calls out as I stare at myself in the mirror. Since my first semester of college, I've adopted a very different style of dress than I wore in high school. Back then, it was baggy overalls and jeans, tank tops in warm weather, hoodies over them in cold. But college gave me a chance to redefine myself. Stifled for so many years by an identity given to me that I didn't want, I left high school and stopped being Feisty, the ass-kicking girl who shaved her head and wore a tough shell of armor around herself.

I became Fiona, all softness and light. It felt easier–it *was* easier–to be vulnerable and hopeful. To talk about emotions rather than defend them.

To explore the space of a different personhood.

As I look at myself in the full-length mirror at a gym owned by the very man who gave me that identity seventeen years ago, I marvel at the synergy. Shedding who I was meant experiencing the painful rawness of new skin.

And here I am, raw again, this time–with him.

Again.

But not the same.

When I exit the locker room, Dia hands me an eyeglass case.

"What's this?" I open it, a pair of lilac and turquoise-framed glasses inside.

"Yours. Rafaela gave us your prescription. Said she got it from you. Our designers determined this was a good fit."

"I thought I'd be training. I don't wear glasses when I train."

"You wore glasses in the viral video," she explains as we head back to the main room.

"I also wore a long, flowing dress."

"The client sells clothing. Not glasses," she says with a wink. "And those are yours to keep when we're done. We have about ten other outfits for you, too. Plenty of sports bras."

"Thank you," I say quietly, fighting a case of the shakes.

"You may end up in all ten today, though. It all depends on Michael's perspective."

"Okay."

"You all right? You're getting quieter."

"Nerves."

"You? Nerves?" She laughs. "Just think of this shoot as one big asskicking of your attacker."

I have zero interest in that, but I'm too polite to say so. "How about I think of it as picking a fight with a guy I've known since we were little? I can't believe Michael wants Fletch in the pictures and video."

"Don't question artists. Michael's damn fine at what he does."

"I'm not questioning it. I just—of all the men in the world to have to work with, Fletch is..."

"The last guy on Earth you'd ever fuck?"

The f-word coming out of her jolts me, making me blush as we turn the corner. I'm not afraid of profanity—I couldn't be Perky's friend if I were—but the sudden image of Fletch and me naked and in bed, sweaty and carnal, takes that electrified word and turns the voltage up.

"You look ready for anything," Fletch says to me, his hands holding boxing gloves.

I blush harder.

"Not yet," Dia interrupts. "Makeup and hair first."

Forty-five minutes later, I'm wearing as much makeup on my face as I have collectively worn since 2009, and my hair makes me look like one of the actresses from that 1980s series about female wrestlers. But we're ready.

And I'm already tired.

"Fiona!" Michael says loudly from my right. "I want you to close your eyes."

"Okay."

"And tell me the story of what happened."

My eyes open.

"The whole story?"

"Not with words, sweetheart. With your body."

"With my body?"

"You're going to re-enact what happened. The moment you realized something was wrong. No words–only use words if they happened in the moment Rico attacked you. Otherwise, you are narrating with your joints and muscles, with your tendons and ligaments, with muscle memory and neurons firing. *Movement* is your scribe."

"You want me to silently re-enact what happened."

"Doesn't have to be silent. Just no words unless they're true to the moment, during the attack."

All eyes are on me. Fletch leans against one of the half walls near the front door. Lights and reflectors are everywhere, about seven crew members in various spots, three video cameras rolling.

I nod.

I close my eyes.

And I remember.

As I breathe, I remember the thin thread of unease that began even before I heard the squeal of tires. I open my eyes and turn my head toward an imaginary window in my classroom.

Then *bang bang bang*.

I look at an imaginary Rico, feel the rush of fear coursing through me, turn to an imaginary Michelle and have her take the kids out of the room. My body moves to the right, away from Fletch and toward Michael as I re-enact, remembering the backs of children's heads, the gut drop as I heard Rico picking the lock.

Tears fill my eyes. I freeze.

"Fiona," Michael says gently. "You're not remembering

this. You are *being* this. Be with the pain. Be with the anger."

"Maybe this is too much," Fletch interrupts, voice tight with emotion. Our eyes meet. I blink hard, willing the tears away, channeling his anger. He's not mad at me.

He's mad *for* me.

"No!" I call out.

"Are you sure?"

"I wasn't saying *no* to you. I was saying no to that rat bastard. No!"

"Did you say no when you kicked him? When he attacked you?" Michael asks, holding his camera up.

"I didn't have time to think. I just... I just—"

"Then *just*, Fiona. Just do that. Don't think. Do what you did. Be nothing but movement and instinct."

"Be Feisty," Fletch says, his voice pitching deep at the end, the word enraging me.

Pumped full of adrenaline and triggered as all get out by this, I turn to him and scream, "NO!"

He moves fast, body behind a punching bag as he braces it. "Here. Channel it all here."

The kick happens so fast, I can't feel the force of the impact, my ankle pushing all of the memory of the attack into the future, as if I can use movement and power to shove emotion through time. Fletch absorbs all the force, body holding steady.

"Again!" Michael shouts, his word unnecessary, as I one-two punch the bag bare knuckled, then kick twice, finally pulling back to do another Thai te tat roundhouse kick, imagining Rico's jaw moving forward in time, as if I could protect every threatened human being in the world with my body.

As if that's my responsibility.

"Now go after Fletch."

I stop.

"What?"

"It's okay," Fletch says, opening his arms as if inviting me to fight. "I can take whatever you've got."

"I don't want to fight you! You're not Rico!"

"No, but I want to catch the *emotion*, Fiona," Michael explains. "We're going for authenticity here."

"This isn't authentic!"

"It's as close as we can get."

"I don't want to beat Fletch up!"

He chuckles. "That isn't happening again, Feisty. Not this time."

The word *Feisty* is a red flag waved in front of a bull.

No, he's not Rico. And manufactured rage really, really isn't my thing. Absurd and over-the-top, the idea that I'm supposed to "fight" Fletch to reproduce the energy of what happened with Rico so a corporation can turn me into a commercial overloads my circuits.

And then I realize how I can use this.

Trauma loops in the psyche precisely because it has nowhere else to go. One of my child psychology continuing education classes taught us that re-enacting the trauma with a safe adult present, or with enough distance to re-imagine a safer outcome, can let the trauma release.

Fletch is about as safe as you can get.

Motioning his fingers toward me, hands out in a fighter's embrace, his eyes blaze and his saucy grin turns me into that very Feisty I've been trying to escape.

Rico crossed a big line. A bold line. Arguably, the line of my life.

Don't mess with people I love.

Especially when they can't fight back.

I charge Fletch, channeling it all, giving him what he's asking for.

He moves as I plow into the bag, my body still unable to attack him directly, his hands on my waist as I spin. Dropping to the ground, I use my lower position to twist out of his grasp, leg cocked and ready, but he's fast.

So fast.

Sweat sprouts all over my body like someone's misting me, the sudden crush of hormones, heat, and the pounding physicality of what we're doing making me wet.

In more ways than one.

I'm a mixture of revulsion and arousal, hating myself for feeling this way as his arms encircle me, my mind split between re-igniting the terror of the preschool attack and the very real, visceral feel of Fletch's skin against mine, welcoming the rutting, animal-like push of his slick thigh muscles against my arm as I fight him, working to pin him.

Failing miserably.

By the time we're done, this scrimmage is a joke, his body pressing me into the ground, arms immovable, my breath heating his nose as he looks down on me with a grin.

And then that fades.

Replaced by the unfiltered expression of a man who is falling. Falling, falling, *falling* into me.

Like time itself has collapsed.

And the sheer force of attraction is how we propel ourselves forward.

"This is great!" Michael shouts from the sidelines, the *click click click* of his shutter breaking the silence, Fletch's hips digging into mine, his hardness making it clear how he feels about me.

He doesn't move. My wrists are pressed into the mat, my hair tugging at the roots, caught under my shoulder blades.

"See?" he whispers in the space between us. "Not

happening again. You kicked my ass in seventh grade. But we're not tweens now, are we?"

As he says the words, my nipples harden, a yearning in the form of flesh centering between my legs. All I want to do right now is wrap my ankles around his waist and be screwed four ways to Sunday.

If that's even really a thing.

"No," I gasp, fighting and failing to be freed. "We're not. And if we're not, then what are we?"

"You tell me, Fiona. What are we?"

All the oxygen in the room rushes out. I'm left in space, floating, aimless and without anchor.

Jolene was wrong.

So wrong.

Space isn't my friend. It's my enemy. It's where everything safe becomes dangerous.

Where Fletch becomes the good guy.

The hot guy.

The I-need-him-in-me guy.

And where it's all caught on camera.

Because this journey started there, with Rico and cameras and people watching me because they *can*.

As Michael shoots photos and dictates angles, all I feel is Fletch's *rum-THUM-rum-THUM* beat, his heart against mine, telling me stories that go back seventeen years.

Before my heart wall had turrets. Before my heart wall had defenses and gun mounts and cannons.

Before I had a wall around my heart at all.

The kiss comes, unexpected but oh, so right. Fletch's mouth is inevitable, lips on mine like fate herself stepped into the frame and ordered us to do this. Logically, it makes no sense, but emotionally, it's what the universe dictates, the kiss aligning so many layers of my being that it's almost painful how perfect this is.

His hands loosen at my wrists, one threading its way through my hair, tugging just enough to break the sensuality of this moment, but also brutal enough to make my hips rise up and beg for more. His tongue is exploring me like no good guy should, nothing but bad and filthy and raunchy and a promise of slick, hot, no-holds-barred sex if I just let him in, just let him try, just let him—

Just plain old *let him*.

But first, I have to let myself.

"Excellent!" Michael shouts, lights suddenly bright and exposed, the kiss's magic ruined by the realization that we've been on camera the entire time, used and manipulated for the sake of a commercial.

Suddenly, the price paid to me for this is not enough.

"Um," he says as I push him off me, eyes jumping everywhere and nowhere, my body so dysregulated, it doesn't know how to act like a human made of flesh and bone.

"No," I whisper, the word getting louder the next time I say it. "No."

"No, what?" he asks, running a hand through his hair, spiking it in places where it's wet.

"Just no."

"Did I... was that not what you... because Fiona, Jesus, I—"

"You didn't do anything I didn't want."

Shoulders relaxing, he smiles at me.

Until I say:

"And that's the problem. I shouldn't want this at all."

CHAPTER 9

*W*e're settling in for morning circle, the children in their slippers, Jahra and Janelle ready to start passing the sacred stone, when Mattie looks at me innocently and asks, "Miss Fiona, are you going to marry my Uncle Chris?"

"Huh?" I'm finishing my sip of tea as Mattie asks. Nineteen children turn to me, eyes curious.

Michelle and Ani's eyes have *questions*.

"My mommy told Uncle Chris that he should kiss you again. When people kiss, it means they want to get married. Are you going to marry Uncle Chris?"

"If she does, then Miss Fiona will be your cousin," JoJo says with the gravity of someone who is completely wrong but has no idea.

"Not cousin. Aunt!" Myles calls out.

Half the students look at him in amazement. He's saying something unscripted.

And it's correct.

"I am not," I say, a frog in my throat, "I am not going to talk about my private life." Unfortunately, I'm not really ready to explain what that means to a group of four-year-olds.

"Is that like our private parts?" Jahra asks, looking at her lap with narrowed eyes.

"No, I don't mean–"

"Did Mattie's uncle give you a safe touch or an unsafe touch, Miss Fiona?" Janelle is in fiery warrior princess mode.

"He–"

"Private is personal! Adults don't touch you in your private places!" Myles shouts.

Michelle and Ani exchange a look.

I wave my hands. "All eyes here," I declare, and they follow my command, which makes me feel, for a shred of a second, like I have some sliver of control. "We are not going to talk about me, or Mattie's uncle. We are here to learn about ferrets and pineapples today."

"Do ferrets eat pineapples?"

"Are ferrets from Hawaii? My grandma went to Hawaii and ate pineapples."

"When I eat pineapples, my tongue falls off."

"Does not!"

"Does too!"

"Then how can you talk? I see your tongue!"

As the standard bickering begins, I breathe a sigh of relief. Whew. Saved from four-year-old curiosity by four-year-old arguing.

Michelle takes the peace stone gently from Janelle, who has dropped it unceremoniously next to her foot so she can enter into the fray, and says in a calm, authoritative, nonjudgmental voice, "I have the stone."

The class goes quiet.

We spend the next two hours moving through work cycles, a group effort to test the hypothesis that ferrets don't lose their tongues when they eat pineapple. Myles's mother helpfully lent me their family's pet ferret for this lesson, though I hadn't planned to feed it pineapple. I've done enough research to explain to the children that ferrets are carnivores and cannot digest fruits easily.

"But can he have a taste? Fairy the ferret really, really, *really* wants some!" JoJo squeaks as the animal wiggles in my hands.

"No!" Myles says, gleeful and excited to know something he can contribute. "He will be sick! We want him to be happy! Sick is not happy!"

"But I am happy when I eat pineapple," JoJo argues.

"You're not a ferret," Ani reminds her.

"I could be!"

Tap tap tap

Every student looks up, so startled as a group that two empty chairs behind standing children pitch backwards and fall with a muted thump on the braided rug. We all follow the source of the sound.

It's the front door.

Through the glass, Fletch waves, a big smile on his face.

"Uncle Chris!" Mattie gasps, running for the door at breakneck speed. Ani opens it.

"He *is* your husband!" JoJo shouts, just as Fletch walks in the door.

Mattie hugs his legs, looks up, and asks his uncle, "Are you and Miss Fiona gonna have a baby?"

Fletch looks at me, eyes wide. "I don't know. Are we?"

Before I can even try to regain composure and respond, Jahra walks to me, places her ear on my belly, and thumps once, hard enough to make me *oof!*

"No," she announces. "She's not fat enough. And the baby didn't kick me."

"But you kissed her!" Miguel shouts, pointing at Fletch

like he's the suspect in a murder. "That's how babies are made!"

Eyebrows up, Fletch looks to me for an explanation.

I got nothin'.

Clap clap!

Ani's gesture saves the day as she gets everyone to simmer down. "It's time to wash hands and get ready for lunch," she says.

"Does Fairy the ferret have to wash hands, too?" JoJo asks as the kids reluctantly leave the main room, Ani and Michelle graciously giving Fletch and me some space.

Mattie, however, remains.

"Miss Fiona would make a good auntie," he says into Fletch's knees.

"Mattie," Fletch says, voice choked with the same embarrassment I feel, the connected energy turning into a flavor. "It's not... well, that's not something you just say."

"But it's true. You told me it's always good to tell the truth."

I bite my lower lip to try not to laugh.

Fletch gives me a begging look that says, *Rescue me.*

I hold up my hands, palms out. *This is all yours, bud.*

His eye roll and sigh aren't changing my reaction.

"Telling the truth is always the right thing to do," he says, peeling Mattie off his legs and bending down to be at eye level. "But it's embarrassing to say that you think I should marry Fiona."

"Hey, now. Why would anyone be embarrassed to marry me?"

Mattie turns his head, blue eyes big as moons, looks at me, and says, "She's so pretty. Don't you want to marry someone pretty, Uncle Chris?" His fingers play with the end of my long hair.

"Yeah, *Uncle Chris*. Isn't marrying a pretty person your primary reason for marriage?" I poke.

"She's sarcastic, too, Mattie. And she has one heck of a kick."

Mattie screws up his face in concentration as he looks at me. "I don't think you should marry her."

"Why not?" I pretend to be offended.

"Because when I'm a grown-up, *I'm* going to marry Miss Fiona."

"I don't know about that," Fletch says, pretending to be mad. "I might have to thumb wrestle you for it."

"My future is going to be determined by the rotation and strength of opposable thumbs?" I interject.

Fletch shrugs. "Two hundred years ago, you'd have been married off for a cow."

"Is that supposed to make some kind of point?"

"You're worth way more than a cow," Mattie says seriously.

Fletch laughs. "Two cows?"

"At least ten," Mattie determines.

"Thank you, Mattie, for upping my value, but nowadays, people marry for love."

"I love you ten cows worth, Miss Fiona."

"Hoo boy," Fletch says, blowing out a long gust of air. "I don't know if I can compete with that."

"You don't think you can love her eleven cows worth? That's more than ten," Mattie asks.

"It's hard to measure how I feel about Miss Fiona."

He ruffles Mattie's hair while I stand there, emotional grid shifting from tentative amusement to an uncertainty that makes me feel like he's entering new territory.

"Then I win! Miss Fiona is mine when I am sixteen!"

"Why sixteen?"

"Because then I can drive to her house!" He runs off,

curious about the kids in the other room all pulling out their lunches.

"Four-year-old logic," Fletch mutters, giving me side-long glances meant to surmise my emotional state.

"Better than most grown-ups."

"Can't argue with you there."

"Nice to see you found something you can't pick a fight about."

"Hey!"

"Fletch," I start, walking into my office, waving him on. As we pass by the children, they snicker and whisper, the girls more stirred up than the boys. We reach the office, I close the door, and ask, "Why are you here?"

"I came to see you because I knew this was your lunch break and you've been ignoring my texts and calls."

"Maybe I need some space."

"I respect that."

"Clearly, you don't."

"Look, Fiona, I'm not here to argue with you. Or to crowd you or upset you. The opposite, actually. I realized our wires have been crossed and it was better to just come to you, face to face, and say what needs to be said."

"You couldn't wait until I wasn't working?"

"If you'd answer my texts and calls, I could."

"Fair enough. What do you want to say? What needs to be said?"

"I would like to ask you out on a date."

"A date?"

"Yes."

"Why?"

"Because I like you."

"That's it?"

"Isn't that enough?"

"After seventeen years of teasing me, of that stupid

nickname following me around like a poltergeist, now you suddenly decide that because I saved your nephew you want to *date* me?"

"It's not like that."

"Then what is it like?"

"I don't know. Let me find out what it's like by spending time with you. Let's both find out what the other is really like. Do we have to define this? Let's explore it." He grins. "Let's explore each other."

"I think you're trauma bonding with me and getting that confused with having feelings for me."

"Trauma bonding?"

"We went through something emotionally intense together. You helped me. I saved your nephew. But that doesn't mean we should date."

"That's not why I'm asking you out."

"Is it because we kissed?"

"That's not why, but it certainly adds to all the *reasons* why."

"You know I'm not a fan of yours," I begin, wavering inside but surprised by my words.

"Because of seventh grade."

"You say that like I should be over it."

He makes a gesture that clearly indicates that's exactly what he thinks.

And he's right. But the part of me that knows that isn't the part that opens her mouth.

"I'm not. I'm also not going to apologize for not being over it. When we were younger, you did a really shitty thing to me."

"Yeah. I know." He leans against my desk and looks down, then up. "And I never thanked you for it."

"*Thanked* me?"

"Getting dropkicked by you taught me about consent."

"That doesn't make sense."

"It makes perfect sense. I was a dumbass twelve-year-old boy who thought when I tried to kiss you and you said no, you meant yes."

"Why would you think that?"

"Because that's what I was taught. Not by my parents," he adds hastily. "By other guys. By media. By all these cultural messages."

"How on Earth did *I* teach you about consent?"

"You said no. I tried to kiss you again. When I did, you dropped me flat. *Bam!* I still remember the look on your face as your foot came flying toward me. You were nothing but sheer power. If it hadn't come with so much pain split seconds later, it would have been unadulterated beauty."

"Get to the consent part."

"You were one hundred percent right. And I've never apologized for not respecting your no. So this is me, the same stupid idiot from seventh grade, saying to you: I am very sorry. Truly. I should never have tried to kiss you that second time. You did everything right and I deserved what you did to me."

I look around the office, the only room in the preschool other than the bathrooms that doesn't have cameras. "Am I being pranked? Does Michael have a camera crew somewhere and this is a paid stunt?"

"No prank. No cameras. Just me offering up my ego for you to poke with the world's biggest pin."

The image of Rico's locksmith pick chooses that moment to invade my mind.

"I don't know what to say."

"Can I tell you about what happened after you kicked the hell out of me way back then?"

"Um, sure."

"I went home. You gave me a shiner. My mom freaked

out when she saw it. Thought I'd been hurt playing middle school football. I was a scrawny thing back then, but I had the height and the width for defense. Coach Szacz saw that in me. Anyhow, I told Mom it wasn't sports. That I'd gotten into a fight. She wanted to call the school and I had to tell her the truth." A wistful smile crosses his face. "The last thing a twelve-year-old dude wants to admit is that the first time he tried to kiss a girl, he got dropped like that."

The first time.

"So," Fletch says, letting out a long sigh as he shoves his hands into the front pockets of his jeans and leans one hip against my filing cabinet, "I told her. And she got very quiet. All she said was, 'Get an ice pack on that, Chris, and let's talk more about this when your dad gets home from work.'"

"Oh, no."

"Right? You get it. To a twelve-year-old, it was her quiet answer and the prospect of Dad hearing what I'd done that made me start to realize I'd *really* screwed up. I thought it was because a girl beat me," he says with a low chuckle that is paternal and wise. It makes time fast forward, allowing me to see him as an older man.

And liking what I imagine.

"Dad got home. Mom asked me to come into his office and tell the story. I did. Dad looked at Mom. She left without a word. And then Dad slowly, calmly, but god-awfully *emphatically* spent the next hour lecturing me on the concept of consent. He didn't use that word. Dad isn't the type to frame things that way. He told me in no uncertain terms that when a woman tells you no, you respect that, because men who don't are the kind you have to protect people *from*."

"Oof."

"Yeah. I mean, look at me now. I'm a paramedic and

firefighter. I own a boxing gym with a focus on teaching people how to protect themselves. The last damn thing I wanted, even at twelve, was to be a bad guy."

"And you aren't."

His eyes narrow. "For some reason, a piece of you still thinks I am, Fiona. And this is me, talking to that piece, telling her it's okay. I'll never do anything ever again that you don't want. I'll never violate your *no*."

"Thank you."

"But."

"Here we go."

"But I'm confused. You kissed me back at that shoot. You told me you shouldn't want *this* at all." On the word *this*, he waves his hand between us, unconsciously stirring energy that is powerful, that wants to divide itself between us and attach connectors, cords you can't see but that have tremendous power.

"I did."

"Then is that a *no*? You don't want to go out on a date? You don't want to kiss me? Because I need this to be crystal clear between us."

Crystal.

He said *crystal*.

Jolene's strange rock is somewhere in here, in my purse? I'm not sure. The piece of me that Fletch speaks to yearns to hold it, listen to it, ask it for advice.

Hold it in the space between us.

"I–I can't go out with you. I shouldn't."

"That's neither a no nor a yes."

"Maybe–maybe for me, this isn't binary."

"You're nonbinary?" he asks, confused. "Which is cool," he adds.

"No. I'm cis het. I mean the issue of whether to say yes

or no to dating you isn't binary. It's not black or white. It's not either/or."

"You don't want labels around whatever this is?"

"I guess?"

"Fiona, I'm a pretty simple guy. I know what I like and I go for it. I know what I don't, so I avoid it. Ever since our high school reunion last year and seeing you again—even though I've run into you over the years and you went out of your way not to talk to me—it's like fate is putting us together."

Fate.

Crystal.

Was Jolene right?

Bzzz

My phone makes me lunge for my purse, the thin silver strip on the side of it a homing beacon.

It's Mallory.

Dress fitting today? First, preliminary one. The big one is later, when Hasty and Raye and Veronica are back in town. But today at 3:30 at Ahern's?

"Everything okay?" Fletch asks.

"Yeah. Dress fitting for the wedding." I text back a *yes*.

Why can I text a *yes* to Mal but I can't say a *yes* to Fletch?

"Dress fitting? Like a tux fitting?"

"Nothing like a tux fitting. You guys go in, they measure here and there, and a few days later you're set. Dress fittings are *events*. Mallory's practically ready to issue invitations and have party favors for them with color-coordinated ribbon and a 4-piece chamber orchestra."

"Don't assume tux fittings aren't traumatic. You ever have a guy's hand up your crotch, measuring?" His eyes drift down my body but suddenly jerk back to maintain eye contact.

"I'm pretty sure someone on the dating app mentioned that as a fetish."

He laughs. I join him. It's tinny and a bit brittle, but that's the sound of breaking the ice.

"Fletch," I say, moving closer to him, liking this. Hating myself for liking this. "I'm glad I taught you, indirectly, about consent. I need you to teach me something now, though. Consider it a fair trade."

"What can I teach you?"

"How to be more than one person at the same time."

"Like, multiple personalities?"

"No. More like having two different pieces of me warring inside. And I can't let one win just yet. So I have a *yes* and a *no* sparring with each other. I'm not sure which one will win. I know that if I pick one now, it'll feel unfinished."

"You're asking me to take a maybe as an answer?"

"I guess?"

Nodding, he looks down, removing his hands from his pockets. The view of his wide shoulders, strong back, and fine, fine ass are enough to make me want to shout *yes!* without a second thought.

And yet I can't.

Not yet.

"Fletch. Chris," I say, using his given name for the first time in… ever?

A child in the background lets out a shriek of joy, others joining in, the backdrop of happiness a blanket of warmth. Add the look in Fletch's eyes as he turns to me, man to woman, heart to heart, and I think my *maybe* is turning to a *yes* damn fast.

"Yes?" he asks.

"I–I don't want to say *yes* for the wrong reasons." My

hand holds my phone, which I put back in my purse, but I keep my hand in there.

"What are the wrong reasons?"

"That's what I need to figure out. It's… I can't put it into words." I brace myself for the inevitable criticism.

"*That* I understand. Some feelings can't be explained. They can just be expressed."

I blink.

I blink and blink and *blink*.

And then Chris Fletcher smiles a thousand-watt grin at me and says,

"You need space. I get it. Space is where we figure out where the edges are."

And just like that, he leaves, the edge between *here* and *there* sharp and distinct.

As the door closes, I feel a pulsing in my purse. I let go of my phone and feel for the source.

It's Jolene's crystal.

And it has something to say.

CHAPTER 10

*M*allory makes a huge deal about the Dance and Dairy festival every August here in Anderhill, but *my* favorite event is the Leaf Peeper Festival, held the third weekend in October, come rain or shine.

And today it's *alll* shine. How kind of Mother Nature to give us blue skies, a balmy fifty degrees even, and plenty of young families we can attract to the Peace Tent for The Grounded Child.

New England festivals aren't that much different from small town fairs in other states, but because pretty much every single town in New England has a town common, there's a festival or a fair or a farmer's market or concert in every single town, nearly every single weekend in autumn.

And for every festival, there are canopy tents in every color you can imagine.

Preschools, churches, the library, real estate agents, vendors selling soap and maple syrup and kettle corn and lavender lemonade and leatherwork and crocheted kitchen towels and… you get the picture.

The Grounded Child has a tent at about six fairs every

year, but this is the big one. Anderhill is the town with more small kids than any around. We have to catch new families now, because they spend the winter deciding where to send their kids to preschool.

And the Leaf Peeper festival is where all the people with kids under five go.

Bouncy house? We got one.

Touch a Firetruck? It's here, with the big ladder.

Rock-climbing tower? More dads than kids use it, but it draws a crowd.

Ice cream truck? Yeah, baby. See that woman coming back from the line holding two cups of ice cream bigger than a newborn's head?

That's Ani.

And she's carrying salted maple caramel in one hand and caramelized peach pecan in the other. From the Hesserman's Dairy VW bus, a rolling hippie palace complete with the best micro-creamery on wheels.

"Here," she says, dropping my pound or so of ice cream in a thump on the folding table. "Hope you're hungry."

"What size did you get?" I goggle.

"Large!"

"This isn't large. This is diabetes in a cup."

"No, that's the next size up."

"What comes after large?"

"What you just said: They renamed extra large 'Diabetes in a Cup.'"

"This will never fit. I can't get all that in my mouth!"

"You just quoted every guy's porn dream," Perky says, appearing between our tent and the one next to us. The festival hasn't even begun yet, which is why Ani got the ice cream now, at 9:30 a.m. By 10 a.m., when it all starts, the place will be packed.

More important to know, Hesserman's ice cream truck

sells out within the first two hours. I learned that four years ago, during our first tent run.

"If it involves this much salted caramel maple ice cream, it's my porn dream, too." For emphasis, I shove a big mouthful in–

And moan.

"That's part of a porn dream, too, Fi. That moan belongs in a Penny Ride video."

"Nah. The pitch of her voice is too high," Ani contributes, turning Perky's face into a mask of surprise.

"What?" Ani says. "Preschool teachers can't watch porn?"

"*Shhhh*," I whisper. "Parents!"

"Who is Penny Ride?" I ask, hating myself for opening this topic even further.

"Search for her on YouPorn. Guy number one comes all over her ass, then the other guys toss pennies at her to make them stick. However many pennies stick is how many guys she then sleeps with."

The rumble of a truck engine mercifully cuts through our conversation as a pickup backs into the space next to us. Two guys in red t-shirts climb out of the back, immediately dropping the gate and pulling heavy equipment onto the grass. I spot a basic festival canopy in a bag, much like ours, and then I see the logo.

Oh, no.

The passenger side of the pickup opens, the door swinging just as I realize who is about to climb out.

Fletch.

I grab the schematic for the festival from the stack of papers in front of Ani. Yep. There he is.

Haverly Fitness. Boring name, but it does the job. Haverly is two towns over, so I didn't expect him here.

Never noticed him here before. How did I miss it? And his tent is right next to ours.

It's like the universe is conspiring to put us together.

Sending me more signs.

"Hey, Fletch!" Perky shouts, waving, as I struggle to process *that*.

Cringing, I turn away and shove more ice cream in my mouth.

Fletch waves back with a smile, all bulging muscles and swift, strong movement.

"I can't believe you turned him down," Ani says with a sigh, straightening brochures on the table that are already perfectly neat.

"I didn't! I said *maybe*."

"You didn't say *yes*," Perky corrects me. "Might as well be a *no*."

"It's not a *no*! It's just—"

They stare at me with too much focused attention.

"Also, I thought Habitat for Humanity was the table next to us! Where's Mrs. Kormatillo? They started coming last year and Mallory said she would try to man the table."

"Quit deflecting," Perky says in a sing-songy voice.

"OH. MAH. GAH!" screams a long-haired teenager a few tents away, her phone's chain jingling as she runs over to my table, gaze pinging between me and the guys setting up Fletch's gym's tent. "It's you two! Feisty Fighter and Hot Boxer!"

"Hot Boxer?" Fletch freezes as one of his guys says the words, the set of Fletch's shoulders making it clear he's prepared to be teased.

"FEISTY FIGHTER?" I scream, unable to control myself.

"Like, duh! From Insta!" Holding out her phone, she shows us pictures of the photo shoot.

I march over to Fletch and get in his face. "You told them to call me *Feisty Fighter?*"

"What?"

"Someone did!"

"Loads of people in town know your old nickname."

"Did you tell them?"

Before he can answer, we're interrupted by half of the tail end of Gen Z.

"OMIGOD, you two are so *hot* when you fight!" another teen screeches, phone pointing at us, clearly recording, two of her friends joining her and whispering. Soon there are about ten girls between the ages of eleven and sixteen, all of them with long hair and phones that cost more than my used car.

Fletch goes back to setting up his canopy tent, three guys in red t-shirts snickering as they hold the other three posts of the frame.

"You're Feisty Fighter, aren't you?" one of the teens says, looking at our sign. "Oh! The Grounded Child! I went to preschool there."

"Ashleigh, duh. I told you that's where Feisty Fighter worked."

"I know, Bella, but you didn't put it all to*ge*ther! I just did!" She squints at me. "I must have been before your time."

While they bicker, I fume at Fletch. In my peripheral vision, I see Perky shooting me weird looks.

Her energy feels... guilty.

"Like, can we get a selfie with you?" one of the teens asks Fletch, her hair flip a talent I'll never possess. How one puts so much volition and emotion into *hair* is beyond me.

"Sorry. I'm working, Miss."

"Miss? Hah! Like, my name is Ashleigh," she replies, giving him her best sultry grin.

Complete with metal mouth.

My heart melts. She can't be more than fifteen, bless her.

"Hi, Ashleigh. I'm not really doing selfies," Fletch mumbles, stumbling through the awkwardness as if her age brings him down to a less sophisticated speech pattern.

"With her? Both of you?" Ashleigh begs. "I mean, it would be *soooo* cool to be the first of my friends to have a post on Insta. Not just a story–a real post! I'll put you in my *feed*."

The uncertainty on Fletch's face makes it clear he has no idea what that means.

"Sure!" I say, gritting my teeth, my smile more the showing of fangs than friendliness as I give Fletch a look that says, *She's just a kid. Come on.*

"Okay, Ashleigh, but remember what your mom said when you came to my gym yesterday?" he responds, giving me back a frowny sigh that makes me see *I'm* the one who misunderstands.

"Like, I know. It's just social media."

"And you don't stalk people."

"I'm not stalking! I'm *trying* to become an *influencer* and this is how it *works!* My mom is so, *ugh*. So BOOMER!"

I reach for her shoulder and curl my left arm around it, Fletch suddenly to my right, hot and a little sweaty, his scent a mix of soap and salt that instantly transports me back to our kiss. His energy shifts, too, as Ashleigh angles her camera, taking pic after pic from above, my body soft-ening against his hard lines, his hand on my waist gripping tighter.

No! No. This is the guy who told Michael and the

sponsor about my nickname. I'm not letting my attraction to him matter.

And then it hits me, literally, the second he touches me.

When I am with him, I am Feisty.

I don't know how to be *Fiona* with Chris Fletcher.

Oh.

My.

God.

We're nearly thirty, two adults who are obviously attracted to each other. I've kissed the guy in a sweaty, hot pile of our bodies on a boxing gym floor, and he's asked me out on a date. Requested the honor of my presence so we can explore each other.

Emotionally and, it goes without saying – physically.

What am I doing?

Why am I letting some old sense of who I am get in the way of this new sense of who I could be?

Of who I could be *with him?*

Just then, as Ashleigh lets go and wanders off to find a shady spot under a tree where the sun's glare doesn't affect which filter she picks for her pic, Mallory's mom and dad appear.

"What a happy couple you two are!" Sharon says, beaming. "That tenth reunion last year was a godsend for you girls, wasn't it? Mallory and Will got together, then Will asked Parker to be in the wedding and Perky and Parker reunited. Now you and Fletch!"

I cough up half a lung and peel myself out of his grasp.

"Uh, no, Mrs. Monahan, Fiona and I aren't, uh... we're not—"

"I wouldn't date him if he was the last guy on Earth," I joke.

Half joke.

Whatever.

"Hey!" he protests.

"What?"

"You kissed me," he whispers in my ear, the words so light, it's like they didn't happen.

"So?"

"That counts for something."

"What does it count for?"

"I wasn't the last guy on Earth when you kissed me."

"Quit saying I kissed you. You kissed me!"

"It was a mutual kiss."

"And your point is?"

"No one mutually kisses someone and then claims they wouldn't date them even if they were the one and only option."

"It's an expression! A turn of phrase. I'm trying to be light here."

"Am I really that bad? You use strong, emotional words when you talk about me."

"Like what?"

"Hate. You said you *hated* me. Now you say you wouldn't date me if I were the last penis on the planet."

"Hey! Language! We're at a preschool table!"

With dawning horror, I realize our voices are louder than when we started, and Sharon and Roy are watching us like we're a live reality television show.

Mal's mom laughs, a loose, wise sound that feels sexy in a way I can't quite comprehend. "You two are *definitely* a couple."

"No, ma'am, I said before that we're–"

She cuts off Fletch's argument.

"Anyone who can bicker like you two is a couple. You just don't know it yet." Patting his cheek gently, she smiles, turning back to catch Roy's eye.

Except Roy's eye is on my rapidly melting pile of ice cream.

"Oh! Hesserman's is here with the ice cream truck." Weaving his fingers through Sharon's, he takes her by the hand, leading the way to their own version of sugar bliss.

"Relationship goals," Ani says with a sigh, watching them.

"Yeah," Fletch agrees, looking straight at me, until one of his guys shouts, "Hey, HOT BOXER!"

And they all fall apart laughing.

"Gotta go set up," he mutters as he leaves.

Ani's already done with her ice cream, eyeing my melting dish. She leans in and says in a low voice, "You know Fletch's other Insta hashtag?"

"Huh?"

"Ashleigh's right. You guys are #hotboxer and #feisty-fighter, but Fletch is also #fletchisacatch."

Before I can formulate a response to *that*, a very pregnant woman appears, hand in hand with a three-year-old, a big, curious smile on her face.

Time to charm the crowd.

Time to meet my future students.

And definitely time to forget what's happened these last two weeks and settle back into some normalcy.

"You're the teacher who beat up that attacker in the classroom!" Pregnant Mom says, covering her child's ears. "I love the Instagram photos with that hot boxer!"

So much for normalcy.

For the next two hours, I field questions from parents, most of them curious about what happened with Rico two weeks ago. Our signup sheet for prospects fills up fast, Ani changing it out for a new one every half hour or so. Compared to last year, foot traffic is definitely higher, which makes me wonder how many of these people are just #feistyfighter rubberneckers.

Meanwhile, Fletch's tent is hopping, for the same reason: Teens and tweens have seen the Insta campaign for the workout-wear company and they want to be Insta-famous.

"Fiona?" Fletch calls out. "We've got a church youth group that wants a picture with us. They say they're doing a scavenger hunt and need a selfie with someone famous."

"I'm not famous!" My nervous laugh should speak for itself.

"FAMOUS FEISTY!" one of the kids screams, the rest laughing.

A spike plunges through my twelve-year-old heart. Fletch catches my eye and shrugs.

"Do it," Ani whispers.

As I walk over to where Fletch stands, in the center of a group of kids, one of the girls shrieks.

"They're kissing!" she says excitedly, pointing to her phone. "Look at your stories if you're following MPOWR2Q! Click on hashtag feistyfighter!"

Oh, no.

Michael released the pictures from when we kissed?

Fletch's arm goes around my shoulder as phone screens are passed around, my glimpses of the shot making me remember how it felt to have him on top of me, our breath hot and hard, his body hotter–

Harder.

"Hashtag a million for children's charity," he mutters.

"Hashtag I hate all the attention."

"Hashtag even from me?"

"New hashtag!" one of the girls says, looking at Fletch's arm around me, how he's whispering in my ear. "Change #fletchisacatch!"

"To what?" someone else calls out. In my peripheral vision, I see Perky appear, running over to be part of the drama.

"How about #fletchiscaught?" Perky mutters, audible to me but Fletch doesn't hear it.

He pulls me close, nose in my hair, and whispers, "You okay?"

I sigh, looking around the chaos, the clutter of Instagram groupies making it hard for families to get through.

And then I whisper, "Hashtag help."

"You got it," he says, surprising me. My words were a quiet joke, meant to riff on the hashtag theme, but he takes my hand, firm in his, and guides me through the throng of excited tweens and teens. We're moving and weaving between canopies, toward the Hesserman's VW ice cream bus, when we come to one of the police cars.

"Hey, Cap? Can we have a minute in the back?" he asks an officer, whose back is turned to us, but when he spins around, I see who it is.

Officer Capobeira gives me a skeptical look. "Is this some sex role play thing? Because your friend already asked."

"Which friend?" I gasp.

Fletch snorts. "Who do you think?" He looks at the officer. "C'mon, Cap. She needs a place to hide from the crowd."

"Sure, Fletch," he says as Fletch grabs the back door handle and ushers me in.

I've never been in the back of a police car.

The cage thing freaks me out.

"Why are we here?"

"You think the teenie boppers will follow us? I wanted privacy."

"There are six churches within five hundred feet. You could have taken me to one of them."

"This was closer. And more private. No one will interrupt."

"Interrupt what?"

If he were the kind of guy to alpha his way through an awkward moment, Chris Fletcher would kiss me right now.

If he were the kind of guy who took what he wanted, he would kiss me right now.

If seventeen years ago, he hadn't overridden my *no*, he would kiss me right now.

Instead, he's staring at me with a hunger that makes it damn clear he *wants* to kiss me right now – but won't.

"Interrupt giving you some peace from that crowd."

"I'm working, Fletch. That's my table. This is our major recruitment event for new families."

"Your preschool is *the* preschool in the area, Fiona. You don't need to recruit."

"How do you think we're so popular? We have to do these events to keep the waitlist churning."

"Are you seriously telling me that the video of you all over social media isn't sending tons of parents to your school?"

I pause. He's right. The air between us changes as I stop arguing, the backseat of the cop car a mixture of scents, some kind of vinyl and chemical odor mixing with after-shave and urine. It's not exactly sexy.

But Fletch *is*.

"Thank you," I finally say in the same second he reaches for my hand. I startle, body moving half an inch off the seat, fire racing through my veins.

"For what?"

"For giving me a break from that madness." We both look out the window to see the gaggle of Instagirls pestering

Officer Capobeira, who is an impenetrable wall of conde-
scension.

"Any time."

He means it, doesn't he? I can *feel* it. The energy
between us weaves like it's drawn to the warp and weft of a
loom, begging to form something bigger, warmer, stronger.

"You know, I didn't choose this, either," I whisper.

"Choose what?"

"This. Being some sort of crusader. Feisty Fighter, the
preschool teacher who kicks ass. I didn't pick this, Fletch. I
didn't pick my nickname in seventh grade, and I sure as hell
didn't pick having Rico come into my class and do what he
did."

"No. Life threw all of that at you."

"That's how you think about it? Life just 'threw' it
at me?"

"Yeah." He's uncertain. "How else do you look at it?"

"I – it's – But – " All the arguments inside me pile on top
of each other until I can't separate them anymore.

"You're right, Fiona. You didn't choose to have me try
to kiss you all those years ago. You sure as hell didn't ask to
have Rico attack you and try to steal Mattie. But when life
tossed that at you, you *acted*."

His words have the opposite effect.

I freeze.

"I'll go out there and deal with the crowd," he says,
patting my knee in a comforting way that nevertheless
makes my pulse race. "You take a break."

Our eyes meet.

"I think you need one."

CHAPTER 11

*H*aving never been in a wedding before, every part of the dress fitting at Ahern's makes me feel like an alien scout, sent to Earth to gather information on these strange creatures. The energy in this fitting room—such a small-sounding name for such a huge space, where the bride comes out and promenades around a large, circular sofa with mirrors on every vertical surface—is filled with decades of emotion.

Most of it pure tension.

You would think that a wedding dress shop, of all places, would be filled with laughter and happy tears, joyous wistfulness and newfound love.

But no.

Will's older sister, Veronica, who is in the wedding, had a last-minute work meeting and couldn't make it. I'm here, of course. Perky had to leave for Texas because of some issue with Parker. That leaves me, Raye, and... Hastings.

Yes–*Hasty* is here. Mallory's evil older sister.

Without Perky, I'm the lone filter, although Raye knows the scene pretty well. She's flown in with her wife, Sanni, for a separate family gathering of her own. The convergence is perfect, Mallory grinning as she hugs us all, even Hasty.

Who hugs her back with an earnestness that surprises me.

"We are four, then," the wedding dress coordinator, Bettina, says to us in a sing-songy voice as she appears with a silver tray of what appears to be mimosas.

"Actually, five," Mallory corrects her. "My mom, Sharon, is here."

"Oh! Yes. I meant the actual bridal party. Mother of the bride is a category of her own!" Bettina has long, jet-black hair and high cheekbones, with blue eyes too perfect to be natural. If I were judgmental like Perky, I would note that her breasts defy physics and her wrap dress begs the question of how many ribs she had removed to make the difference between her waist and hips so tremendous.

But I'm not Perky. I don't judge.

And Bettina's smile is genuine.

Some people love the satisfaction of lining details up just so, of design that seems more like fate than art. Physical comfort isn't enough without aesthetic pleasure. Mallory's an interior designer and that's her goal–for people to feel like their environment is perfect in every detail, yet comfortable and casual to inhabit.

Weddings are the opposite, it seems. Stiff and regal, we create fairy tales out of uncomfortable traditions.

And fabric.

Mallory and Hasty's mother, Sharon, is a total sweetheart. Kind and good-natured, she's nothing like either of her daughters when it comes to managing details. Mallory is nearly OCD about certain specifics, while Hasty runs her life like it's one big project management checklist. A born delegator, Hasty is all about being the boss.

Which is great, when she *is* the boss.

In regular life? Not so much.

"When Burke and I got married..." I overhear her say for the third time as Raye stifles an eye roll and reaches for a second mimosa. A huge wave of sadness hits me as I miss Perky something fierce.

Feeling sheepish but not caring, I pivot around a big, white pillar and grab my phone.

You're missed here. If Hasty mentions her wedding to Burke one more time...

Perky texts back, *I'm on my way.*

Ha ha, I wish.

No—really! Flight cancelled. Plane had mechanical failure. Give me twenty minutes in this Uber and I'll be there. It was going to be a surprise!

Before I can answer, I'm interrupted.

"Fiona, how are you doing with your newfound success?" Hasty purrs, hugging me like I'm a talisman she can touch to bring good luck. A mover and shaker, Hasty is drawn to attention and drama, as long as it gives her leverage and helps her move up in society.

"I'm fine. Happy to pay off my student loans and see children's groups getting a million dollars."

"That's *it*? That's all anyone gave you? Small reward for putting your life on the line."

"I'd have done it for nothing."

"Pushovers always say that."

"So do preschool teachers. Occupational hazard!" I chirp. Years ago, I figured out the best way to get under Hasty's skin, other than calling her Hasty. Like me, she hates her nickname.

She hates having her putdowns met with positivity.

"Altruism doesn't have to be divorced from money," she sniffs. "Corporate altruism is a thing."

"How?" Raye asks pleasantly, a little crinkle at the bridge of her nose adorable and simultaneously a bit threatening. "The entire mission of a corporation is to provide profits for shareholders. What does altruism have to do with that?"

Hasty gives a haughty huff. "Plenty of corporations have philanthropic divisions, Rayelyn."

"You didn't say philanthropy. You said altruism. The words have different meanings," Raye points out.

"I know what they mean," Hasty replies in a voice so cold, it could be used in a cryogenics lab.

"Then–"

"These mimosas are delicious!" Sharon interrupts, nearly elbowing Hasty as she inserts herself between her daughter and Raye. "I wonder what that extra flavor is?"

"A mimosa is literally two ingredients, Mom," Hasty declares, half disgusted. "Orange juice and Champagne."

"Then the extra flavor must be joy, because I love having both my girls here with me, and all of you lovelies as well."

Hasty deflates slightly.

"Actually, good palate, Sharon," Bettina says smoothly. "We put the tiniest drop of pomegranate syrup in our mimosas, for a hint of something special."

Sharon gives Hasty a look that shuts her up.

"Fiona!" she says, turning to me, letting Hasty off the hook. "Halloween is almost here. That must be so much fun as a preschool teacher!"

"It is," I agree. "I get to dress up in costumes and run around having fun."

"What are you this year?" Sharon asks.

"Internet famous," Hasty mutters.

"A pineapple."

"How cute! Will you dye your hair yellow?" Sharon's interest in my costume seems to piss Hasty off.

So I stretch this out.

"Oh, I love that idea, Sharon!"

She beams, then her smile drops. "After the terrible attack, your classroom needs something cheerful. How are the children?"

It occurs to me that very few people ask me that question. How *are* the children? So far, they've been fine, but Mattie's most negatively affected.

Before I can start to explain, unfortunately, Bettina appears.

"Hastings, Raye, and Fiona? We have your dresses over here," she says, gesturing to a back hallway. "While you're trying them on, we'll get Mallory ready for her dresses. This is going to be so much fun!"

Sharon's hand presses on my wrist. "We'll catch up later. I really do want to make sure you're fine." A quick side hug from her makes me relax.

Or maybe it's the mimosa.

Pretty sure it's the little bit of Mom love.

We form a line, Hasty in front, me next, Raye last, our high heels silent on the ivory carpet. Each of our separate dressing rooms has our respective dress on a mannequin, a new experience for me. I stand behind it and unzip the dress, moving the spaghetti straps over the mannequin's shoulders, wondering how this works.

Do I put the dress back on the mannequin when I'm done? Do I hang it on the single hanger on a long horizontal pole to the right of the mirror? Do I go out to the bigger fitting area and show my dress? Mallory's voice carries down the hall as she excitedly talks to Sharon about some special guest book made from pressed bamboo pulp.

The dress is exquisitely simple, each of us in the same

style, but each a slightly different earth tone. Mine is a gossamer pink, like a Himalayan salt lamp in fabric form. When Mal told me my color, Perky smirked, as if the two had some secret joke about salt lamps I didn't understand.

Once I slip into the dress, though, I don't care.

It's perfect.

"Oh!" I hear Raye exclaim next door. "Wow! This fits perfectly."

"Of course it does," Hasty calls back. "It's tailored."

Raye's tone changes. "Then the seamstress is at the top of her field, because this is the best tailoring I've ever had done. I sent pictures and my measurements, and she had a Skype call with me because she was nervous about the specifics, so I'm impressed!"

I don't mention that this is the *only* tailoring I've ever had done.

Tap tap tap.

"Fiona? How's the fit? I'm Lana, the seamstress." Her voice is lightly accented and pleasant.

"It's perfect!"

"May I check?"

"Sure."

The door opens, a woman with dark, clearly dyed black hair walking in, smiling wide, her red lips stretched across a broad jaw, eyes surrounded by deep wrinkles from years of being friendly. Her hands touch me across my shoulders, my waist, and a rapid series of movements leads to a satis-fied nod.

She departs as quickly as she arrived.

In her wake, I stare at myself in the mirror, hearing the chatter of my friends around me. Perky's talking about Parker's apartment and what it'll be like to redecorate his living room with beanbags. Mallory's telling her mother all about how Will wants to alternate holidays with her family and his, in Florida.

They're talking about houses. Lives. Even children.

They're all more anchored, more settled, more adult than I am.

A creepy-crawly feeling starts in my stomach, radiating out to the third chakra, making it creak and groan as it tries to move. I'm stuck, aren't I? Unlike my friends, I haven't integrated my past into my present, which means I can't really see the future. Or move toward it.

Does the future have thick forearms and kind, wide eyes that tell me to breathe?

Does the future smell like salt and soap and coffee and kiss with his whole body?

Does the future sit in a car outside my preschool class-room to sooth the worries of a tiny boy?

Does the future vibrate on a higher plane that I'm too stuck in my old patterns to feel?

Tap tap tap I hear next to me, then the seamstress has the same conversation with Raye she had with me, but as they speak, I tune out the words, my palms smoothing the dress I'm wearing, my legs turning weak.

We're all dressed in form-fitting, elegant bridesmaids dresses to stand at the front of a church with our friend, to welcome her across the threshold of a new life with the man she loves. Mallory will commit herself for all her remaining days with Will, their love a testimony to something greater than each of them as individuals. The energy they radiate will potentiate and strengthen the whole world.

"PERKY!!" Mallory shouts from down the hall, her scream followed by shrieks.

Hasty, Raye, and I poke our heads out of our respective fitting rooms.

"Oh, goody," Hasty mutters from two fitting rooms

over.

"Do we go out there?" I ask, still in my dress, admiring the cut.

"We're not the ones on display today," Hasty says with a grunt and the sound of fabric brushing against itself. "Mallory is. This is just a pro forma fitting to make sure our dresses are fine. Don't gain any weight for the next eight months!"

Raye and I ignore that.

I undress, careful not to pop stitches, and replace the dress on the mannequin. It feels foreign, like I'm a little girl playing dress up, like one of my four year olds pretending to be a princess.

As I take in my friends (including Hasty, who isn't even close to being a friend, but I'll be charitable), I can't help but compare. They're sleek and smart, confident and centered.

So are you, my wise self whispers deep inside. *Release that which does not serve you.*

My shoulders drop. Tension rolls off me like rain.

I can release anything that holds me back.

Including this grudge against Fletch.

Mallory is spending the rest of her life with a man she's loved from afar – and, now, near – for most of her life.

What kind of man will I spend most of my remaining life with, if I'm lucky enough to find him? Where will we live together? Is he going to respect my values? Broker in kindness as his primary goal in all interactions? Will he understand that my teaching is a calling, a divine message that the lessons I must learn in this life come from the children entrusted to me?

What will our children look like?

What will our shared love feel like?

How will I meet my life partner? My soulmate? My

true love?

What if you already have? my wise self whispers.

I stare into the mirror, my own eyes latched onto their reflection, the gaze deepening as those words ring out in my mind.

What if you already have?

Giggles a few dressing rooms over snap me out of the daze I'm in, Perky being a rabble-rouser, the laughter infectious.

"Let's see the bride!" she calls out.

As I walk back down the hall, I see Perky sipping a mimosa. Mallory is inside a dressing room, saying something to Sharon, who stands in the doorway wearing the look of an eager squirrel that just found a stash of nuts.

"There is nothing better than spreading your legs, lifting one up, and kicking as hard as possible with all your core," Perky says, looking at me with a funny expression.

"Are we talking about kickboxing or sex?" Mallory calls out. "What kind of sex are you having if it involves *kicking?*"

"Don't judge me."

"Edgy," Hasty intones, forcing Perky to glare at her. "How is Parker these days, when he's not at the mercy of your violence?"

"How did you know about the bite marks?"

She reddens, opening her mouth to respond.

"*Shhhh*," Sharon says, surprising Hasty, who seems stunned that her mother would reprimand her.

Then Mallory steps out of her bride's fitting room, and we all gasp.

Tears fill my eyes at the sight of Mallory in a fitted ivory lace gown that flares out at the knee into a dramatic mermaid train, her fiery red hair setting off her creamy skin against the color. The dress is a modern cut, her full figure an ideal form for the nipped waist, the wider hips, and the lush form-fitting bodice that dips between her breasts. Sheer illusion sleeves appliquéed with lace frame her shoulders, creating a look that somehow manages to be both tastefully modest and dead sexy.

Raye and I exchange a look that digs ninety-seven layers deep in an instant, burrowing back in time to middle and high school, when we knew Hasty all too well.

There are many insults on the tip of Mallory's sister's tongue, and we can imagine them all:

THAT DRESS WILL LOOK wonderful once you've lost fifteen more pounds.

No—make it twenty.

You always look washed out in white, but a good make-up artist can fix that.

Off-the-shoulder dresses are soooo 2018.

BRACING OURSELVES, we're ready.

Hasty stands, reaching for Mallory's hands, holding them out and looking her up and down with a teary smile that must be about the booze, right?

And then she reaches for Mallory in an embrace, whispering, "You look so beautiful, Mallory. Will is a lucky man."

Raye, Perky and I exchange shocked looks.

"Who took out Hasty's true chip and replaced it with a benevolent program?" Perky quips.

I elbow her. "She's beautiful. Let's focus on that."

"Will is going to cream his pants when he sees you," Perky declares.

"So classy," Hasty murmurs, though she's still smiling at Mal.

"You look gorgeous," I gush, eyeing Mallory, who smiles at me. "I can't believe you're really getting married!"

"I know!" Perky wails. "It's going to change everything!"

Everything is changing.

Every*one* is changing.

Everyone but me.

Within ten seconds we're a sobbing, gushing mess. Bettina offers tissues and little squares for patting under our eyes and catching mascara runs. She has everything. I suspect, in a pinch, the woman can make a sterile field on an end table and perform the Whipple procedure if someone needs it.

Anyone in the wedding business has to be prepared for all things dramatic.

It's like preschool, only you don't have the benefit of nap time.

On the other hand, you have mimosas.

"I love Will so, *so* much!" Mallory gushes as we all cry.

"He's perfect for you," Raye says. "Always has been. He just needed time to figure that out."

"Look at you! The first of us to get married!" Mallory chokes back, hugging Raye. "You and Sanni are so happy."

"We are." Her eyes cut over to Bettina and Sharon. We all know she's married to a woman, but you never know how the older crowd will react. Bettina's somewhere between an older millennial and a younger Boomer, so...

"I can't wait to meet Sanni. Why didn't you bring her here?" Mal's mom asks.

Raye smiles, the expression hiding all of the reactions she was prepared to call to the forefront, just in case. "I didn't think it was the right thing to do. Spouses aren't in the wedding party, right?"

"No, of course not. Imagine Burke here!" Sharon titters.

Hasty looks like she swallowed her mimosa flute.

Recovering quickly, though, she points through the glass storefront and says, "Hot damn, that is one fine set of legs on that biker."

We all turn to gawk, because while we are a bunch of enlightened millennial feminists, we're not untouched by beauty.

Except the fine set of legs belongs to someone I know all too well.

"Fletch?" Mallory squeaks, laughing as we all realize the hot set of carved muscles in tight bike shorts we're ogling is my—

My *what*?

"He's the one you did that photo shoot with. The video on Instagram of you two sparring was viral gold," Hasty croons.

"Nothing's as good as Perky's tits," I blurt out, earning a glare from my friend, who shares the love with Hasty.

"Quit saying that word," Perky hisses.

"What word? Tits?" Hasty repeats with relish.

"Stop," Perky mutters.

It seems to charge Mallory's sister. "Mmmm, he's fine. Too bad I'm married." She eyes Fletch like a hungry praying mantis looking for her next head to eat.

"Burke wouldn't give you a hall pass for good old Fletch?" Perky snarks.

"A hall pass?" Sharon asks, completely unaware of subtext. "Like in high school?"

"*Exactly* like in high school, Mom," Mallory jumps in just as Fletch, completely oblivious to being turned into eye candy, pulls on the hem of his shirt, angling it up to wipe his brow, showing off a torso of well-honed, perfectly curved washboard abs, and a happy trail that would send me hiking down it every night.

Every. Single. Night.

Sharon sounds deeply confused as she asks, "Why would someone need a hall pass–"

"Fletch!" Hasty shouts from the doorway, waving him over. He's chaining his bike to a rack in front of the coffee shop next door. All slick and sweat, he comes over with soaking hair, a big, bemused grin, and a body chiseled by a sculptor whose muse must have worked for *Sports Illustrated* in another life.

The Julian Edelman Body Issue has just been kicked to my number two favorite thing to look at.

No! No! I can't objectify him like this.

Well, I *can*.

I just feel like I shouldn't.

"Hey. Hastings, right? Mallory's older sister? What are you–" The second his eyes land on me, the confusion disappears. "Wedding dresses. Right. How's it going?"

Mallory disappears in a *swoosh* of fabric, Sharon on her heels, gushing about how gorgeous she is, Mal dissecting some specific detail about how the shoulder dart is off on the left side.

"We're debating whether Perky's tits or your photo shoot kiss is better viral material. What do you think?" Hasty asks, leaning against the doorway, making me hate her more and more with each word out of her mouth.

"I think this is one of those moments when a man knows that keeping his mouth shut is the safest response," Fletch says smoothly, eyes on Sharon Monahan, who gives him a thumbs up.

"You got yourself a smart one," she says to me with a nudge.

"No, Mom, I told you. Fletch and Fiona aren't dating," Mallory reminds her.

"I know. They told me at the Leaf Peeper festival."
Sharon's knowing grin reminds me of Jolene.

"What are you doing here, all sweaty and in tight shorts
and... sweaty?" Hasty asks, losing her point as quickly as
she lost her morals – the second she met her husband.

"Just finished a century bike run."

"Century?" Hasty asks.

"Hundred miles."

"You rode a hundred miles on a bike?" Sharon asks.
"Did your car break down? Cellphone battery dead?"

"No, Mrs. Monahan, I do it for fun."

"First of all, Christopher, how many times do I have to
tell you it's *Sharon* now? You're twenty-nine years old, for
Pete's sake. And second, who rides a bike for a hundred
miles for fun? There are so many other activities you can
engage in that are fun!"

"Like going out on a date with a nice person!" Perky
pipes up, elbowing me.

"Thank you, Mrs. Monahan–Sharon," he chokes out.
"We all have different ideas of fun, don't we? I like long,
punishing rides where I use my body to accomplish my
goals." Eyes darting to catch mine, he burns me with one
long look.

Hasty begins fanning herself with a veil brochure.

Bzzz.

Somewhere in those painted-on bike shorts, he has a
phone. Reaching behind him to pull it out of a zipper
pocket, we all get a nice big eyeful of all the ways Fletch's
body *accomplishes* his goals.

"Why are you not screwing this man senseless?" Hasty
whispers in my ear. "I would ride him like a butter churn."

Holding the phone to his ear, he waves to us all before
walking back to his bike. Then he stops, turns around, and
shouts, "FIONA!"

"Oh! It's like the end of *The Graduate*, when Dustin Hoffman begs Elaine to run off with him and–" Sharon whispers.

"You left a sports bra at my gym. Cleaning crew found it, along with a six-pack, in the box from the sponsor. You can come and get it any time."

His grins makes it clear what *it* really is.

And then he's off.

"Hoo boy," Hasty mumbles. "You're crazy not to tap that."

"If I were thirty years younger and single..." Sharon says, voice dropping off at the end.

Maybe I *am* crazy not to tap that.

Raye just laughs at us. "I had such a crush on his sister, Candi, when we were younger. The Fletcher attractiveness genes are strong."

Hasty's stomach growls. "Mom? Time for lunch? We just got quite a show in, didn't we?"

"Yum! Yes, let's get ready for some great food from Pedro!" Sharon announces.

"Please tell me we're not going to Taco Cubed," Perky says, alarmed. I grip her shoulder in solidarity.

Sharon gasps and says, "Of course we are! It's Mallory's favorite and you know how she is about her Mexican food." Just then, Mal emerges from the dressing room, out of the perfect dress and back into street clothes.

Raye slides a look our way and mouths, *What's wrong?*

"The perfect dress," Mal says as we shrug into our coats and grab purses. "The perfect future husband. The perfect wedding party," she adds, and as we pour onto the sidewalk and wait for her to exit.

Just as the door closes, she whispers conspiratorially in Raye's ear, just loud enough to send shivers down my spine:

"And now – the perfect ratio."

CHAPTER 12

*S*ports bra, huh?

I know that in the rush to get the hell out of the gym on the day of the shoot, I may have left a bra there, but a follow-up text from Fletch last night, after the wedding dress fitting was over and I was back in my apartment making schedules for parent-teacher conferences, mentions a six-pack.

Six-pack. Mmmm, Fletch's six-pack. Or is it an eight-pack? I try to remember the scene of him wiping his face with the hem of his shirt.

Eight. Definitely eight.

Squeezing my eyes hard, I try to banish the image.

I fail.

"Stop it!" I chide myself, working hard not to think about Fletch's hard body.

There's only one car in front of his gym, a white compact in a handicapped spot. No divining rod needed for this small shopping center. Free parking galore is the name of the game when you locate your business in a glorified strip mall. I pull in next to the white car and look at

Haverly Fitness.

Am I really back here? What am I doing?

No, really. What am I doing *not* dating him? The Leaf Peeper festival drove some of that home. The wedding dress fitting made it clear he's objectively hot (not that I need anyone else's opinion on that). My jealousy at the mere idea of Hasty getting her hands on Fletch leaves me with a surprising amount of uncontrolled energy inside.

Of all the weeks for Jolene to be attending a past-lives regression workshop in Tahoe.

We've reached early November weather, where New England moves out of "crisp" season and into "remember that year we had 148 inches of snow?" territory. My leggings and tunics and long fall dresses aren't cutting it anymore. It's ski jackets, jeans, and shearling boots time.

As I open the door, classic rock plays on the sound system, a heavy beat that makes me want to jump on a Stairmaster and climb my way to heaven. The only people in the small gym are Fletch, who is wearing a tight-as-hell, long-sleeved red workout shirt, and an older woman about my mom's age, with mostly grey hair, a very pain-filled face, and the sweaty look of someone who's about to clutch her chest and drop from a coronary.

"Stephanie, you can do it," Fletch says, the two of them completely focused on whatever's going on behind the boxing bag blocking my view.

"It—my arm doesn't want to do it."

"But your mind does. Let your mind do it. Let go of the anxiety."

"It doesn't work! The doctors were right," she says in a defeated voice. I sense she's losing because she's giving up, and not the other way around.

"The doctors don't have to be right, though. Prove them

wrong," he urges, voice encouraging but tough. "Lift it. I'm spotting you if something goes wrong."

"I don't want to hurt my wrist again. What if that happens?"

"What if it doesn't?"

The kindness in his voice melts me. Tipping her face up, she gives Fletch such a vulnerable look, the kind of hope that requires the other person to give a little piece of themselves, a mere loan of willpower. Motivation. Sheer grit.

Which Fletch has in spades.

"What if what doesn't?"

"You're prepared to fail, Stephanie. More than prepared. But I want to see that you're prepared to *succeed*."

Blinking hard, she looks down, taking it in. As I step closer, I see the walker, an aluminum contraption with bright pink tennis balls on some of the feet. Stephanie is far too young to need one.

Which means this is a more complicated training session than your average client.

"Everyone tries to tell me I can be the exception," she whispers, wiping away a tear as Fletch bends down and makes eye contact, his presence so solid, so strong, so willing. Most men shy away from emotion, but he's drawn to it.

"You can."

"But it feels like so much pressure. Always being the one who beats the odds. And then when I admit I feel this way, it's like—it's like I'm ungrateful. Like I don't get to feel whatever I really feel about having this stupid condition. Like I'm supposed to meet everyone else's expectations, be an outlier and overcome obstacles, and do it with a smile on my face and record it on Facebook and Instagram, too!"

She gives a half smile that Fletch mirrors.

"Have MS. Recover from an MS flare. Beat the odds with MS. Become the poster child for women over 50 with

MS. And make sure your eyelashes are perfect," she says quietly. "Hashtag self-care."

"Hashtag self-care," he repeats, musing over it.

"Hashtag *bullshit*. Self-care feels like yet another thing I'm supposed to put on my to-do list and then fail at, too." She shoots him a cynical smile. "Bitter Gen X-er here. I shouldn't be so jaded around a millennial."

"Eh. We're jaded, too. But before we bond over our shared cynicism, you need to do these reps with eight pounds. I know you can. And the stronger you make this arm, the easier it'll be to use it for mobility. Legs are next week. You're not leaving here until you get this arm exercise done."

"I'm due for my four o'clock coffee!"

"Then I'll use caffeine as a hostage to get those reps."

"You are a bully! A java bully!"

"If you say so." He hands her the weight. "Come on. Five reps."

Her arm shakes as she tries, barely getting one rep in.

On the second, she pauses, but gets the rotation in, the curl jerky but done.

"Two," I say aloud, making them turn. Stephanie nearly drops the weight.

"Fiona?"

"Hi, Fletch. Just here to get the–"

"THREE!" Stephanie grunts, the word loud and exhausted, but done.

"You can do it," I encourage, her entire arm shaking as she goes for four.

"Make sure there's no pain, no tearing. Shaking's okay. You're re-connecting neurons and muscle fibers here, Stephanie." He cheers her on. "This is great–"

"FOUR!" I shout with her as she gets it done.

"I don't think I can do five."

"Then don't think," he orders. "Just do it."

"Now you're a Nike spokesman?"

"Is that what it'll take to get you to do five?" he asks her.

"I'll run out and get you a coffee now if you do five!" I inform her.

Shaking her head, she grits her teeth and raises the weight, bracing her feet on the floor. Sweat practically pours off her face and she adjusts her posture, clearly working to draw strength from her core, something Fletch must have taught her.

Up, up, up the arm comes, and then:

"FIVE!" I scream, Fletch shouting, the two of us doing an impromptu dance as Stephanie drops the weight, propping her hips against the walker and moving to our imaginary victory song.

And then she gives me a good, long look.

"Oh, Fletch! Is this the girl you were telling me about?"

His eyes get big. Caught!

#fletchiscaught, all right.

"I – "

"The one who saved all those kids from an attacker at the preschool? The lucky girl who got to kiss you in those Instagram photos?"

"Uh – "

She winks at me. "Good for you two. I've been married for twenty-seven years. Find the person who grows with you and never tries to tell you who you are. My Sal is that way. He married one version of me and has had five more over the years as I changed. As long as we change together, that's all that matters."

The front door opens and in walks a guy about her age, wearing workout clothes, a paunch where his waist once was, gold-rimmed glasses surrounding friendly dark eyes.

Laugh lines dot his face and he gives Stephanie a big grin as he holds two to-go cups of coffee.

"Caffeine fix!" he announces, turning to Fletch. "Did she earn it?"

"Hell, yeah!"

"Sal, if you don't hand over that latte in the next tenth of a second, I will fry you with my laser beam eyes."

"Again? I still have burn marks on my ass from the last time. You really need to stop admiring it so much when I'm turned away."

She swats him with a towel as he hands over her coffee.

"Good workout?" he asks, eyes jumping from Stephanie to Fletch, finally landing on me with a silent question mark.

"Hi. I'm Fiona."

"His..." Sal's eyebrows go up, clearly expecting me to say *girlfriend* or *wife* or *fiancée*.

"Nemesis," I finally fill in.

Every set of eyebrows except mine rises higher.

"That's a new one. Relationship status: nemesis," Stephanie cracks.

"It could be useful," Sal says, earning another swat.

"What are you here for?" Stephanie asks me pleasantly.

"I left my bra here last time we..."

As I say the words, I realize what it must sound like.

Stephanie and Sal give us both *hubba hubba* looks. Stephanie leans on her walker and starts to stand, Sal practically leaping across the room to help.

"I'm fine," she insists, standing while holding onto the walker with her left arm, right arm shaking like crazy as she brings her coffee cup to her mouth and sips through the top.

"You're shaking from exhaustion, not tremors, but that's great control. I haven't seen you use that arm with weight in a while," her husband marvels.

"Blame Fletch."

"I'll *thank* Fletch!" Sal claps Fletch on the back a few times. "Steph's been trying this new diet approach from a doctor in Iowa who has MS herself, and we're at six weeks. This is more functionality than she had two years ago. This is *awesome!*"

Unaccustomed to effusive praise, Fletch seems to dial down a bit in the face of it. "Yeah. It is. She did all the work."

"*Pffft*. I just whined and you pushed me through," she says, letting Sal take her coffee as the two slowly make their way to the main door.

"You're describing marriage, Steph. Not personal training."

"See you on Thursday, Fletch! We'll get out of your way so you can do whatever you're planning to do with Fiona's bra!" A series of chuckles follows that, leaving Fletch and me in a state of awkward laughter.

The door closes.

We're alone.

"What was that about?" I ask, voice filled with marvel.

"Stephanie has multiple sclerosis."

"I gathered that. But, wow."

"Nothing's *wow* except her work. She came to me about two months ago. She's fifty-three, a few years out from being diagnosed. Heavy-duty meds caused kidney problems, so now she's taking a holistic approach. Found a neurologist to support it. I'm just here to work on balance and maintaining muscle mass."

"You were so encouraging with her. So kind. You pushed her, but you did it in a way that made her want to do the work. Like you're part of her team, urging her on."

"I *am* part of her team. When I work with people, that's my mindset. We're in this together. I'm not just standing there barking orders and watching. Their win is my win."

"That's how I feel when I teach. The connection *is* the lesson."

"Then we're not so different, are we?"

"No. We're not."

Heavy silence stretches between us, dark and full of unarticulated emotions. My attraction to him isn't just physical – though there's plenty of that to go around. It's energetic, a pull I can't explain, one I feel more than I think.

If Mallory or Perky were feeling what I feel right now, I'd admonish them for being a fool for not bridging the gap between their hesitations and their joy.

Fletch could be my joy. He could be that one man I wondered about, back at the wedding dress fitting.

Why am I saying no?

He's respecting my *no*–all my nos, going back seventeen years.

What if it's time I respect my *yes*, though?

"Fletch?"

"Hmm?"

"Does the offer still stand?"

"Offer?" Now he's just messing with me.

"To go out."

"Are you asking me out on a date, Fiona?"

"Not technically. I'm asking if your offer to go out on a date still stands."

"Sounds like you're asking me out."

"I'm asking if you are still interested in asking *me* out."

"Why not just–"

Crossing the space between us, I take his hands in mine, shutting him up with the touch.

"Fletch. Do you still want to date me?"

"Yes."

"Then... I accept."

"You accept that I still want to date you?"

"Fletch."

"What?"

"You're as annoying now as you were seventeen years ago!"

"But I'm not trying to kiss you without your consent right now."

"What if I consent?"

"Do you?" He moves closer.

I don't answer with a word.

I answer with a kiss. A kiss *I* initiate. My glasses lift up as our faces meet and I reach up to pull them off, holding the stems in my hand as it lingers at his neck.

If a kiss can be perfect, this one is, crossing time and space to pull emotional tendrils together. I'm kissing him for seventeen years of confusion and craziness, for seventeen years of rejecting a piece of me that was just fine to begin with, for seventeen years of being defined by a fellow tween's impulsive move.

He's kissing me back for his own reasons, and whatever they are, they're mighty fine, as his mouth takes mine and tells it stories that make my heart smile. Hands around my waist, he pulls me close, belly to belly, my coat still on but unzipped, the press of his flat torso and muscled terrain achingly tactile. My hands go up behind his neck, fingers brushing the ends of his short hair as his tongue uses a kind of energy I have never encountered before.

Breathless, we break apart, then come together again, the world spinning slowly without us, our bodies here but the rest of us, on every plane, lost in each other.

The cool air against my lips is the first sign that he's pulled back. I open my eyes to find him so close, staring deeply, chest rising and falling as the scent of him mingles with the frankincense and rose oil I put on earlier today.

"So?" he asks.

"So... what?"

"Is that a yes?"

"You think that was a *no*?" One arm still around him, unable to let go, I cover my mouth with my hand, laughing.

"I think I need a clear yes, Fiona."

On tiptoes, I kiss him lightly, then drop back, body pulsing.

"Yes, Chris. Absolutely—*yes*."

CHAPTER 13

*H*e told me to dress in workout gear and to bring a coat, hat, mittens, long johns, and ski pants.

But lightweight shoes.

This is brutal.

The suspense is killing me.

And that doesn't even include any of the anxiety around going on a first date.

Yesterday I said *yes*.

Yes to a date.

Yes to a kiss.

Yes to the idea that my two warring identities could somehow, inconceivably, co-exist inside me. I'm not planning to shave my head and go back to wearing Doc Martens just yet, but it's nice to smile when I think about Feisty.

When Fletch arrives to pick me up, he's driving his work truck. Two bikes are attached to a rack in the back.

Bikes.

In early November? I'm going to need a balaclava.

"Hey," he says as I walk down to his truck, his hug like embracing a down comforter with a face. "I forgot to mention a balaclava, so here." The thin fleece and nylon garment looks like he's offering me a chance to rob a bank.

It's also eerie that he read my mind.

"Thanks." So much for my hair. "What kind of date is this?" I ask as I adjust my glasses around the balaclava, tucking my long hair in and under the neck of my coat.

"The fun kind."

"That will be a distinct departure from my experience of dates."

He tilts his head slightly, studying me, the Patriots knit hat on his head topped with a red, white, and blue pom pom that bounces. "The bar's that low?"

"I've had fun ones. But I've never had one that required a balaclava."

"Then let me rock your world."

How? You're not naked, I almost blurt out, laughing at the thought, bringing more scrutiny from him. He grins, my laughter infectious.

"What's so funny?"

"I'll tell you later." *Like, at our wedding.*

What is going on in my mind? This is Fletch. Chris Fletcher.

Just like that, I'm imagining him as the *one*.

Jolene says when we break patterns, it's like shattering glass, not like eroding a rock. No steady drip when your consciousness shifts and frees yourself from old looping behaviors that calcified. The turning of a lens yields a completely different perspective, she says.

And it leaves you lighter. Freer. Untethered.

Unchained.

Could it really be this simple?

Moving to the back of his truck, he begins unloading the bikes.

"I thought we were going somewhere."

"We are." He points to a thin strip of woods behind my building. "You live on the rail trail. I almost rented an apartment in this complex, you know? Just because of that."

"That?" I don't have it in me to confess that I have never, ever–in four years of living here–used the rail trail. Not even for a walk. I prefer dirt trails, not asphalt, for running and hiking.

"Yeah. One of the best resources here. If I lived this close, I'd use it twice a day."

"We're going to bike on the rail trail? In November?"

"Best time. You don't overheat. The trail is sparsely populated. The leaves are gone but the snow hasn't hit. And the small businesses along the way are happy to see you when you break for coffee or ice cream."

"Now you're talking my language. Coffee. Ice cream. Mmmm."

Handing me a bike, he pauses, hand covering mine on one of the handlebars. "I assumed you'd be fine with this. You're in fantastic shape, and–"

"How would you know whether I'm in fantastic shape?"

"Uh, the mineral springs. Remember?"

I freeze, chest rising and falling as I keep my breath even, the rush of sexual longing almost unbearable. "Right," I finally say. "I guess the mystery's gone?" I joke.

He takes that as an invitation to move closer, his breath a white cloud in the cold. "I don't need a mystery, Fiona. Remember? I'm a simple guy. I appreciate quality, hard work, and kindness. You're the whole package." He kisses me slowly, sweetly, then grabs my ass. "And you've got a really nice package."

Before I can smack him, he pulls back and jumps on his bike. "Climb on!" he urges.

Repressing a much dirtier image of what that means, I do as he says, straddling the bike seat. "It's too high!" I call out. Circling back, he pauses, rotates his hip so his leg comes over his bike, and reaches in his pocket, kicking his kickstand at the same time.

All of his motions seem synchronized.

"Here," he says, removing his gloves, his hot palms on my jeans-covered leg enough to send electricity straight up my thigh and into my core. Head down, he pauses, the corners of his mouth turning up as he realizes the effect he's having on me.

"You need to spread your legs a little further if I'm going to make sure it fits just right," he says, caressing my thigh.

Holy Mother Gaia, I think flames just shot out of my clitoris.

"Isn't that always the case?" I gasp as I slide back off the seat, breaking contact, smirking back.

"It's so tight," he says as he uses a small wrench to loosen the seat's bolt.

"Flatterer," I mutter.

He looks up with a wink. "If I don't screw this in just right, you won't be able to sit properly."

"Make sure you don't strip the nut. I hear that can hurt."

"Nuts serve a good purpose but are definitely a problem if they get in the way."

"Not if you know how to handle them properly."

Fletch stands, staring me down with a grin that makes dimples appear in his cheeks. "Is this how it's going to be?"

"What?"

Pulling lightly on his waistband, he inhales slowly, then

sighs. "Until now, *my* bike seat was a perfectly fine fit. I need a few minutes for that to be true again."

I climb back on the bike, the seat just right. Pressing the ball of my foot into the metal, I begin biking toward the trail. "Then have fun catching up!" I call out as I take off, laughing maniacally.

"HEY!" he shouts, moving a little slower than he should to his own bike.

This is fun.

For the next five minutes, I'm in the lead, until a blur passes me on the left.

Ah, well. I was ahead for a short time.

For the next ten miles, we bike next to each other, Fletch graciously slowing down to my pace. Our speedometers measure speed and distance, so I know how far we've gone, and as we hit ten miles, I realize nervously that I have to be able to make it back as far as we've come.

A flag on the path, with the logo of a local coffee chain, calls my name.

"Ready for a snack?" he asks, nodding toward an old factory building, the brick exterior still painted with flaking antique signs.

We stop, my legs a little wobbly as we walk in after racking our bikes. Inside, the coffee shop is cozy, a big blackboard behind the counter with the rainbow-chalk menu that's a staple in every funky little place like this.

We approach the counter, and I reach for my wallet in my coat pocket.

"What's your drink?" Fletch asks me.

I look at the board. "I'd love a macchiato. Hazelnut." I glance around, as if getting away with something. Perky hates that I love hazelnut coffee.

And then I change my mind.

"Actually – wait. A Golden milk latte, please." Something about being here, with Fletch, makes me crave more warmth. More comfort.

And a little spice.

"Depth charge," Fletch says to the clerk. He pulls out his card and swipes before I get a chance.

"Uh, thank you," I stammer, the truth of this day sinking in. I'm on a date. With Fletch. He's being a grown-up, and we're flirting and kissing and...

I'm on a date.

With *Fletch*.

"You okay?" The level of attention he's giving me is swoony. "You suddenly went pale. What's up?"

"We're on a date."

"You're just figuring that out now?"

"Shouldn't this be more awkward?"

"No."

"That's it? Just... no?"

"Yes."

"You don't think this should be more awkward?"

"I think this is perfect." A kiss on the cheek punctuates his sentence, the server giving an *awwww* as she slides my golden latte forward. His depth charge, a black coffee with a shot in it, is up next.

We migrate to a booth near a Jøtul wood stove. The scent of burning wood and the uneven heat radiating from the small hearth make it feel like we've rolled back time about seventy years.

"Does dating me bother you?" he asks.

"Millennials don't date."

"But we are. Dating."

"We're on a date, but we're not dating."

"I don't understand."

"If we're on a date, which is a noun, it doesn't mean we suddenly take it all the way to dating, which is a verb. We haven't made the leap to verbing. We're still in the noun stage."

"You sound just like Mallory when you talk that way."

I sip my latte. It's spicy and warm, the thick milk and the yellow turmeric blending with the ginger and a little cayenne to heat me up.

Fletch's look has the same effect.

"Mallory is right much of the time."

"And here she is, verbing Will on a regular basis."

In all my years of thinking about Chris Fletcher, the phrase *dumb jock* was the one that came to mind the most. I was wrong. Sharp and funny, he's a low-key guy who knows how to banter, but who doesn't have to be in the spotlight. His kindness with his sister and nephew, the patience he displayed with his client, Stephanie, and his overall way of making me feel like I *matter* are blending to replace some stilted, outdated view of him that I'm carrying around.

"I wouldn't know," I say between sips. "We don't talk about their verb life."

He laughs, drinking more coffee, stretching out on his side of the booth, the tip of one boot hitting my ankle. "How're your bones?"

"My bones?"

"Handling the ride all right?"

"Oh, sure. Ten miles is nothing."

The grin spreads. "I knew you'd say that. Let's go for fifty."

"FIFTY!!"

"Round trip. Not one way."

"Forty more miles," I say, nodding. "I can do that. Are we pausing every ten miles?"

"How about we do fifteen more after this and take a nice, long break at the midpoint. I brought food."

"You did?"

"It's on my bike. No need for a cooler."

"You thought of everything."

He takes my hand. "I've been planning this date for a long time."

"Since the attack?"

"Before then." Swirling his cup, he stares into it. "Not for seventeen years, but Fiona, you're a damn fine woman. I couldn't run into you and not notice you."

"I'm sorry."

He jerks his head up. "For what?"

"For not noticing you."

"Why would you? I'm just a guy."

"You're more than that." I squeeze his hand. "I'm seeing it now."

"Are you?"

"Yes."

"What do you see?"

"A guy who thinks fifty-mile bike rides are a great first date."

"Weeds out the weak." As his thumb strokes the back of my hand, my belly warms.

"Most guys just test women in bed. You test them on a bike trail," I say, standing as I finish my golden milk latte.

"Wait. The bed thing was an option? Because I want a redo."

Jokingly, I rush to the cup bin, leave my mug there, and race to my bike. I'm too slow, though, because he's behind me, arms around my waist, our playful fun turning quickly into an inspired heat as he kisses me against the brick building, my ponytail caught between my shoulder blades, the tugging sensation barely registering as our tongues tangle with each other, his body so warm, so powerful, so fine.

Pressing in and up against me, Fletch's body has an

urgency in the way he kisses, as if this is his one chance and he needs to milk it for all it's worth. My legs part slightly and I feel his erection against my thigh, the undeniable recognition of his sexual maturity colliding with the part of my brain that's stuck in seventh grade. A giggle starts in the back of my throat, quickly–and rightly–snuffed out by a moan as his hand slides to cup my breast.

Forehead against mine, he suddenly says, "Jesus, Fiona." A quick breath, hot against my stinging nose. "How the hell am I supposed to make it fifteen more miles without touching you?"

"The same way you made it the first ten."

"That was torture."

I press my hips forward, the cold brick chilling my ass cheeks. "So is this."

He groans. He pulls back, hands on his hips, looking down at the ground as he takes deep breaths. "You're right. This should be more awkward." Searching eyes meet mine. "Why isn't it?"

"I don't know."

We grin at each other like idiots.

And then I'm in his arms again, the kiss harder, more poignant, more intense.

"I want to make one thing clear," I say, taking a pause.

"Hmm?"

"I'm not sleeping with you today."

Every muscle in his body turns to stone, especially the giant part pressing against my hip. "Huh?"

"I'm managing expectations."

"I never expected that on a first date."

"Okay. Good. We're on the same page."

"I only sleep with women after the thousandth mile."

"The what?"

"Once we've biked a thousand miles together."

"Ha ha."

"I'm serious. How can I get naked with someone I haven't had saddle sores with?"

"You're a true romantic, Fletch."

"See what you've been missing all these years?"

Bzzz.

I reach for my phone, my hand accidentally touching his erection through his jeans. He makes a frustrated sound. I pretend I didn't do it, and look at my phone.

It's a notification from the dating app.

Pressing the app icon, I wait until it jiggles, then I tap the X to delete it.

"What're you doing?"

"Oh," I say, pocketing the phone, then kissing him. "Just making space."

"That was the dating app."

"You have really good eyes."

"I'm slightly farsighted."

I touch the stem of my glasses. "I'm not."

"Your glasses make you look intriguing."

"Intriguing?"

"You wear these big frames. Lots of color. It's so different from when we were in school together." One hand reaches for my brow, a finger running along the line of my hair. "And you have hair. Purple and platinum now."

"You don't like it?"

"I didn't say that. Just that it's different. When I look at you, I have these completely different images in my mind from memory. They have to merge. Takes some effort."

"Effort?"

"You're worth the effort." A long, slow kiss comes next, crowding out the questions on the tip of my tongue. When I look at him, I see the same guy, only better, than I knew when we were kids. How he views my younger self and my now self is, to use his word...

Intriguing.

"I'm both, you know," I gasp as I pull out of the kiss.

"Both?"

"Old Fi and New Fi. I'm both. I went off to college and decided I didn't want to be a kickass kickboxing hard-edged chick. I wanted to be softer. To feel instead of think or kick. To slow down and appreciate all the ways kids can teach us. They have pure little hearts and their energy is like water to a parched man in the desert for me. Being around them means no hard edges."

"Soft." His hand rubs my shoulder. "I can see that."

"But Fletch, when you look at me – who do you see? Because I'm a bunch of different versions of myself inside. And I think one of them really, really doesn't like you. That one was the part of me that came to the surface every time I saw you."

"And now?" he asks, eyes searching my face. "What part of you is here, with me?" He kisses me gently. "What part of Fiona Gaskill just kissed me?"

Energy warms my blood, flowing like heat and light in every cell of me, the feeling radiant and real, so hopeful and happy I can taste it.

"Every single part," I whisper.

"Good. Because that's the part I want."

"Which one?"

"All of them. I see *all* of them when I look at you, Fiona." He smiles, eyes narrowing, the brown depth of them too hard to describe. I can only feel them, the emotion behind what they say touching all the years of who I am.

"I'm sorry," I tell him, the words like bricks I have to lift out of a thousand-mile deep well. But I do it. I lift them and offer their weight to him in the form of apology.

"For what?"

"For carrying around this crazy idea that because I couldn't get over something, it was your fault. You've been taking up a lot of energy inside me, Chris Fletcher. For someone I thought I couldn't stand, I thought about you a *lot*."

"How about you keep thinking about me a lot, only in a different way?"

Our mouths meet, his lips soft and full, his arms hard and unyielding as we kiss into each other, burrowing with intensity, the cold wall no longer there, the freezing gust of wind a welcome intrusion to help sweep away the past. We're spinning and spinning, each other's center of gravity, and as I lose myself in him, I realize I've found myself, too.

Finally.

Energy doesn't lie. People do. People can fool themselves, use denial as a tool, create defense mechanisms that look like artwork.

But energy? It just is.

And when you fall for the right person, it's the same way.

It just... *is*.

CHAPTER 14

*W*e've been on five dates in just a few weeks, logged 175 bike miles together (turns out he's serious about that whole 1,000 mile thing!), and now it's the ultimate dating test: eating at Taco Cubed together. The technical name for the restaurant is Taco Taco Taco, but Taco Cubed is easier. The best Mexican joint in the region, it was founded the year we graduated high school, and I've been a regular ever since.

Plus, flirting with the owner's son, Pedro Jr., is a fun pasttime.

My eyes cut over to Fletch.

Was. *Was* a fun pasttime.

"There's a parking spot right there." Fletch points to a paid municipal lot as I navigate my little electric car through the streets of Anderhill. I'm fully charged, so it feels wrong to take one of the free charging station spots in town.

"But it's a *meter*." I curl my lips and shudder.

"So? I've got quarters. Or we can use that parking app to pay. It's all set up on my phone."

"Hand me my divining rod."

"Your *what*?"

"It's a piece of wood."

"You'll have to be more specific." He looks down at his crotch.

I blush. This is the stage of dating we're in. We haven't had sex yet–actual intercourse, that is–but there's a running exchange of double entendres. Mostly clever, sometimes silly, a few groaners.

"It's shaped like a Y."

"This?" He holds it up, then holds his palm up. "Man, the sunlight is ginting off that crystal hanging on your rearview mirror. What is that?"

"Energy vampire talisman."

"HUH?"

"Just give me the rod." Fumbling a bit, I take it from him.

"What does that thing have to do with parking?"

"It's magic. And energy. Not that there's any difference between the two."

"What does it do?"

"Guides me to free parking."

"That is weirdly specific."

"It's better than a more general intention."

"What's that? Witchcraft?"

"Not quite, but you're getting close."

"You're a witch? Like Salem?"

"No. But I use energy to find energy."

"Sounds circular."

"Only if you view it on a single plane, in a single universe, and believe in entropy."

"I, uh..."

"AH HA!" The car pulling out up ahead, one of the six

spots without meters on Central Street, couldn't have timed it better.

"Coincidence," Fletch murmurs.

"My divining rod creates a lot of coincidences."

"You just point this thing at whatever you want and you get what you want?"

"It's not quite that simple, but in a way, yes."

A quick grasp of the Y and he points it at me. "Huh. What do you know? It works."

"*I'm* not free parking!"

"I will not make a joke about putting something in your garage."

"Chris!"

The kiss he gives me curls my toes, but the gear shift between us pokes painfully at my hip as my stomach growls.

"Are you sure you don't want to go straight to Thai Me Up?" he asks, arms still around me.

Heat plumes in me, sudden and fierce.

"What?"

Jutting his chin, he points behind me. "You know. The Thai place. Thai Me Up?" I follow his line of sight and see the sign for the restaurant.

"Oh. Right. That. No. Taco Cubed is good," I mutter, suddenly squirming.

We separate and leave the car, walking into Taco Cubed, the scent of cumin and cilantro tickling my nose in a delightful way as we make our way to the counter.

Tatted-up Pedro Jr. is there, head down, eyes darting across the food prep area. "Hey, Feisty Fighter," he says in an understated way, looking up briefly at Fletch. "And Hot Boxer."

We both groan.

"About time someone started dating her," he comments

to Fletch with a look that says he approves. "She's a goddamned goddess and deserves to be worshipped."

I go mute. Fletch's hands turn into fists.

"Uh, thank you, Pedro," I say as I touch Fletch's arm.

The grin Pedro flashes me shows a little wistfulness. "You're batty with your magic crap, but you remind me of *mi abuela*. She was into that voodoo, too."

"It's not voodoo, actually."

Waving a spatula in the air, he says, "It's all voodoo eventually. Whatcha want?"

I turn to Fletch. Here's the real dating test. Will he pass? The theme to *Jeopardy* plays inside my head.

He looks at Pedro and says, "Triple hard shell with two guac, one sour cream, extra green chile salsa, and peanut butter." Hand on the small of my back, he leans in and adds, "Fiona?"

That's an order I've never heard of.

"Did you just order *peanut butter* with your tacos?" I ask gleefully.

"Yes."

Pedro shrugs. "Weirdo, but he's not wrong. I tried it after my dad lost his shit when Fletch asked for it the first time. It's not bad."

Fletch gives me a triumphant look. "Try it with me."

"I don't have that level of taco courage."

"You want your normal order, Feisty?"

I grit my teeth. "Yes. No peanut butter." Fletch squeezes my hand.

"You don't know what you're missing." He kisses the back of my hand as Pedro cocks an eyebrow and steps into the kitchen to get something.

"Guacamole and peanut butter do *not* go together."

"Why not?"

"Because they have distinctly different mouthfeels."

"So do our tongues."

"What do our tongues have to do with—*oh!*"

Not caring one bit who sees, Fletch takes me into his arms and kisses me, a full-throttle, no-holds-barred, public-claiming kiss that leaves me thoroughly wet, physically boneless, and a bit disoriented by the time he's done.

"See? Different tongues have different feels but they taste perfect *together*."

"Right," I say, struck dumb. "Yeah."

Pedro brings our two trays and moves on to the next customer, giving Fletch the evil eye.

We move, my body floating, and settle into a booth.

Fletch surveys his tray for a moment, then moves the guac, salsa, sour cream, and peanut butter in alarmingly familiar ways, aligning them and arranging a series of four knives in specific patterns. His precision comes with an intensity that's making me hold my breath.

A ball of lead forms in the pit of my stomach. He reminds me of—

"Fiona! Fletch! Imagine running into you here!" Mallory is wearing a stylish black wool peacoat, her arm hooked into Will's elbow. The two of them are sporting red cheeks from the cold, but other than that similarity, the they couldn't look more different.

Mallory is excited.

Will looks like someone took him hostage.

Taco hostage.

"Hey," he says glumly, making Fletch cock an eyebrow.

"Hey, man. You okay?"

"Oh. Sure. Just, you know," he says, thumbing toward the menu board and ordering counter. "Getting tacos."

"*Real* tacos," Mal notes, eyeing my soft tacos like they're evidence in a Hague trial.

And then she looks at Fletch's plate. Cocks her head.

Narrows her eyes. One of her longer curls picks that moment to *boing* up, brushing against an increasingly tight jaw.

Will watches, more wary than I like.

Moving slowly, she sits down on the edge of the booth next to Fletch. Her eyes don't leave his tray.

"Is that... what is that?" she asks, pointing to the peanut butter.

"Peanut butter," Fletch answers happily, picking up the first knife and–

No.

Oh, no.

I move over so Will, still in his zipped-up winter ski jacket, can sit down, too.

Fletch plunges the clean knife into the container of guacamole and carefully spreads it on the edge of his taco. He picks up the second knife and moves on to the peanut butter, doing the same. Third knife, sour cream, same.

Salsa, same.

The four layers are evenly distributed, of approximately the same thickness, and have a visually pleasing appearance.

And then, with Mallory eyeing him like Perky with PMS eyeing a menthol cigarette, Fletch takes a perfectly composed bite of the edge of his taco.

As he chews, her eyes drift to my plate, where one of the soft tortillas flops like a homeless man's threadbare blanket.

Finishing his bite, he swallows, reaches for mineral water, takes another gulp, and looks at Mallory. "You seem overly interested in my tacos." He glances at the counter. "Why don't you guys order?"

"Peanut butter?" Mal says in a low, breathy voice, like a homicide investigator viewing a novel way someone's been murdered, as if a perp has killed a human being using only an expired Starbucks gift card and an IUD.

"Yeah."

"Is it… what does it taste like… I'm intrigued!"

"Really?" Will grunts, standing up. "I'll go get our orders." He leaves quickly, almost guiltily, abandoning me with these two weirdos. Pretty soon they're going to start talking about—

"The ratio," Fletch says pleasantly. "It's all about the ratio."

Seventeen generations of terrified ancestors start screaming in my astral plane.

"YES!" Mal gasps, moving closer to him. "The mouth-feel has to be perfect."

At the word *mouthfeel*, he grins at me, my tongue still tasting that kiss.

"My perfect ratio is about micro and macronutrients," he starts, though it's hard to hear his words over all of my past lives scrambling in an effort to blameshift the torture I'm going through right now. What karma did I incur to deserve this? I finally fall in love with a guy and he's—

Hold on.

Love?

"The corn shell has the carbs. I'm trying to convince Pedro to carry cassava-flour tortillas. They're gluten free, too, and…"

I project my consciousness into 1842 on the Dakota prairie during a snowstorm that causes widespread famine, to give myself some relief.

Sadly, it doesn't work, so I pick at my taco until Will comes back with their orders.

Fletch looks across the booth at me. "You okay?"

"Fine."

Will does a double take. "Uh oh. When they start saying *fine*, you know the honeymoon's over."

For the next ten minutes, Will and I sit next to each other and eat our food like normal people. Which is to say, we don't count out macronutrients, talk about manganese and folate micrograms in avocado, or discuss how combining peanut butter oil and green chile salsa does something to brown fat.

Which you want more of.

I guess. It's hard to understand Fletch's words over the sense of despair that changes my blue-light aura into a broken yellow taco shell of doom.

I cannot believe I am watching my bestie and my new boyfriend bond, word by word, bite by bite, over the perfect ratio.

"This is crazy," Will mutters to me as he wipes his mouth, balling up his napkin and tossing it on top of his failed taco. My own failed taco mocks me, as if it's turned grey and is dissolving into a cloud of ash, to be carried off by Thanos's finger snap.

It didn't make the cut.

"How can they do this to food?" I say out of the corner of my mouth. "It's like they're D&D nerds with dairy and legumes."

"I heard that," Mallory says sharply, then she grins. "You two are just jealous."

"Jealous?" Will and I say in unison. Then we snort.

"Of what?" I ask.

"That we have elevated mere calorie consumption to something with more meaning."

"You've taken a positive emotional experience and deconstructed it to the point of despair," I counter.

Will nods. "Thank you for putting it into words," he says, patting the back of my hand.

Fletch's eyes narrow as he watches that gesture.

"Well, I, for one, am thrilled to discover one of your friends is as smart about taco ratios as I am!" Mallory says in a voice I know is joking, but Fletch might not. She looks at Will. "How about we invite them to come on our trip next weekend?"

"Trip?" Fletch asks.

"We rented a two-bedroom cabin in Maine. Middle of nowhere. There's skiing nearby, but snowshoeing right at the cabin. Plenty of fun sledding. Parker and Perky were coming, but he had to cancel–some subcommittee assignment about concrete road dividers or something. You guys want to come?"

"We're second choice?" I ask, a little hurt. Mal's eyes catch mine and widen.

"No, of course not! We asked Parker and Perky to join us, before you two were..." She looks at Fletch, who looks at me, then down at Will's hand, then up at Will.

Who removes his hand.

Huh. I've got a possessive one, don't I?

"Before we were *what*?" I ask Mallory, but my gaze holds Fletch's, and we sit there, soaked in the energy of definitions.

"Before we were a couple," Fletch finishes.

Definition achieved.

"Are we?"

"You're my girlfriend," he says, making Mallory practically pee herself with joy.

Will just nods slowly.

"As long as you say yes, of course," Fletch adds.

"How can I say no?"

He reaches across the table for my hand. "That's not a yes."

"Yes, Chris," I say obediently, happily. "I'll be your girlfriend. Not that we need a label, because labels don't define people, but..."

"Fiona?"

"Yes?"

"That's better. Just yes."

"Then it's settled," Mal says. "Next weekend is going to be so much fun! We'll make tacos for dinner one night."

Will and I groan.

Fletch and Mal just laugh.

CHAPTER 15

"*W*hat do you mean, we have to *hike* up that hill to the cabin? Why can't we drive?" Mallory asks as we stare at the large sled next to us. Will hands her a printout of the email from the owner, a friendly explanation of how this remote rental cabin works. It's been a week since we ran into her and Will at Taco Cubed and here we are, the four of us, on a weekend getaway.

Adulting.

"Even an SUV with chains can get stuck. It's only a quarter mile. No problem," Fletch responds. "My grandparents have a place in Rowley on the beach, and when it rains bad enough, the road washes out and we use a cart. This is nothing." Meanwhile, Will's pulling suitcase after suitcase out of the back of his Volvo SUV, a fairly new vehicle he and Mal bought this year, in preparation for having a family fairly soon.

It's really been helpful for all her luggage.

"We have to walk up *that?*" After two days of pouring rain, the hill is nothing but mud.

"There's a sled." He points. "The owners covered it all."

"Is there internet?" Her nose crinkles up as her mind races to explore all the possibilities.

"There's a dish. Some kind of satellite internet. But you have to be really close to the cabin for a signal," Will says as he acts as her sherpa, loading suitcases and bags. He peeks into one. "Is this grocery bag full of nothing but bacon, brownie mix, eggs, and coffee?"

"Yes."

"And this one is taco makings?"

"Uh huh. The refrigerator stuff is in the cooler."

Will and I share a look only Taco Hostages would understand.

"Good thing I brought steaks and asparagus," he mutters.

"I LOVE ASPARAGUS!" I shout, a little too loud.

"Are you a stinky pee person?" Mal asks as we lock up the car and start our ascent up the muddy hill.

"Huh?" Fletch asks.

"You know. Asparagus pee. Some people have that gene. Like cilantro. It tastes like soap for some people. Genes."

"I don't know. I don't smell my pee," I confess.

"What does it smell like?" Fletch asks, grunting as he pushes the sled out of a rut, helping Will.

"Like asparagus," Mal says slowly.

"Never noticed," he says, and then that's the last we hear from the guys, other than grunting, until we make it to the top of the hill.

When we're on the porch, which is soaking wet from the rain, I take a moment to turn around and appreciate the sweeping, panoramic beauty of this place at twilight. The three-hour drive was worth every minute. It feels like we're at the tippy top of the world, the road down below the only sign of civilization. To the right of the cabin is a huge lean-to full of wood. Solar panels, separate from the house, are in an array to the left, facing south. The front door is unlocked, which surprises me.

Then again, thieves would have to work damn hard to get here.

"Never knew bacon and coffee could be so heavy," Will complains as he unloads the sled, flashing an ungrumpy grin at Mallory, who bats her eyelashes. They're cute together, a study in contrasts that have come together to be a comfortable combination.

Is that what Fletch and I look like to an outsider?

Our boots are covered in muck, and we each take turns scrubbing them on the boot scraper, then carefully step inside the door. Lifelong New Englanders, all of us, we're trained in boot etiquette when it comes to mud and snow.

No one wants to step on a lump of wet mud in socks or slippers later.

Three trips from the sled to the house and we're done. I kick off my boots, unzip my weekend bag, and find my purple furry slippers, a gift from Mom and Dad last year.

"Cute!" Mallory says, eyeing her three suitcases. "I'm not sure where mine are."

"Which bedroom do you guys want?" Will asks. There's a big living room, the kitchen to the left, all of it open. A small table with four chairs between kitchen and couches serves as a dining room. Straight ahead is a hallway that bisects the two bedrooms. An open door at the end of the hall shows me that's the bathroom.

The place is small, cozy, and very rustic. Fletch is kneeling in front of the woodstove, lighting it, and it's already putting out a wonderful woodsy scent.

And now we're deciding which bed he and I are going to share, to sleep together for the first time.

"That one," Fletch says without ceremony, hauling his

duffel bag and my carry-on into the room. I follow him, Mallory smiling at me as Will starts moving her luggage in, piece by piece.

The guy's going to need some time.

In our bedroom, Fletch puts my bag next to the closet, dumping his duffel on the floor at the foot of the bed. Before I can say a word to him, I'm on my back on the quilt, his mouth on mine, our bodies still encased in thick coats.

"This is fun," he says, looking down at me with eyes that feel like I'm being invited into eternity.

"It is."

"I'm happy to be here with you."

"Me, too. With you."

And I am. Every breath I take when I'm near him feels so grounded and centered. Reading his energy is easy. It's neutral in a freeing kind of way, not too frenetic, not too mild. He just *is*, and how many people have that kind of presence?

"Hey! Not yet, you two!" Will jokes as he leans against the door frame. "How about an early dinner and a moonlit walk later?"

"We can make tacos!" Mallory calls out from the other room. "I brought all the fixings!"

Fletch climbs off me as my eyes catch Will's.

"STEAK!" he shouts, practically sprinting. "I brought fresh herbs and your favorite manchego so Fletch and I can grill steak and asparagus. Let the guys make dinner tonight," I hear him urging as I smother my smile with my gloved hand. Fletch stands near the coat rack, peeling off his layers.

There's an old-fashioned radio, the kind with a dial. I turn it on. Nothing but static.

"Getting a signal out here will be hard," Fletch says,

turning to the CD player next to the radio. "Man, this is old school. Love it."

"But there's internet, right?" Mal asks, a bit nervously.

"There's a DISH satellite," Will patiently explains. "It's in the instructions. We're limited to two hours of internet a day, though."

"*Two hours?*"

"Why are you worried? We didn't come here to be online," he says, nuzzling her cheek.

"What if we want to binge Netflix?"

"What if we—*what?*" he asks, tickling her, Mal's curls bouncing as she giggles. "You think we're here to binge-watch Netflix? I'm here to binge on *you*."

Fletch's arm goes around my shoulders as he reaches for one of the beer bottles in a six-pack, pops the cap off, and offers it to me. The cool rush of good beer and the laughter make me relax. With the rest of the weekend ahead of us, time feels endless.

In the best way possible.

Setting himself up with his own beer, Fletch drinks and watches our friends. Sometimes I forget he and Will have a completely independent relationship outside of Will's connection to Mallory. I've been in school with Fletch since sixth grade. Graduated from high school together. Lived in the same town since college. We've tangentially crossed paths, but as we hang out in this cabin and I see the easy, casual way Will and Fletch are—like Perky, Mallory, and me—he becomes more real.

And when I'm with him, I'm more real, too.

Will lets Mal go and grabs two more beers, popping off the tops and offering one to her gasping form.

"I'll get you back for that!" she vows before taking a sip. Both Will and Fletch wander away from us, taking in the rental. It's rustic to say the least, with brown leather couches covered in thick throw blankets. Two small wood-stoves are positioned strategically, a small kettle on the one near the kitchen. Depending on where you stand in the living room, you're either comfortably warm or ice cold. But the place is well insulated, and a welcoming basket of snacks sits on the counter next to the owner's instruction sheets.

We're here alone, for two nights, to do nothing.

My eyes jump to the bedroom door.

Well, not... *nothing*.

"They have quite the DVD collection," Fletch notes, using his finger to poke through the jewel cases. "Hmmm. Sally Field in *Not Without My Daughter*. Kurt Russell in *Overboard*. Chevy Chase and Goldie Hawn in–"

"Who?" I ask.

"Kate Hudson's mom," Mallory explains.

"No, I know her, but who's... Chevy..?"

"A comedian? I think he was on *Saturday Night Live* a really long time ago? And some cheesy 1980s Christmas movie my dad likes."

"Oh."

"Those don't sound like the most recent movies."

"Every season of *The Muppet Show*!" Will says in the tone of a young boy. "Wow! My grandpa loved these!"

"Hey!" Fletch says in a tone of surprise. "My signal works!" He wiggles his phone.

"Mine doesn't," Mallory pouts.

I look at my phone. No bars.

"Mine, too!" Will says, fist bumping Fletch.

I turn mine off. "Happy not to be tethered to it or get all my notifications. I'm still gaining about five hundred Instagram followers a day!"

"I'm running at about a thousand," Fletch says.

"What?"

He grins. "That sportswear campaign has been fabulous for the gym."

Will's stomach growls. "Hey, Fletch. Let's fire up the grill and get those steaks going."

For the next twenty minutes, Mallory and I sit on two separate leather chairs under down blankets, drinking beer and watching our guys make dinner. It's a sight to behold, not because I've never seen a man cook—my Dad does it all the time—but because these are *our* guys.

I have a boyfriend.

And we're here with our good friends, being adults, on vacation, having fun.

No pretense. I don't have to impress him. There's no constant internal judo going on. It's just me and him and our buddies, spending time together.

This is everything I ever hoped for.

How did it fall into my life so fast? Not much more than a month ago, I was in my classroom, perfectly fine. Life was okay. Dating was a pain. I wasn't searching for the right guy.

But the universe was searching, for me.

Was it? Did I attract the right energy to make me see Chris in a new light?

Or did he find *my* light?

The guys shrug into their coats and head outside with asparagus wrapped in tinfoil and a plate of steaks. Within a minute, I smell cooking meat.

"This is amazing," Mallory says in a tone of awe. "We're here. They're here. You're dating Fletch. *Fletch!*"

"I know!" I drink more beer. It's turning warm, my pace decidedly slower than everyone else's. Truth be told, I'm not a huge beer fan. It's fine and I like it well enough, but not enough to drink too much. "All those years I wasted."

"Wasted?"

"He's so wonderful. Kind and smart and competent."

"Competent is attractive?"

"Of course! Competent is the new sexy. *People* magazine should have a World's Most Competent Man issue."

"When I think of a competent man, I think of my dad."

"Not Will?"

"Competent feels flat. Like, do you want just a *competent* guy in bed?"

"Ew. No."

"Then why would you want a competent guy in another area? How about exceptional? Awe-inspiring?"

"Because competence in daily life is hard to find! He's dependable. Can assess a situation and take action. I trust him to fix stuff. Don't underrate competence."

"Will's like that, too. He's not a paramedic or a fire-fighter, but he just does what needs to be done. He knows how to keep pushing to get the right answer or solution. Does it on his own."

"Exactly!"

"And he's *wayyyy* more than competent in bed!" Mal squeaks as she finishes her beer and gets another.

"I heard that!" Will calls out as he and Fletch come back inside with cooked steaks. "Who says I'm competent in bed?" The look on his face makes it clear he's not pleased with that label.

"Not me," Fletch cracks. "Every time we've had sex, you've been the best ever."

Will freezes mid-stretch, the plate of steaks still in his hand, hovering over the counter. Their eyes meet.

"We said we would never talk about that," he says tightly.

Mal and I instantly sit up and lean toward them.

And then Fletch laughs.

Mal throws a pillow at him, hitting his face square on, making him chortle even harder as Will shields the steaks.

"What happens in the football locker room stays in the football locker room," they intone together.

"Oh, my God. It's like high school all over again," I call out as Mal and I trade eye rolls.

And yet, it's not. At all. Not even a little.

In high school, Fletch and Will were the closest thing to gods, because they were football players. Popular jocks who were smart, too. Will was the top guy—the quarterback on his way to the Ivy League, blocked from being valedictorian only by Mallory.

Fletch was a good-enough student, the football defensive linebacker recruited by Endicott College. He majored in Exercise Science, came back home, worked for the town, and founded his own gym.

Chris Fletcher is a townie through and through, accepted by all.

Back in high school, we were so different.

"Never in a million years did I imagine this," Fletch says as he and Will set the tiny table, Mallory and I standing to come over for dinner.

"Imagine what?" I ask.

"That Will and I would someday go on a weekend getaway with our girlfriends, and you two would be the women."

"Fiancée," Mallory corrects.

The word *girlfriend* makes me smile.

He tips an imaginary hat to her. "Yes, ma'am."

"I imagined it," Will said. "Not like this, but I wondered about Mallory."

"You never dreamed about being married to me. Settling down. Having a family," she adds.

Fletch gives me a glance that carries so much meaning, I feel the weight of its energy in every cell of my body. It's so heavy, I have to instantly sit, plunking down on a hard wooden seat, the jolt rattling my bones from the ass up.

"No," Will agrees as we all take our places. "But I liked you. We've talked about this before."

She just smiles as she flattens a paper napkin in her lap.

"I wondered about Fiona," Fletch says, my arm pausing in midair as I bring the rest of my beer to my mouth.

Everyone goes silent, Will smirking at him.

"Wondered if she'd flatten you again if you kissed her?"

"For the record," Fletch says in an arch tone, "that hasn't happened."

"Yet," I mutter.

Will is in the middle of eating his first slice of filet and practically chokes. Mal bites her lower lip, while Fletch looks at me with an *I dare you* expression on his face.

"If you want a fair fight with me, Missy, I'll give you one. My studio. Next Wednesday. Day before Thanksgiving."

"You're on."

We drink and eat, and Mal and I make all the appropriate praising comments, but in truth, the steaks are expertly cooked, the asparagus is roasted to perfection, and somehow they managed to grill fresh pineapple in a way that makes me want to moan with orgiastic wonder.

Oddly enough, I'm reminded of ferrets, who cannot eat this delicious treat.

By the time we're finished with the meal, I'm ready to find a blanket, curl up on the couch with Fletch, and watch some silly comedy until I fall asleep.

"Dishes!" Mallory calls out, looking at me as she stands, double-fisted, holding Will's empty plate. "They cooked. We clean up."

I fake whimper and stand, reaching for Fletch's plate. "Fair is fair."

He threads his fingers behind his head and leans back, biceps bulging as he flexes and says, "I could get used to this."

Our eyes connect, held a beat longer than is proper, the deepening look making me swoon. "Me, too," I tell him.

As I walk away, he pats my ass.

"You two are adorable," Mal whispers as we figure out the kitchen, the layout very homespun and simple. No dishwasher. Mal starts scraping plates into a composting jar on the counter and I rinse them, finding a scrubbie sponge and some grease-cutting dishwashing liquid.

"Thanks. I still don't get it," I say before realizing she walked away and is coming back with the rest of the dishes. Will and Fletch are now on the couch, fresh beers popped open, chatting.

"What?" she asks brightly, taking a clean dish from me, ready with a towel to dry.

"I don't get it. How he and I have settled into being together so easily. It's too easy, Mal. Like something's wrong."

"You're not like this, Fi. You never worry about the other shoe dropping."

"No—it's not that. I'm not paranoid or worried. It's more that I'm perplexed."

"Perplexed?" We become an assembly line of dishwashing, the clean plates moving steadily as I wash and she dries, the stack growing until we're done. Silverware next.

"I spent so much time angry with him for what happened all those years ago. Why? How could I take such a nice guy and create this caricature of him in my head?"

"Because we were twelve when that happened. And then the rest was the teen years. Fletch wasn't this easy-going and fun and nice back then. Neither was Will." She makes a huffing sound. "And you and I weren't the same then, either."

"So this feeling I have of missing out–of wasting years– is unnecessary?"

"What does Jolene say?"

"She told me to make space. That the universe would send what I need into the space, but I had to clear it out for that to happen."

"And it did."

"But Mal–I'm really falling for him."

"Falling? In love?"

The word *love* makes me shiver, a literal vibration with a frequency that feels so good to have in my body. "Yes."

The *maybe* that almost slipped out felt too timid, too old-Fiona, too uncertain. What rises to the top with my *yes* is a blend of the old and the new, better and stronger, more assured and resilient.

The truth always wins out.

The sound of glass on glass makes us both turn. Fletch is standing within hearing distance of us, his arm up, the empty beer bottle having just landed in the recycling bin.

The look on his face makes me wonder if he just heard us.

Love.

"Fiona," he says slowly, each step toward me making that frequency inside stronger. "Let's go for a walk."

"A walk?"

Mallory smiles to herself. "I can finish up," she declares.

One of Fletch's hands lands on my hip, the way he pulls me into him a grounded act. "If we had bikes, I'd go night-time trail riding with you." A press of his lips on my temple should be a quick kiss, but he lingers.

Mallory rinses her hands, then dries them, leaving the kitchen with a wink.

"Nighttime riding? Would those miles count?"

"Count?"

"I thought we had to bike a thousand miles together before you'd sleep with me. By my calculation, we're only at 455," I tease.

"How about we move our legs in bed and that counts?"

"How many miles do you expect to accumulate from *that*?"

"More than you could ever dream of, babe."

A low, throaty laugh that comes from a piece of me I didn't know I had but that is thoroughly delighted to step forward makes me feel warm and liquid, ready for hours of naked fun in bed with a man I am falling for more and more.

A man I wasted all those years avoiding.

"How about we just walk for a mile or so?" he suggests, thumbing toward the door. "It's a full moon and the night sky up here is spectacular."

"Don't go too far. There are bears out here, you know," Will warns us.

"We'll stay on the path down to the car. I'll take a stick."

"A stick isn't going to protect you from a bear."

"No, but it'll buy me enough time to get you to safety," he says to me.

"I suddenly have zero interest in going for a walk."

"But we need wine!" Mallory says, winking at me. "There's some chilling in the car. You two should definitely go for a walk."

Does she know something I don't? Did she overhear something Fletch and Will were discussing?

"Okay. I'll take the chance," I say slowly.

"I'm really not worried," Fletch says, "and I wilderness camp. If you want, I can make a spray bottle."

"A spray bottle?"

"Of urine."

"That's up for debate!" Will calls out. "Lots of people think it's bullshit that black bears don't like human urine."

"Every time I've camped, I've sprayed a urine perimeter around my tent and never had a bear come near," Fletch argues.

"You're fighting about your *pee*," Mallory points out.

"We're settling the terms of the debate," her fiancé replies.

"About pee. Urine. Piss. Tinkle."

"Tinkle?"

"That's my grandma's word for it, God rest her soul."

"'Urine perimeter' is so sexy," I whisper in Fletch's ear.

"You got a kink I need to know about?" he asks, slightly alarmed.

"No! Can we stop talking about pee and just go?" I grab Fletch's arm and pull him to our coats. We dress quickly but carefully. That whole lifelong-New-Englander thing teaches you to respect the cold.

The temperature has dropped radically in the last few hours, a steady, light snow coming down, already blanketing the ground, layering on the wet trees, making the land around us cast an ethereal glow as the evening light takes on a hazy, almost silvery cast that makes me think of between times, energy diffuse and wanting, waiting to find its rightful place. As we walk, Fletch pokes the ground with his stick, one arm around me as we walk in tandem.

The car isn't far. We take two four-packs of micro-brew beer, and for good measure I grab bottles of white wine. The trek back is short, the snow still falling, the crunch of our footsteps all we hear. When we are almost back to the cabin, we stop. The light spilling out onto the snow, the scent of woodsmoke in the air, creates a classic scene of warmth and comfort. Falling flakes whirl and glitter in the air all around us.

He's right. The scenery is spectacular.

Especially because I'm looking at him.

And he's looking right back.

Swept up in his arms as we drop what's in our hands into the snow, I'm transported by his kiss to another layer of existence, where my feet don't touch the ground and my heart never, ever stops beating with joy. His lips are warm and wet and the way he touches me makes me feel like we've met before, as if splintered pieces of past lives have assembled themselves into the souls we are now, and we're hugging hello, reacquainting ourselves with a deeper love that transports across time.

We're covered head to toe in outerwear, so my gloved hands can't touch his hot skin or feel the silken strands of his short hair, but our mouths, our tongues, the intensity of our embrace is more than enough.

I have more than enough, now.

"When I saw you in your classroom after Rico tried to take Mattie, something in me broke and grew at the same time, Fiona," he rasps against my cheek. "I knew Mattie was safe, over in the woods with the cops, but they wouldn't let me over there yet. So I came upon you and so help me, Fiona, the first thought I had was *Please don't let her be hurt*. Because I knew I'd have to kill my own brother-in-law with my bare hands if he hurt you or anyone else in that classroom."

"He didn't."

"Because you are *you*. I know you hate that stupid nick-name I gave you back in seventh grade, but you are Feisty. Feisty with a big F, feisty with a little f. You're fierce and you fight and you're so goddamn free, Fiona. I saw it in you when we were kids. It's like you glow, even when you don't have a reason to. You just can't help it."

He presses his palm against my heart. "I've never met someone so easy to be around. Someone who I know is pure *good*, no matter what. You had that since the day I met you. You'll have it until the last day on Earth I see you. I want that day to take as long as possible to happen. I want to be in your life for as long as you'll let me."

I shut him up with a kiss, tears streaming down the sides of my face, the need to touch his skin greater than the need to hear him say another word. We're on the precipice of saying the word *love*, and as much as I feel it, it's too soon, too rushed, too *something*.

I need more time, even when it feels like we've known each other in past times, and what I want more than anything is to show him how I feel, with my body, with my bare soul, with my naked lust. His hands slide around my waist, pulling me up, into him, splitting my thighs until the full thickness of him is hitting the perfect spot, making me rise up, up, up, gasping as a climax begins, his mouth on mine, his lips suddenly at my nose, biting my earlobe, then stopping.

He licks his lips. "Salt. Are you crying?" His hold on me lessens. "Fiona, I don't want you to do anything you don't want."

"No! The tears–they're happy tears." On tiptoes, I kiss him, his uncertainty melting as I decide to be bold, stroking him outside his jeans, eliciting a groan that vibrates straight between my legs.

"You're killing me. I'm ready to make love to you right here, in the snow."

"I'm not exactly interested in having a popsicle inside me."

"For as much blood as I have in there, no way is it anywhere close to frozen."

"How about we go back to that nice, warm bed at the cabin?"

"You're on," he says, stiffly lifting one boot, then the other, as we waddle-race back to the cabin, grabbing his bear stick, the beer and wine and hauling it back.

As we approach the cabin, a loud thump on the wall on the left gives us pause.

"That was loud," Fletch says, brows knitting. He opens the front door just as we hear Mallory scream a muffled, "Oh, my GOD!"

Thump!

Our eyes meet and we burst into laughter, Fletch grabbing my arm as if he needs me to keep him up as he folds in half.

"They're loud in bed, huh? Who knew?" he hisses.

"Will! Oh, my GOD!" she screams again.

Thump thump!

The wall seems to shake, a giant thump making pictures in the hallway quiver on the walls.

"I can't make it stop!" Will cries out.

"Can it get in?" Mallory squeals.

"I don't think so, but it's determined!"

"Where are Fletch and Fiona? We need them to see this!"

"No. No, we don't," Fletch says, horrified. "Were we invited to a swinger's weekend and didn't know it?"

In unison, our phone notifications go nuts. I guess I can get a signal here after all.

I look at my screen. It's nothing but texts from Mallory.

THUMP!

"Bear?" Fletch says, squinting at his phone.

I look at mine.

There's a bear in our bedroom. And we're trapped in the closet. Help!

"What does she mean, bear? Is that a euphemism for–"

"MALLORY!" I scream as Fletch raises his stick behind him, like a parking lot barricade, holding me back. "WILL!"

"FIONA! HELP! BEAR!"

And then their bedroom door opens two inches, the brown snout of a small bear poking out.

"Holy shit," Fletch says, holding onto the stick, inserting himself between me and the–

Bear?

CHAPTER 16

*Y*es.

Bear.

"MALLORY!" I scream as the bear backs up. My shout scared it.

"FIONA! FLETCH!" she shouts back. "Thank God! Help!"

"Where are you?" Fletch yells.

"IN THE CLOSET!" Will bellows.

The door's cracked slightly, the glimpses of dark fur roaming back and forth making it clear the bear's not full grown. Which means there's a mama nearby.

"That's a cub," Fletch says, as if reading my mind. "An older one, maybe a year or so. I need to get him out of there. *Fast.*"

"The mama is close, isn't she?"

"I guess. All I know is they stay with their mothers for about two years." He turns toward the door. "HOW DID IT GET IN?" he shouts.

"WILL WAS CLEANING THE GRILL AND IT APPEARED!" Mallory screams.

"We ran for safety and hid in here!" Will adds.

The bear startles, banging against the open door, shutting it again.

"Hang on!" Fletch says. "Stop shouting! Just text!"

He pulls out his phone and starts a group text with: *We're scaring it and keeping it in the bedroom with the screaming.*

OK, Mal texts back. *But I'm scared too. And I think it peed in my shoes.*

"You," Fletch says to me as he holds the hiking stick like a baseball bat. "Go in our bedroom. Lock the door. Shove the bed against it. And don't come out until I tell you it's okay."

"What?"

"I don't want you getting hurt."

"You think you can single-handedly He-Man your way through getting a bear out of the cabin? No way. You need my help."

Bzzz

Use a stick to open the bedroom door. It wants to leave and can't figure it out, Will texts.

I'll lure it out the front door with some food, Fletch replies.

Use the taco stuff, Will answers as I type, *Use taco fixings.*

Will and I are on the same wavelength. I see I have a Taco Ally.

Fletch gives me a funny, incredulous look.

None of this would be happening if we'd gone to that ski resort with the couples stone massage and the CBD-oil options! Mallory texts, adding nine red angry faces after.

You said you wanted to try something new, Will replies.

THIS IS NOT MY IDEA OF NEW! she answers in all caps.

"Aren't they sitting in a closet right next to each other? Are we seriously stuck watching them textfight?" I ask Fletch, who moves to the fridge.

"I'll get the damn bear out of there and ignore the rest," he sensibly states. "Must be feeding before hibernating at the end of the month. Biggest worry is the mama. If she shows up, we're toast." He eyes the front door.

I walk toward it.

"No!"

"Why? I'm looking to see if she's out there. We have to open the door to get the baby out. Right now, we're all reasonably safe, Mallory's shoes aside. If we open that door to shoo the baby out and she's there, we escalate this."

He tilts his head as he looks at me. "You would make an excellent first responder. You can triage a situation damn well."

"I'm a preschool teacher. My entire day is nothing but triage."

THUMP! THUMP!

The bedroom door shakes on its hinges, the young bear making huffing sounds, the distinct scrape of claws on wood making my back teeth ache.

I close my eyes.

I imagine the bear.

I ask my ancestors for help.

I summon the energy and light force of all beings and I synchronize.

Slowly, I walk to the window, eyes barely open, and look out. Fletch is holding a container of blueberries and a piece of frozen salmon.

"No, mama. Stay away, mama," I tell the mother bear.

"You see her?"

"No. I'm telling her to stay away."

"Why are you—"

THUMP!

"It's safe," I tell him, hand on the front door.

"You open the door and run into our bedroom. I'll throw the food on the porch, then I'll open Will's bedroom door and run. You got that?"

"Yes."

He grabs my arm. "I mean it. You RUN into our bedroom and lock the door, no matter what."

Adrenaline races through me, the feeling old and familiar. My arms and legs feel numb and electric at the same time, Fletch's protective intensity making it hard to argue.

Because he's right.

"What about you?" I beg, worried sick that something could go wrong.

"I'll be fine. I can run outside if I need to, or tip the couch over and get under it. I'll grab that pan," he points to the clean cast-iron skillet on the stove, "and bang it against something metal to scare it. The thing just wants to leave."

"Okay."

"You ready? Open the door, run to our bedroom, shove the bed in front of the door. That's all you have to do, babe."

I nod and grab the doorknob.

"One, two, THREE!" he shouts, my hand turning the knob, opening the door all the way, hoping it doesn't ricochet back. Sprinting to our bedroom door, I look back to see Fletch fling the food outside, then run to Will and Mal's bedroom, opening that door and leaping back with the stick, grabbing the skillet and–

The bear comes rumbling out, sniffing, racing toward the door. Musk, thick and pungent, fills the air, making me stare, encased in a cloud of energy that feels wildly present yet dangerously distant.

The animal makes a beeline for outside.

Without thinking, instinct makes me race back to the

front door, Fletch beating me to it, shutting it hard, his back against it.

The bear, I see through the window, devours the food on the porch and sniffs at the door.

"GO AWAY, BEAR!" I shout, slapping the window a few times.

It runs off, looking back once with a sad face.

"JESUS CHRIST FIONA THAT WASN'T THE PLAN!" Fletch yells at me.

"I COULDN'T EXACTLY DROPKICK IT!" I scream, shocked by his fury. Being yelled at by someone I'm close to isn't in my repertoire. In my family, we don't yell.

Ever.

"IT COULD HAVE COME BACK AND HURT YOU!" He grabs my shoulders, pure fear in his eyes, his energy a ball of fiery orange, like sunspots.

"STOP IT! STOP SCREAMING AT ME!!!"

And then I'm in his arms, my face in his chest, his heart beating so fast, it's like a freight train, the thump of it against my eye socket like a ball peen hammer to the skull.

"I wasn't there the day Rico went nuts and almost got Mattie. Candi never told anyone what was going on. I couldn't stop him from hurting her, or Mattie. *You* stopped him that day. You and you alone, Fiona. But you don't have to be alone anymore and I have a hell of a lot more to lose now than I did a month ago. So damn it, don't do that again. Don't put yourself in danger right in front of my eyes when I can't do a damn thing about it. Please. *Please,*" he says, voice choked with emotion, as Will and Mallory emerge from their bedroom, wide-eyed and completely freaked out.

Mallory clings to him, her shock evident. "Did that just happen?"

"It did," Will says definitively, holding a large lamp in the hand not touching her. "Bear's gone?"

"Completely gone," Fletch informs him. "We got him out. Door locked."

I'm sobbing, the tears coming hard, so hard, as he holds me. It's difficult to breathe and I don't care, because every moment from that day in my classroom rises up, the safe sanctuary of his arms, his visceral fear, his abject horror at all the possible ways harm can come to those we care about finally letting me face it all.

"I–I didn't want *you* to get hurt," I finally say, pulling back and hitting his chest with the heel of my hand. Our eyes meet and his are a bit teary, though he's not crying. "You ever think of that, Chris? That maybe *I* had something more to lose just now, too?"

"I lost my really nice Canada Geese jacket Will got me for my birthday," Mal says. "The bear decided to pee on that and missed my Uggs."

I love you, I think, blocking out Mallory's mournful ode to a coat.

"Holy crap, that really just happened," Will says as Fletch stares at me, the words I said sinking in, his eyes becoming kaleidoscopes of emotion. With his fingers, he strokes my cheek, running his index finger down a tear-soaked trail of skin.

In the periphery, I see Mallory open the bottle of wine, the screw top a godsend in the moment. Unceremoniously, she drinks straight from the bottle, guzzling enough that Will stops her, but only to take it and have a few chugs, too, before handing it back and reaching for a beer.

"Fiona... "

THUMP!

Mallory screams as the front door rattles, the metal handle shaking.

"We're safe. It can't come in," Fletch assures her. Will moves toward her out of instinct, their arms wrapping around each other's waists.

"It can't break the window, right?" she whispers.

"No," I say. "It knows we have food. We just need to scare it off."

"Is the car safe?" she asks.

"We locked it," Fletch assures her, our own communication set aside for the sake of the moment's urgency. "It can't get in, and there's no food in it. But now's as good a time as any to do this." Letting me go, he walks over to the window on the far side of the room, opening it.

"What are you doing?" Mal asks.

And then Fletch begins to undo his belt.

Eyebrows flying up, Mallory looks at me for an explanation.

As if I have one.

Ziiiiiip

Fletch undoes his fly, his jeans loose at the hips, the tip of his butt crack showing. Perfect dimples top each buttock, the columns of muscle along the sides of his spine so well defined, they look carved.

"Are you—is he—Fletch, are you *peeing* out the window?" Mallory hiss-screams.

Yes.

He is.

"Urine perimeter," he calls back over his shoulder. "Will, come on, man. Let's do this. Male urine is what we need."

"Male urine?" Mallory says, incensed. "That's sexist!"

Will looks down at his crotch, then shrugs. "Might as well. The bear damn near scared the piss out of me, but not quite."

My emotions feel like they're attached to bungee cords and I just BASE jumped off a radio tower.

Fletch sniffs the air. "Ah. Now I get it. Asparagus pee!"

Will opens the window adjacent to Fletch's, undoes his pants and pulls them down enough to unleash that which needs to be unleashed. The sound of a second stream of urine fills the air.

"Spray it in an arc, man. We're going for the perimeter. Can you stop your pee midstream?"

"Why?" Will asks, the sound halting.

"Nice. Now, let's move to the bedroom window in our room."

They pull back, moving toward the door to Fletch's and my room, pants still undone.

"*What on Earth are you doing?*" Mallory yells at them.

"Making a pee perimeter," Fletch calmly explains, he and Will turning toward us, their penises tucked in but pants undone. "The scent of human male urine keeps bears away."

"Maybe," Will reluctantly adds. "I'm not convinced."

"Then why are you doing this?" Mallory asks him.

"Because it's a thing to do and I drank a little too much beer at dinner."

And with that, the guys disappear into our bedroom.

A flaming ball of emotion, Mallory walks over to the kitchen, grabs the half-chugged wine bottle, and offers me some. I take it, the dry white wine helping slightly.

"Tapped!" Will calls out.

"We need more beer," Fletch announces. At least they had the decency to zip up this time before moving into a new room.

How did we get from making out in the moonlit snow, to fighting off a bear, to screaming at each other, to–

A urine perimeter?

"You're going to drink more beer to produce more urine for your pee line around the cabin that will keep the bears at bay?" Mallory asks in a tone that makes it clear she thinks they've gone batshit crazy.

"Yes," they answer in unison.

"What if we want to be part of the urine perimeter?"

"First of all," Fletch explains as Will hands him a cold one, "it only works with male urine. And second–"

"How would you aim?" Will arches his hips. "Your stream would go all over the place. You'd pee down your leg. We're not being sexist, Mal," he says, holding in a burp. "We're just being *pragmatic*."

And then he grins.

How much beer, exactly, have these guys had?

When you've been friends with someone for as many decades as I've known Mallory, you know what they're thinking by the simplest of details. The way the corner of her eye twitches, how her lips push out before she bites one. How she cracks her fingers just by tightening her hands into fists, then relaxes them.

But mostly, I know exactly what Mallory's thinking because she yells: "ARE YOU INSANE, WILL?"

"Cheers!" Fletch says to his old football buddy as the amber necks of beer bottles clink in the blissfully bear-free space of our weekend getaway, Mallory's words hanging there as we all process far too much near-death energy, the residue clinging to our skin, in our eyes, lining our noses. It's everywhere, like a dusting of ash after a fire.

Time to clean the room.

Quietly, I walk into the bedroom and find my suitcase, the search for the small muslin bag quite quick. Inside it, there's a series of other bags, the scent of sage and pau d'arco wafting up.

"Can you believe those two? They're out there saying wait till Ramini and Osgood find out they warded off a bear with their bare hands," she says, incensed. "And now they're going on about the bear/bare pun. So much for a romantic weekend of fun! They want to finish off all the beer, leave us the wine, and pee their way to wilderness man status. *Grunt grunt*," she punctuates, until hysterical laughter is the only sound she makes.

Cool air hits the tip of my nose, inviting me to breathe in deeply, so I do. It takes four long, slow, methodical breaths for Mallory to join in, the impulse like a yawn. In my classroom, this works.

Turns out adults aren't all that different from four-year-olds.

"Are you okay?" I finally ask her, putting my hands on her upper arms, my light touch about giving her healing energy. Whatever I've got is hers, my higher self working to bring us both up to a better, calmer, more nurturing vibration.

"No. That was horrifying. Will bolted into the cabin and tried to close the door behind him but the bear was too fast and strong. I was tidying the kitchen counter and suddenly, Will was shoving me into the bedroom, trying to lock the door, but there aren't any locks! The bear somehow got the door open, so we hid in the closet. It didn't seem to want us—it just wanted food. Everything in the kitchen was in the refrigerator or put away. We had our phones and texted you."

"We were out of range until we got closer to the house."

"That's what Will said. And then we just... well, we screamed. Tried to get it to leave. But it was big and Will said there could be a mama and–"

"Deep breath." We breathe together. Her energy cools, slightly. I take the sage stick and light it, not to drive bad energy away but more to cleanse the space.

Also, I just like the scent of sage.

"Will said we just needed to wait it out. Bears don't eat humans, and this one was small."

"He's right."

"But that was scary as hell."

"It was."

"How are you? I saw you two fighting."

"It's—that was our first fight, I guess. First fight before we even sleep together."

The way Mallory's mouth makes an O when she's surprised cracks me up. She looks like the AlwaysDoll, a sex device Perky protests against because of the use of toxins in the made-in-China products.

"You haven't had sex yet?"

"No. This weekend was supposed to be it."

"And now we have two cavemen out there drinking pee juice to make the bears go bye-bye."

"Right. So sexy."

The two of us make caveman grunts and then devolve into laughter. Ah, the energy *is* changing.

Here we go.

The unmistakable sound of a window opening some-where in the cabin makes us look at each other.

"Hey! Fletch! Bet I can write my name in the snow!"

"Oh, God," Mal groans.

"It's a perimeter, Dickhead! Not a dick cursive lesson!"

"They're getting pretty drunk, aren't they? Fletch is using Will's stupid nickname from high school. He called him Dickhead and Osgood called him Lowman."

"BET I CAN PEE FURTHER THAN YOU!" Will shouts. "LET'S SEE WHO'S GOT THE LONGER—" a distinct pause hangs in the air until he finishes, "—STREAM!"

"We've descended into whose dick is bigger," Mal sighs. "They're pretty drunk."

I drop my voice. "Whose dick do *you* think might be bigger?"

"*This! This* is why the females can't do this! They don't have the arc!" Fletch's voice stretches out into a hint of a Boston accent, the word sounding just a bit like *ahk*.

"I think our date is going to be with Netflix – not dicks – tonight," Mallory sighs. "Only two hours of internet per day?"

"I don't think they'll be awake in two hours at the rate they're going," I whisper, my arm around her shoulders, the gesture turning into a tight hug we both need.

"I'm so sorry, Fi," she says into my hair.

"Me too, Mal."

"No, I mean–you haven't had sex yet? With *him*? Have you looked at him? He has a body to die for."

"*Mallory!*"

"I might be engaged, but my eyes still work. You two have been dating for how long?"

"Three weeks or so."

"And no sexytimes?"

"I didn't say *no* sex. Just not *the* sex."

Her eyes dart all over the place as she leans in and asks, "What is *the* sex? Like, anal?"

"NOT ANAL!" I shout.

"Aw, man!" groans one of the guys from the other room, in a tone of serious disappointment.

"Who said that?" we hiss at each other, my heart jamming in my ribs as I look through the open bedroom door and see Will and Fletch in the kitchen, opening yet another beer.

"Might be better if we never find out who, exactly, said that," Mal whispers.

"One more, Dickhead, and I think we get the job done," Fletch says, lifting his beer bottle to toast with Will.

They miss.

"Eye-hand coordination is lost," Mallory bemoans, pulling out her phone. "What do you want to watch?" she asks, opening the app. "I don't even want to think about what my bed smells like after that bear was in there," she says with a shudder.

"We should go check."

"No. I'll do it later, after Peefest is over. This is Will's phone, so we can use his data if we need to."

"Movie or television series?"

"Movie. A rom com where the guys don't get drunk and pee the bears away."

"I think we can find something that meets those criteria."

"It's harder than you think."

They overhear her, because someone shouts, "That's what he said!" and two guys fall apart laughing.

Mallory quietly closes the bedroom door. We crawl into bed.

"You're shaking!" Mal says, face tight with worry.

"I'm just remembering one of my past lives."

"Your what?"

"I went to a workshop where we did regression via hypnosis. In a past life, I ran a camp in Northern Canada. I died in a polar bear attack."

"Fi!"

"And now I think this is why the bear came. So I could relive it, survive, and have Fletch save me."

Skepticism radiates from Mallory's brow. "I think the bear was just hungry."

"If you say so." I can't stop shaking, though.

"You really believe that woo stuff? *Really*?"

"I don't *not* believe it. Why?"

"Because you're smart. Educated. You have a master's degree and – "

"You think the way furniture is positioned in a room can make someone go bankrupt."

"Feng shui is an ancient art that – "

"Or cause them medical harm."

"It's a study of energy that – "

I cut her off with a palm. "I only told you about the polar bear because I needed a friend."

"I *am* your friend!"

"Then support me. You don't have to believe what I believe. But can you respect the feelings I feel?"

"Of course!" We dissolve into a hug.

"You always smell like frankincense," Mal whispers into my neck. A long sniff, then she pulls back.

"Better than asparagus pee."

We both look at the back of the bedroom door as Fletch and Will make some He-man sounds.

"You're not who I thought I'd be snuggling up with, watching rom coms," I confess as I get up and pull two quilts from a stack on top of a cedar chest in the corner.

"Me, either," she murmurs, squeezing my arm. "But if I had to pick anyone but Will, it's you. Don't tell Perky."

I snort. "If Perky were here, you'd say the same thing to her and tell her not to say anything to Fiona."

"I would."

We laugh.

And then we watch.

We watch until the DISH internet hits two hours and expires.

And then we use all of Will's remaining data before we walk out into the living room to find the guys fast asleep on separate couches, pants mercifully buttoned and zipped, bear successfully kept away by the power of rented beer.

Each of us takes one of the quilts from the bedroom and covers our respective guy, then goes to bed.

Where I try to weave my tangled energy back into a coherent whole before I drift off to sleep.

CHAPTER 17

*M*oonlight on snow outside casts a glow in the room, and as I wake up, I notice three things.

1. The digital clock says four a.m.

2. The curtains are open, which is why the glow is so bright.

3. Fletch has one hell of an erection and is currently kissing the back of my neck.

"Mmmm," I say, turning over, wondering what we're going to talk about. His hand is on my hip, sliding up over my ass, rounding the curve, and moving up my ribs. I'm wearing a long, thin nightdress and panties, since I went to bed assuming nothing would happen tonight.

This is a pleasant surprise.

"Sorry we fell asleep in the living room," Fletch whispers in my ear. The warm rush of his breath coupled with his hand on my bare breast under my nightgown makes every word in my brain spark like a firework.

"How many beers did you drink?"

"Enough that it took a gallon of water to balance it all out."

"A gallon?"

"Yeah. We've got a foot-thick yellow perimeter out there now. I made Lotham drink a shit ton, too, and whizz it out before we both went to bed."

"You really know how to talk to a woman in bed, you sexy whizzer, you."

A deep, amused rumble from his chest cuts through the weirdness. He pulls back, the touch gentle, his breath smelling like mint toothpaste. "Let me try again."

"I'm all about redos."

"This is one do-over I have to get right."

"Given that I'm half naked and your hand is on my breast, I think you're already in a good position."

"I'm looking for an even better one," he says against my neck, but then pulls back, eyes serious. I can see he's fully present, the beers long gone from his brain, his attention focused and full, all aimed at me.

"I don't understand. It just can't be this easy," I blurt out.

"Why not?"

"Because you've been here all this time. All these years." I rotate in the bed, the sheets pulling from my waist as I twist to look him in the eye. "I avoided you for so long. We live in the same town. You work two towns away. Your nephew is one of my students, Fletch."

"*Chris*. I like it better when you call me Chris. Especially in bed."

"Don't like nicknames?" I say with an over-the-top affect. "Imagine that!"

"I see you're feisty in bed, too." The comment comes with a nice squeeze in the right place.

I squeeze right back and he laughs.

"Fine. *Chris*. And if you call me Feisty again, all bets are off. I've spent a long time trying to escape that name. Trying to escape *you*."

He smiles and brushes a long piece of my hair off my shoulder. "Yeah. How do you think it felt, carrying a torch for you all these years, knowing you couldn't stand me?"

"You dated plenty of women. You weren't pining away for me."

"First of all, Fiona, how would you know I dated 'plenty of women'? I thought you didn't pay me a whit of attention all these years."

Damn it. Caught. "I didn't. But I knew. People talk."

At the mention of other women, the air between us changes. His confidence drops, a tentativeness in him emerging that feels a little shaky, less secure. I've cracked open a conversation most people wouldn't touch when they're naked with another person.

"Maybe I *was* pining away for you. Maybe you didn't notice *that*."

"Ha ha."

"I don't want to talk about anyone but you." Our lips touch as he leans in for a kiss. "I don't want to think about anyone but you." Another kiss. "And I certainly don't want you talking or thinking about anyone but me, *ever*, Fiona."

This kiss is different.

"I'm sorry I yelled at you earlier," he says, cutting the kiss short but punctuating it with another. "I shouldn't have done that. It was reckless and unfair. I was just so damned pumped. Seeing you run toward the door, toward the bear, it was..." He sighs.

"You already said enough. We're fine. It's fine."

"Are we?"

I answer with a kiss, my hands encircling his waist, palms seeking the heat of bare skin at the base of his back.

"I know," he says between open-mouthed kisses that make the cool air where we're not under the warm down comforter feel even icier, "that I keep saying this." Kiss. "But damn. I can't believe I'm in bed with you."

"Why?"

"Because I'm about to have sex with *Feisty*."

Instead of being angry, my belly curls in with laughter, his fingers on my breast moving down to catch the movement.

"You're about to have sex with Fiona. A twenty-nine-year-old woman who is the grown-up version of that girl who fought for her no," I say, the words coming out with confidence.

His hand halts, but doesn't pull back.

"You always have your no with me, Fiona. Always."

"I know I do. But right now, that no is sound asleep, blissfully dreaming about how it will rise up when called forth. Now is not one of those times, Chris. Make love to me. With me. I just want you. I can't believe it either, that you were here all this time, and I rejected you. This is me *not* rejecting you, right here, right now." My hands move up the bare skin of his back, memorizing the hard curves of muscle as he touches me, his shoulder blades and lats like gears in a machine.

"I love—damn," he says, cutting off what he was about to say, pulling one hand off me to rub his hair and breathe out through his nose. "Too soon, right?"

"I don't know. Is it?"

"I love being with you. It's so easy, like you said before. Too easy. Almost like all that energy and universe and abundance stuff you talk about is real."

"It *is* real!"

"You're turning me into a believer."

And with that, our lips meet, the kiss deep with hunger,

words we're so close to saying caught on our tongues, behind our teeth, in our throats. Our bodies will have to say them instead.

The first time you make love with someone is always its own form of art, a blank canvas you fill in with whatever your heart, eyes, and hands guide you toward. He tastes like mint and beer, the softness of his mouth so pleasing, so different from the hard lines of his body. Chris is thick, a former football player who has only hardened and broadened over time, his wide bone structure layered with strength coiled in his thigh muscles, which I touch openly as I tug at the waistband of his boxers.

Duly noted. He's a boxers kind of guy. Suits someone whose nickname is Hot Boxer.

Sitting up, he lifts the down comforter, letting a shock of icy air into the warm cocoon we've created as he peels off his shirt, the moon nicely approving of the display. With the window behind him, the light makes the hair on his arms and chest glow like a halo, as he looks at me with encouragement.

Peeling off my nightgown takes a bit more effort, but as I succeed and fling it off the bed, the cool air tightens my nipples.

"You look even better than the last time I saw you naked, in the hot springs."

"I do?"

"Yes. Because unlike then, now I know I get to have you. Be in you. Make you come and come inside you. We get to be together this time. Last time was an accident. A gorgeous, wet, beautiful accident. But this? *This* is so much better."

I didn't know *words* could push me so close to climax, but his do.

His mouth is on my nipple now, the fiery heat making

me gasp as his body stretches and he's over me, full and powerful, only the thin strips of our underwear keeping us from being fully nude. I reach down to fix that, pulling mine off, leaving them under the covers and kicking them down.

He does the same.

The thick, raw heat of his erection makes me want to open myself immediately and guide him in, but it would be too quick, over too fast, and that's not what this is about. Sensing my hesitation, he stops the swirling on my nipple and looks up, eyes vulnerable, expression so open, it's like looking into the eyes of a soul you've known for thousands of years.

And loved for thousands more.

"You okay?"

"More than okay. Just thinking."

He kisses the spot between my breasts. "About this?" A kiss on one nipple. "Or this?" The other nipple gets some attention. "And this?"

I moan, parting my legs by instinct. "I'm thinking a piece of me is going to explode if you aren't in me, now."

"Mmmm," he says, kissing a trail down. "How about we make you explode without me in you, and save that for a second explosion?"

"I don't know if there's enough energy in the world for me to handle that."

"Then let's generate more."

Before he slips completely out of my grasp, I run my hand along the rolling waves of his ass, the muscle hard and taut, my mind making a map of the terrain, his movement lower leaving me only his shoulders to explore. The second his tongue touches my clit I am electrified, a whimper escaping because it's been too long since anyone's done *that*.

And *this*.

And holy hell, no one's ever done *the other thing* before.

Whatever maneuver he's doing now, he's right—it's generating some vibration I didn't know could be created.

We're making a new kind of energy. Wet, hot, slick, filthy, naughty, *dirty* energy.

And who knew Chris was so good at it?

Baring my body feels right with him, the glide of skin against skin, the permission to let my hands go where they want to, the dropping of boundaries so perfect. His mouth is on me, fingers in me, his whole self focused on giving me what I need, and that is what finally tips me over—knowing that in bed, as in regular life, Chris Fletcher gives his all.

Every last piece of himself.

We're quiet, the sound of my orgasm released as sighs and groans, his work finished as I fist his hair in my hands and pull up, one more second of attention on me a painfully exquisite sensation that I have to stop. He kisses me until I pull away and slide down, wanting to give him what he just lavished on me, hoping the reciprocity holds.

"Ah, Fiona. That mouth of yours," he murmurs as I slip under the covers, the dark cave warm and heady. His body is my only roadmap as I blindly find what I need and give, give, give, focusing my mouth and tongue and fingers on this man who electrified me, nerve endings still shivering as if in awe.

He's full and hard, the tip of him so hot, it's like I'm plugging into an energy source, my tongue licking a line up the sensitive underside, his hands finding my breasts, pinching a little too hard, a little too rough, with just enough brutality to make me nearly come again.

Then his hands are in my hair and I find a rhythm, one that allows me to use my palms to cover his body, to travel the lines of it up and down, a cartographer in bed, my mouth milking him.

Or trying to.

"No," he says abruptly, stopping me. "You wanted me in you, and I want to be in you. Save that for next time," he says with a grin that's almost spiritual, the look a message to come back to him, as if yet again there's a connection that goes further back than I ever dreamed.

Turning to his right, he pulls a condom from the bedside drawer, one he must have planted when we first arrived. The forethought makes me smile, the rip of the wrapper and his quick work of it understated and gentlemanly.

"I want you on top," he says. "I want to look at you. I want your hair in my face, tickling my chest. That's how I've imagined this when I've dreamed about you."

"You've—what?"

I comply, because how could I not? Moving up, I straddle him, careful not to get too close, my hips pulled back enough to hold the connection at bay, but it's becoming impossible to control the impulse to ride him.

And ride him hard.

"Do you have any idea how many nights I've been in my bed, alone, and thought about you? Imagined sleeping with you? Giving you pleasure? Having sex outdoors, leaned up against a tree, my only view your fine ass and that long, gorgeous hair?"

"You... have?"

"I have, Fiona. Especially since that day at the preschool. And now you're here, inches away, and you're luminescent. You glow. Let me make you glow even more."

His words guide me to him, the feel of his hands on my ribs, riding down to my hipbones as I center myself and anchor. He's big, but I'm so wet and ready that the feeling of fullness is its own form of pleasure, the long, slow pull up from my knees making me ache with joy.

Chris sits up and pulls me to him in a kiss that feels desperate even though it isn't. Feels urgent although we have all the time in the world. Feels amazing and like every-thing has converged in the multiverse across time and space in the feel of his mouth against mine.

Because everything has.

As I lower myself onto him, our thighs meet, mine outside his, the stretch required to move around such a strong guy more intense than I'd ever imagined. His hands move to my breasts and I arch back, reveling in his touch, in the freedom to move like this, in the unbridled sense that my every act, every motion, is unjudged, uncontrolled, unrivaled.

We just are.

He's deep in me as I look down at him, my hair brushing against his chest, his eyes so intense, it's like they burn. I'm lost in the emotion, the energy wrapping itself around and around into a rope, a cord, a cable strong enough to power time itself.

Every bit of my skin is flushed and tingling, my core on fire as his eyes–oh, those eyes–take in my body, appreciative and smoldering, making me feel like everything around me exists in orbit.

And we are the center.

His face changes, the intensity deepening as his eyes close and his breath hitches, my own orgasm taking over, making me shut out the world, making him my only connection with it. A rhythm starts between us, unspoken but quickly joined, until we're coming together, the sensa-tion startling and integrative, his ass pushing up as my hands find his hips and urge him to take me some place where we can just do this, be this, feel nothing but this.

And then I collapse on him, completely gone yet present at the same time, split and united, vulnerable yet strong.

"Jesus," he whispers into my hair, hands on my ass, rubbing in circles. "You're amazing."

"Mmmmm," is all I can manage.

By the time I realize I should climb off him, I don't care, his hands pulling the down comforter up over my shoulders, my words thrown without caution into the space we've made.

"I love being with you, Chris."

"I love being with you, too, Fiona."

And then we fade off, because we're right.

This *is* easy.

Which is how it should always be, for everyone, in whatever lifetime they're living.

WAKING a guy up with a blow job shouldn't involve getting a knee to the face, but I take full responsibility.

"*Ow!*" I burst out as my lips, formerly on his limp shaft, move sharply against him, working hard not to bite down as his knee hits my cheekbone.

"Wha? Oh, God! I'm so sorry," he says, crawling under the covers to meet me, removing the object of my attention. "Did I just knee you?"

"Yeah."

"What were you doing?"

"Spinning alpaca fur. What do you think I was doing? I asked if you wanted a little morning wake up."

"I thought you meant coffee!"

"You'd rather have that? Okay," I say, rubbing my cheek, starting to crawl out from under the covers.

"No! NO!" he shouts, laughing, body shaking with mirth. "I just misunderstood your naughty intent, Fiona."

"Ah." I poke my head out from under the covers, the cold air a bit of a balm on my red cheek.

He kisses the spot I'm rubbing. "I'm sorry."

"It's okay."

"HEY FLETCH! GET OUT HERE," Will shouts. "Mallory says we have breakfast duty and the women have all the other meals!"

We turn toward the door, Chris's face falling.

"Breakfast duty?"

I shrug. "Sorry. I guess I'll swallow bacon and eggs for protein instead."

Eyes wide, he gives me a look that is hard to decipher, given how new we are to each other sexually.

"Don't tell me I blew my only chance?"

"You blew my chance to blow you."

"FLETCH!" Will bellows.

"Damn it," he mutters, climbing out of the bed naked, fine body on display.

"Raincheck works for me," I assure him.

He stops, one leg in his boxers, the expression on his face in between two emotions.

"I really do love being with you, you know," he says.

I blink. I breathe. I smile. "You said that last night."

"So did you."

"I meant it."

"So did I."

"Good. Because it would suck if you didn't."

"And you're saying you'll suck at a future date?"

I throw a pillow at him. He nearly loses his balance, flaccid penis bouncing like a slinky, making me laugh more.

Somehow, he manages to put on his pants, then a shirt and sweater, crawling back under the covers fully clothed. A long, slow, hot kiss makes me wish he were still naked.

Another kiss on my injured cheek and he says, "This is it, isn't it?"

"It?"

"Us."

"Yes," I say slowly. "It is."

"You kicked my ass when we were younger. Now you appreciate my ass."

"Maybe," I say with a smile.

"There was no maybe last night."

"I get to decide whether there's a maybe or not!" I declare as he climbs out of bed, Will yelling again from the other room.

"Tell you what," he says as he turns the doorknob. "Let's work through the maybe."

"How?"

"Come to my studio again. Let's do a real workout."

"Oh—you *literally* mean let's work it out."

"Right. Remember I challenged you to a bout on Wednesday? I meant it."

"You're on. Prepared to have your ass kicked." I blow him a kiss.

He grins. "I wouldn't have it any other way, Fiona."

And then he leaves, calling out to Will, asking where the bacon is.

Jolene was right.

Go have your date with Fletch.

Speaking of Jolene, I follow the scent of sage back to the windowsill, where I find the strange crystal she gave me.

When I touch it, it's warm.

And the vibration it sends through me feels like a happy chant.

All I had to do was make space. Be proud of my old self. Invite all the pieces of who I am to come together into a whole. An empowered, loving, strong, gentle, smart, tender, kickass whole.

A whole lot of feisty.

CHAPTER 18

"My brother's coming into town for Christmas," I tell Chris as he comes back inside his apartment, an arm full of wood making it hard to shut the door. Jumping up, I help him. It's not entirely selfless, after all.

I get a cozy fire in exchange.

His apartment is the left half of a converted older home, a duplex with its own yard. Chris put a small fence in place out there so his basset hound, Gloria, can run around in peace.

Yes, he has a dog. I didn't know until we got back from the cabin two weeks ago, and he had me over. Gloria took to me instantly, tail wagging, eyes mournfully accepting.

Plus, I don't kick her out of the bed when she wanders into the room as dawn breaks and she wants to snuggle at Chris's feet. He was hers first, so I have to defer.

It's early December now, the awkwardness of Thanksgiving over with. Mom and Dad are back from their cruise with pictures and stories galore. We split the holiday in half, which meant Chris and I had two Thanksgiving meals.

I'm pretty sure we're still half-stuffed.

"Tim? Or Dale?"

"Oh. Tim. Dale has to stay in Wisconsin because of Claire's family. I guess this year it's their turn. Dale said they'll come out next summer."

In the past, these sorts of scheduling arrangements struck me as something other people deal with. My brothers try to both be here for Christmas every three years or so. But from now on, Chris and I have to juggle it all, too. Yes, we live in the same town and so do our families, but this year, it feels different.

Because it *is* different.

Suddenly, I want Tim and Dale here. I want the whole nine yards. Big family celebrations and nieces and nephews and... all of it.

Because Chris represents it *all*.

"Sounds good. My mom wants us here for part of it. Maybe Christmas morning? We've all spent the night at Mom's since Mattie was born. Everyone gets to watch his excitement."

"You mean everyone's woken up at 4:57 a.m. by a screaming child shouting that Santa came and wanting to open presents."

"That's.... uncanny how accurately you describe it."

"Sounds like so much fun!"

"Only a preschool teacher would say that. Mattie doesn't even let us get coffee," he grouses as he sets the frame for a solid fire, kindling just so, crumpled newspaper and a wax firestarter thrown in for good measure.

"I'll be in charge of coffee," I say as I bend down to kiss him, my hand unable to stop touching his tight ass.

"I'm about to pitch forward into the fire if you do that again, Fiona."

"That's what it would take for you to be hotter than you already are, Chris."

His laughter is gratifying.

Gloria looks up from her dog bed behind us, a snuffly sound coming out of her as she stands. The old girl gets around just fine, but she's a little slow. The heat of the growing fire draws her in, the light from the new flames illuminating the pattern on her fur, large tan and auburn splotches in a sea of snow.

"Listen to her, Gloria!" he says as he pets her, giving extra good scratches along the dog's neck. "She's objectifying me!"

"*Snurf*," Gloria says, nose up, neck straining to get as much of Chris's attention as she can.

"You're the only woman in my life who doesn't make fun of me," he says to her, kissing the top of her head.

"That's not true – " I start, then think about his sister, his mom, me, and...

Chris just clears his throat and lavishes Gloria with more attention.

Bzzz

"Whose phone?" I ask, searching the living room with my eyes. Chris's place has the high ceilings of an older home, with original fireplaces in three rooms, but only this one really works. Big windows with painted radiators under them bracket the large space, thick leather couches and chairs everywhere. His great-grandmother's hand-knit afghans cover two chairs, and though I'll never meet her, when I crawl under one with Chris and we watch the fire, sipping mulled cider, I feel like the love that came from her hands and heart in each stitch crosses time.

Love becomes energy that infuses whatever we choose.

"That's you," he grunts. "My phone's charging in the bathroom."

That's the other thing about his apartment – he has no wireless internet, and charges his phone on a large stand in his bathroom, behind a tall screen.

I look at my phone and see someone's called, from a number I don't know. No voice mail.

I ignore it.

"Here we go," he says, still crouched down, the fine pull of denim around his ass its own form of entertainment. The mugs of coffee with a splash of Irish cream call my name. So does a nice, warm quilt. We're experiencing a big, unexpected cold snap in early December, the single digit temperatures at night making it easy to snuggle up.

As he stands and turns around, our eyes meet.

"You were looking at my ass again, weren't you?"

Gloria lets out a long sigh and rests on the floor by the fire, paws under her chin.

"Again?" I bat my eyelashes. "How would you know if I were?"

"It feels hot."

"Your ass *is* hot."

"You know the expression 'my ears were burning' when you know someone's been talking about you? Same principle."

"Then get that hot butt of yours over here and warm me up."

Taking me at my word, he climbs in my lap. Gloria watches us, head up suddenly, tail starting to wag as I giggle, Chris burrowing his pelvis down into my crotch.

"Chris!"

"What? I'm warming you up!"

"Not like this!"

"How about like this," he says before kissing me, towering over me in my lap, the dig of his bones and density pushing me deep into the couch, his hands in my hair, cradling my face. Normally, I'm in his lap, so the role reversal sets me on a collision course, hands unsure where to go, mouth completely consumed by his.

Lost in the kiss, I slide my hands under his shirt and sigh with deep contentment as I cup my hands at his ribs, loving the feel of his broad back. Exploring a person's soul and heart is a lifelong journey, but the body is the same. It changes with time, energy shifting the feel of it, how we move and hold ourselves, how we feel and breathe making what looks like the same assemblage of skin and bone an ever-changing landscape.

"Hmph," Gloria says from behind us, Chris's mouth spreading into a smile as we kiss. He pulls away and twists to look at her. Craning my neck to see around him, I understand why he smiles.

She's asleep, lost in rabbit dreams.

Chris's hands seek the hem of my shirt, pulling up with a quick movement that makes it clear we're not just playing. The easy slide into making love on his sofa is part of the newness of this, the simplicity of this relationship, the subtle goodness of time together as a luxury we define by how we choose to use it.

I open one eye as my shirt disappears and I'm in Chris's arms as he pivots, pulling me on top of him now. Gloria stands, the *clink clink* of her dog tags echoing softer as she leaves the scene.

Good roommates know when to get lost.

"This isn't balanced," I whisper as I make Chris take his sweater and shirt off, pulling them over his head as his arms lift up, the turtleneck comically caught as he laughs, my fingers unable to stop touching his bare chest. Each rib has a muscle line along it, for goodness sake.

Who wouldn't touch him?

In a hot second, his face is clear again and his tongue is in my mouth, my hair caught in his fist, the press of his body hovering over mine too much, not enough.

As I reach for his belt, Gloria runs to the front door, tags jangling.

I freeze.

"What's wrong?" Chris whispers.

And then –

Tap tap tap

"Shit," he mutters, holding steady. "Probably just a UPS delivery or something. We can hide and – "

A different kind of jangling happens. This time, it sounds like a key.

The front door opens, a hallway the only thing separating us from whoever's here.

"Chris?" It's his sister, Candi.

And the distinct sound of a sobbing, hysterical child.

"UNCLE CHRIS!" Mattie moans as I roll onto the floor by the fire. Fletch tosses a quilt at me for modesty, thank God. I wrap myself in it like a burrito, covering my face, legs exposed, and I stay still.

My heart rams against my breastbone, empathy centers on fire, because Mattie is in distress.

Seeing me half-naked won't help.

"What's wrong?" He asks Candi, who sounds very, very close.

"Why aren't you wearing a shirt – oh, never mind," Candi says. "I'm so, so sorry. Mattie is having one of his moods, and nothing I do will calm him down. He keeps talking about how scared he is, and only Uncle Chris can help. He wants Gloria, too."

I reposition the quilt so I can see them. Chris is holding Mattie in his arms now, Candi next to him, both of them behind the couch. I'm on the other side, looking up. All I see is a sliver of the room with them in it.

"Shhhh, Mattie. It's okay. You're okay."

"I – I – I don't wanna be like dis!" he wails. "I – Mama says I need to just – just- breeeeve."

In sympathy, I take a long, deep belly breath, pushing my spine against the hardwood floor, hoping my energy will connect with his and bring him up.

Inhale.

Exhale.

Inhale –

And something tickles the back of my throat.

Sniffling comes from Mattie and Chris's soothing undercurrent, his voice murmuring words I can't hear but certainly feel. My throat threatens to cough, my neck spasming as I fight the impulse, biology and modesty fighting in a blood match.

Biology wins.

"*Coff*," I choke out, the sound closer to a death rattle than a release.

Candi's neck jerks to the right, her eye catching mine.

Mattie looks over the couch. "Was that Gloria?"

At that exact moment, the dog walks right up to Chris, lifts up on her front paws, and licks Mattie's foot.

"Oh, my God," Candi groans, the sound making Mattie panic, wails resurging.

With no choice now, I grab the quilt and hope it doesn't slide off me as I sit up. Fortune is on my side as I move to a standing position completely covered, though it's super obvious what we were doing.

To Candi, at least.

"M-m-miss Fiona?" Mattie squeals, his meltdown subverted by my revealed presence. "Why are you here?"

"She was, uh, visiting me," Chris says.

"Visiting," Candi coughs into her hand, suppressing a laugh, taking in his shirtless form and my quilted self with a new eye.

Scrambling out of Chris's arms, Mattie walks over to me, climbing on the couch seat to stand nearly eye-to-eye. "You visit Uncle Chris? But how?"

"What do you mean, how?"

"You live at the school," he says emphatically. "They let you leave?"

"Remember how we talked about this, honey? You saw me at your grandma's house last week at Thanksgiving," I remind him.

"But that was a holiday! I thought you were there just for that."

"No, sweetie. I am allowed to go wherever I want and do whatever I want when I'm not teaching."

He frowns, then turns to Chris. "Did you kiss her again?" he demands.

Candi makes a snorting sound.

"Yes," Chris confesses.

"Then you have to marry her!"

"Okay, buddy," Candi says, pulling Mattie off the couch as Chris puts his shirt back on. I'm remarkably jealous, because I can't do the same.

Gloria gently bites the edge of my quilt and starts pulling. Oh, sure, doggo. Now's the time to be playful.

"Listen, Mattie," Chris says, bending down, hair mussed but eyes serious. "You can come over here any time. Just, you know, don't let your mom use the key to get in without knocking a few more times." A patented sibling glare shoots from him to Candi.

"How was I supposed to know you and Fiona would be — "

"Would be what, Mommy?"

"Would be giving Gloria a bath," I improvise.

Candi openly laughs. No pretense. It's long gone.

Mattie's eyes light up as Gloria drops her bite on the quilt and canters off, tags like jingle bells.

"A bath! Can I help? I've never given a dog a bath before. Does Gloria have bath toys?"

Chris shoots me an incredulous look. "We were giving the dog a bath?"

"We... were planning on it. But we could bake cookies instead!" I say, a little too cheerfully. "Christmas is coming. If you have sugar, flour, butter, and..."

"COOKIES!" Mattie screams. "I'm gonna bake cookies with Miss Fiona at Uncle Chris's house!"

"Right. Bake cookies," Chris says, grabbing his lukewarm coffee and drinking it down fast.

Candi composes herself and looks at me. "If you want to bake cookies and give the dog a bath, do you mind if I leave Mattie here so I can run some errands alone?"

"That's how it is?" Chris grunts. "Interrupt us while we're – "

"GIVING THE DOG A BATH!" I say in an arch tone as Mattie plays with Gloria's ears.

"That would explain why you're not wearing shirts," she challenges him. "You know. The bath part. Might get wet doing that."

Wink.

"I wanna make cookies. Gloria can have a bath tomorrow," Mattie declares.

"Looks like lots of stuff has to wait until tomorrow," Chris mutters, though he ruffles Mattie's hair and looks at him, taking his thumb to wipe away his nephew's tears. "How are you feeling now, champ?"

"Better. Lots better. I always feel better when I see you."
Flinging his arms around Chris's neck, Mattie gives his
uncle his all, a full-contact hug that comes with every ounce
of his energy, too.

Tears fill my eyes.

Chris is going to be the best father someday.

And then my shoulders drop, ribs expanding, arms and
legs and torso and head all attached by a completeness, a
connective vibration that makes my heart float like a helium
ballon.

Chris is going to be the best father someday.

To *our* children.

"I love you," I blurt out, because once you realize who
you're meant to spend every waking moment of eternity
with – and even the sleeping ones – you have to tell them.

Have to declare.

Have to say it, loud and proud.

If you say so, Jolene told me a long time ago.

Well, here I am.

Saying it's *so*.

Candi's jaw drops as Chris looks at me from over
Mattie's shoulder, love in his eyes.

"I love you too, Miss Fiona!" Mattie shouts, beaming.

Candi, Chris and I laugh, but Chris's eyes stay on me, a
cord of energy connecting us that grows and thickens,
strengthening with each breath.

"You do." His words are confirmation.

Not a question.

"I do."

"I love you, too, Fiona. With all my heart."

Mattie wriggles in his arms and stands on the back of
the couch, putting his ear up to Chris's chest.

"It's a big one, too, Miss Fiona." He frowns. "Wait. Do I
get to call you Auntie Fiona now?"

"Hold on there, bud," Chris says, throat working hard with emotion, eyes on me. "Not yet."

"Not *yet*," I echo.

But someday.

CHAPTER 19

*E*pilogue. Or Stinger. You Decide.

"IT IS TIME TO DANCE!" Philippe shouts, the word DANCE! always capitalized in my head when he says it. The middle of January turns out to be a great time to take dance lessons for the wedding. The post-Christmas crowd has enlarged Philippe's class, using their holiday gift certificates and filling the room with new faces. But there's not much else to do this time of year in Anderhill, so Wednesday nights have become something fun for Chris and me.

And tonight, it's the six of us. Perky and Parker, Will and Mallory, Chris and me.

CLAP CLAP!

Chris is in mid-bite, eating his second chocolate chip cookie. He shoves the rest in his mouth and drinks his lemonade, a guilty look on his face as I eye him.

"Carbs. Can't help it," he mutters as he brushes off his

fingers on his jeans and moves over to the rest of us. We've formed a semi-circle at the edge of the highly polished dance floor.

"I still can't believe you two are together. Last time we had a dance lesson, Dancy had a heart attack and you looked like you wanted to climb on top of Fletch and beat him to a pulp."

"Well, you're half right. I do enjoy doing half of that."

"Which half?" Chris whispers, rubbing his rib. "Because you got one hell of a kick in last week when we were sparring."

"Fair's fair. I couldn't walk straight for a day and a half after that night in your apartment."

"STAHP!" Perky shouts, plugging her ears. "I can't take it. Fiona's got a boyfriend and she's talking porny to him!"

CLAP CLAP!

"Persephone," Philippe says in his accented English, the lilt light but clear. "Can you please have one DANCE! lesson without using the word *porn?*"

"Um—no."

Aggrieved sighs from both Mallory and Philippe make our crew laugh, the rest of the class bemused.

"Take a partner!" Philippe calls out, Chris's hand on my waist in an instant, his two left feet threatening my toes like copperheads on a hike near a river. For a guy who teaches boxing and kickboxing, he's remarkably inept on a dance floor. As I put one hand on his shoulder and one in his hand, I step up on tiptoes and whisper something unspeakably filthy, so raw and hot it makes his neck turn red.

His hand flattens on my sacrum and pulls me in. He's hard as a rock.

"Nice mouth for a preschool teacher," he murmurs,

reminding me of the exact same words he said to me at our high school reunion. "You shape young minds."

"Apparently, my words shape other things," I say, rubbing against him.

"Fiona," he grunts, the sound threateningly sexy. "Don't make me take you into the coat room and–" This time, he's the dirty talker, his threat turning into a promise as I start throbbing between my legs.

"DANCE!" Philippe shouts, the music starting.

But we're frozen in place, thrumming with need.

And then suddenly, Parker's phone buzzes, along with Will's and Mallory's phones. Two ringtones begin seconds later, the sudden cacophony of communication making the tension in the room skyrocket.

"I'm so sorry!" Mallory gasps, half leaping across the room to grab her phone from her purse. Will's is ringing, too, so the combo is worrisome. Are Sharon and Roy okay? Did something happen to Will's parents?

Parker's phone is buzzing, too, though.

"Oh, shit," he mutters, pointing to the glass screen as the six of us form an impromptu huddle by the door. It's hard to see, but Parker has live news feed from a major international news outlet on his phone.

And the image is of Mallory's older sister, Hastings Monahan, and her husband, Burke Oonaj, complete with their names and headshots. Not mugshots–professional headshots like a CEO of a company would have.

The caption: *Bay Area venture capitalist arrested in...*

"*What?*" Mallory cries out, her phone against her ear. "Mom? Is that really her on television being arrested?" Will appears to be on the phone with Roy, explaining that Parker's here and we'll figure something out.

"Does this mean she can't be here for my bridal shower?" Mallory whimpers.

"I think she has bigger things to worry about, Mal," Will says gently, one eyebrow up as he looks at Parker, who is tapping away from the video and over to his phone, making a call he has to leave the room to complete.

"I've got a lawyer friend in California who can step in and triage," he says to Will and Mal as he leaves. I pull out my phone and tap to a news station.

Yep. Mallory's sister is being perp walked, handcuffs and all, out of a sleek, high-end restaurant in Presidio Heights in San Francisco.

Hastings Monahan in handcuffs.

And the bridal shower's in a month.

Chris leans down and says, "I hope she didn't do anything too–"

"Don't say it," I groan, knowing the Dad Joke is coming.

"Oh, God," Perky intones, Mallory thankfully out of hearing range.

Chris shrugs.

He does it anyway:

"Hasty."

THE END

HUGE THANKS to readers for joining Fiona and Fletch on their journey in *Feisty*!

THERE IS one more book in the "Do-Over" series coming next— yes, *Hasty* gets a book! Watch for *Hasty* wherever you read.

OTHER BOOKS BY JULIA KENT

Suggested Reading Order

Shopping for a Billionaire: Boxed Set

- Shopping for a Billionaire 1
- Shopping for a Billionaire 2
- Shopping for a Billionaire 3
- Shopping for a Billionaire 4
- Christmas Shopping for a Billionaire

Shopping for a Billionaire's Fiancee

Shopping for a CEO

Shopping for a Billionaire's Wife

Shopping for a CEO's Fiancee

Shopping for an Heir

Shopping for a Billionaire's Honeymoon

Shopping for a CEO's Wife

Shopping for a Billionaire's Baby

Shopping for a CEO's Honeymoon

Shopping for a Baby's First Christmas

Her Billionaires

It's Complicated

Completely Complicated

It's Always Complicated

Random Acts of Crazy

Random Acts of Trust

Random Acts of Fantasy

Random Acts of Hope

Randomly Ever After: Sam and Amy

Random Acts of Love

Random on Tour: Los Angeles

Merry Random Christmas

Random on Tour: Las Vegas

Random Acts of New Year

Maliciously Obedient

Suspiciously Obedient

Deliciously Obedient

Our Options Have Changed (with Elisa Reed)

Thank You For Holding (with Elisa Reed)

Little Miss Perfect

Fluffy

Perky

Feisty

Hasty

ABOUT THE AUTHOR

Text JKentBooks to 77948 and get a text message on release dates!

New York Times and *USA Today* Bestselling Author Julia Kent turned to writing contemporary romance after deciding that life is too short not to have fun. She writes romantic comedy with an edge, and new adult books that push contemporary boundaries. From billionaires to BBWs to rock stars, Julia finds a sensual, goofy joy in every book she writes, but unlike Trevor from *Random Acts of Crazy*, she has never kissed a chicken.

She loves to hear from her readers by email at jkentauthor@gmail.com, on Twitter @jkentauthor, and on Facebook at https://www.facebook.com/jkentauthor . Visit her website at http://jkentauthor.com

CPSIA information can be obtained
at www.ICGtesting.com
Printed in the USA
BVHW032203160420
577785BV00001B/115

9 781950 172031